THE DAY I DIED

This is speculative fic
humdrum imaginatio
tainment of a unique
words will feel for a
your memory for a certain hour, discover a pleasure that is like a dream on the fringe of recollection.

'Maybe you sense that there is someone nearer than beside you, who without foul intent has for a spasm of eternity usurped your mind and body, and mated with one unknown to you, whose eyes are vivid with laughter. Have I been, am I, perhaps, in you?'

Coming soon from Star Books
also by Walter Harris

DROOP

LIFE WITH THE ASHES

VAMPIRES REST

Other books by Walter Harris

CLOVIS

THE DAY I DIED

Walter Harris

A STAR BOOK
published by
W. H. ALLEN

A Star Book
Published in 1974
by W. H. Allen & Co. Ltd.
A division of Howard & Wyndham Ltd.
44 Hill Street, London, W1X 8LB

An original Star Books publication

Printed in Great Britain by
Richard Clay (The Chaucer Press), Ltd., Bungay, Suffolk

ISBN 0 352 300221

For Eileen and Julian

‘Wilt thou marry me?’ asked God;
Satan replied: ‘I will.’
Mating, they bound me in limbo,
In limbo I dwell still.

MY LIFE 1759–1815

CHAPTER ONE

My Aunt Brennan had three breasts, none of which was much service to her. Perfectly equipped to suckle Cerberus, had that three-headed guardian of the underworld been more than a myth, she was condemned by our village as a witch and chained to a wall, till it fell time for the Gloucester Assizes.

It was not only her mammalian abundance, however, which brought misery to Aunt Brennan, but her indiscretion. She confided in various folk, most of them gossips, that she had been visited at midnight by a talking mouse that had coupled with her.

The rodent's name was Bergamoy and he was immortal, having been born into the world in its beginnings, sometime between Genesis and Deuteronomy. Being the only creature of his kind, Bergamoy had wandered the world in extreme frustration for several aeons, unable to find a mate, until he had at last come upon a beast which in spite of its peculiar aspect presented an opportunity for satisfaction of the mouse's rabid appetites.

Two hundred years' pondering of Aunt Brennan's description have convinced me that Bergamoy's light-of-love was a duck-billed platypus.

We Hazells were tied farmers, and had been resident in the Gloucestershire village of Pepton Harbinger for centuries. Although we considered Aunt Brennan's three breasts strange and on the face of it no gift from God, we were aware that nature sometimes produces an eccentricity, such as a five-legged calf or two-headed chicken. In fact, had it not been for Bergamoy, who seemed to be a genuine and inexcusable incubus although none of us ever saw him, the natural magnanimity of our village might have spared Aunt Brennan.

As it was she was blamed for divers local catastrophies, such as the murrain which smote many cattle, and the death of a farmer at the horns of a bull hitherto deemed placid.

I remember, the night before Aunt Brennan died, going to

see her as she languished in chains, fettered to the wall of the poorhouse.

'Ah, Wheatcroft, come to see the witch, have you?'

'I don't believe you are one.'

'If I were I wouldn't be here, would I, boy? I'd be cavorting above the heads of the people on my broomstick, wouldn't I? And sending down curses that would satisfy Satan at his most vengeful. Not only dead cattle everywhere there'd be, but dead childer. I'd bring back the plague, I'd call the Black Death to perch here like the summer swallows, so I would. I'd pick the hay in the fields and turn it into jewels, streaming through my fingers while the devil and I watched them melt; I'd fly with Satan, clinging to his back and gladly inhaling the sulphurous stink of him.'

Her voice dropped. 'But I'm not a witch, boy, I'm just a poor woman, and if there were any justice or any reason in the world I would never have been accused.

'I used to believe in God, but now that He has forsaken me, and the devil too by the look of it, who shall I believe in? It's unjust that I should have to leave this world without comfort.'

'Leave this world? But you won't be condemned to death, Aunt Brennan.'

'No one's going to have a chance to condemn me, not at the Assizes. I've heard whispering, Wheatcroft, and I've seen sniggering, I've seen the twisted faces of people who fear me as they mock. I know what's in store, and there'll be no mercy from any high quarter here; Squire's away and his bailiff lost some of his own kine to the murrain that I am blamed for.'

I was afraid for her. 'What will happen, Aunt Brennan?' I whispered. She shivered, her chains clanking.

'I've seen it before, boy. The ordeal by ducking. The bailiff will come, smirking, and dangle his keys before me. "Come, my fine one," he'll say, "we're going to make you clean, we're going to wash away your sins in the lake yonder."

'So I shall be taken, and strapped into the ducking-stool, and heavily dipped until there's more water in me than air, and I shall be drowned.'

'I'm sure there's a God, Aunt Brennan,' I said, trying to reassure her; the Reverend Adam Herrick, our priest, sounded so confident about Him, interpreting His Word three times on Sundays with the intensity of one who broke bread with Him each morning and was privy to all His plans.

'Ah, you're still too young to think any different,' trying to raise her hand to pat my cheek. 'God lives in the young, but He leaves them later. You mark my words, men cease to be godly when they lose their innocence.'

'But you've often called me a little devil when I've thrown a stone or dropped an egg.'

'Happen I have, but you won't be really evil till later on.' She stared at me through the gloom, and shivered. 'Pray for me tomorrow,' she muttered.

'I will, Aunt. I'll pray for the comfort of your soul.'

'Pray also for the comfort of my body, child. Pray that by some miracle I shall not drown.'

'Perhaps they will not come at all.'

'They'll come, boy. I can already hear their laughter surging through the air—'tis a terrible thing, the laughter of tormentors.'

I had to ask my aunt a question ere I left her. 'Aunt Brennan, did you really take a mouse to bed?'

'Why, I'd be too great a fardel for such a small beast.'

'They say that the mouse was your familiar, a gift from Satan; they say that Bergamoy came to you and lusted for you and was taken into the warmth of your couch.'

'He came to me in a dream, and asked for comfort. "Comfort is in woman," he told me, "and in a chill world every woman is a refuge." '

'They say also in the village that Bergamoy is evil and corrupts, and seeks sanctuary up a nun's skirt when he can.'

'Then surely he is a mouse of God, not of Satan,' Aunt Brennan laughed. 'After all, boy, God is in all things, is He not? He was a brown mouse,' she added.

The air was moist with evening; I shivered.

'Be you gone now, boy,' Aunt Brennan murmured, ' 'tis no good the two of us dying through dampness. Off with you, my dear, and remember: pray for me tomorrow.'

'I shall,' I promised. I stared at her as she crouched in the shadows, and wondered at man's cruelty, that sought to snatch away the life of Aunt Brennan; as I walked away she became a rustle, a panting and a muttering and, as I walked farther away, a weeping.

A few further paces towards my home and Aunt Brennan was already become a memory.

CHAPTER TWO

AUNT BRENNAN died an oblique death under an alchemist's sky, dark gold and menacing green, overlaid with cloud mauve as a bruise. The sun was furtive in its rising, as though not wishing to cast its light on the mob about to torment my aunt for their own devilish amusement and the love of God.

Down to the pond with her, poor pale woman, her dignity blown to tatters by their ridicule. Into the ducking-stool, strap her into this parody of a child's plaything, this evil see-saw, and plunge her into the water. I watch from a distance as my father's sister is drawn up, weed streaming green from her sodden bonnet; time for a glance at the sky and a half-breath before again they duck her, and watch as eagerly for the bubbles of her breath as for salvation. How often I have noted since, that there is no fertilizer like human misery to bring to blossom human merriment.

The people of the village, Aunt Brennan's friends, turned as though by the magic of which she was accused, into demons, indulged implacably their urge to hurt by not raising her from the water.

The diminishing bubbles climbed desperately to the surface, each beseeching Brennan's tormentors for mercy, but each was denied. When at last Brennan was brought up, she was dead.

Great was the disappointment of the mob, for had they not had her trial to look forward to? As she sat, head hanging loosely, the water dripping off her, her clothes clinging to her thin old frame, the laughter turned into cries of disappointment, which in turn, at last, quieted, suffocated, under a thick mantle of shame.

They untied Aunt Brennan, bent her over and watched the water pour from her; I saw a minnow that she had drawn into her lungs writhe on the ground before managing to cast itself back into its element.

I moved away, turned awhile later to watch the crowd surround Aunt Brennan as if in a strange, compulsive reverence, and though as I watched I felt the hatred die from me I knew that I must leave the village, for I was young enough to believe that one could flee the sins of this world and that Utopia might be found beyond the next hill.

My father and mother I loved, but I had regarded them as gods, being immortal, and they had quailed before their neighbours' determination to extinguish Aunt Brennan as though to defend their own flesh and blood would be to deny that of the Lord Jesus, which my aunt had allegedly profaned.

When I took up my belongings no one tried to forbid me, save my mother with tears; my father raised his fist as though to strike me for my impiety in deserting him and the future he had thought to have in me, but saw in my eyes the futility of his gesture and opened his fist to offer me, instead of a blow, a blessing.

Lonely is the road from evil, lonelier than that other road I had to take, the road from childhood, yet I felt that to stay with my family would be to expose myself to an even greater solitude.

I set off on the road to London.

CHAPTER THREE

LONDON lay ahead of me under a parasol of charcoal smoke. I had not seen so large a town in my life, although I remembered, five years before when I was in my ninth year, going with my mother and father to Cheltenham. London, however, was vast, and I approached it with apprehension and wonder.

Just outside the village of Kensington I saw a highwayman laughingly hold up a coach; I hid trembling behind an oak as he sat with the grin beneath his mask watching valuables landing to the right and left of his horse's forefeet; his companion rode out of the bushes behind him and gathered them up, and with a shout of thanks the two galloped away.

I came to Chelsea, with its roads ringing harsh music from the wheels of carts and carriages, and the rich ripe smell of midden overwhelming in the hot mid-morning. The stench hung over the city as it had done in Pepton Harbinger over the cesspit; London it seemed to me was itself a cesspit, with its open drains in the centre of the streets and the ordure steaming everywhere, fresh from the bowels of men and horses.

The people, too, had the look of fungus about them, being white and altogether less healthy in aspect than country folk; wherever I looked there were men voiding themselves against walls or over the drains, and ladies emptying chamber-pots with a great splash on to the cobbles.

Yet there was a magical majesty about London; the boats on the river, the church steeples reaching everywhere up to God as though at the same time wishing to point Him out and attract His attention and favours, the great egg which Sir Christopher Wren had laid atop St. Paul's glowing and glistening in the distance, the shouts of the carters and hackney coaches, and the cries of the street vendors with their 'lily white vinegar', 'strawberry ripe' and 'physic for your digestion or a tormentor for your fleas'.

The flies formed a loud, shimmering screen about my

head, swooped away to riper attractions steaming on the cobbles, dispersed their squadrons to attend to a mackerel barge under full sail nearby. At this moment I nearly turned back, but a gust of wind blew away flies and stench long enough for me to realize that London was my opportunity, London my personal adventure. I would return to Pepton Harbinger only when I was rich and could build myself a house of grandeur, and call upon the respect and the penitence of those who had drowned Aunt Brennan.

Here in London I need not feel too homesick for the countryside and its attractions; I was tripped up by a squealing porker which had hurled itself from a nearby house, its owner bearing a knife in loud pursuit of his dinner.

'Stop the beast!' he screamed at me, as I picked myself up, 'the animal is demented! Sight of the pot in which he was to be cooked has quite deranged him. Stop him!' Without waiting for me to apologize for my inability to obey he rushed down the street brandishing his knife and calling upon Heaven and Hell alike to deliver back to him his pig; laughter flowed like slops from the upper storey of the houses which leaned as though to kiss across the street.

There was a distant scream, and soon the pig was borne back across its owner's shoulder, its throat cut and its fair lashes lying along its cheek as if grinning at its prank.

'You look hungry, boy—now that we are to feed perhaps you would like to join us?'

'Thank you, sir,' but how he stank; I decided that he must be a dye-maker, or possibly a boiler of soap. Nevertheless, I was more than ready for a slice of pork or fat bacon, having finished my own provisions the previous evening.

The inside of my host's house was dark, not so much owing to the absence of windows as to the thick greasy smoke which weaved about it; it turned out that I was right and that he was a soap-boiler by the name of Jenkins.

'This is my wife, Mrs. Jenkins, and this is——'

'My name is Hazell, Wheatcroft Hazell.'

Mrs. Jenkins, who bore a remarkable resemblance to the porker which her husband flung into her arms, gave a dry sniff and went into the kitchen. Several fowls strolled about, one of which, flapping on to a table to excrete over a loaf, was soundly kicked and fled squawking into the yard.

In the soap room, vats of boiling and putrescent liquid

heaved and spat, the air being so dense that I felt suffocated.

'I need an apprentice, boy,' said Jenkins. 'Can you afford to pay me five shillings a month in order to learn the trade?'

Fortunately I did not have to lie about my money, having none; I have never liked to lie, perhaps because we enjoy most that at which we are best, and I have only ever been good at lying when other people's happiness depended on it, such as when I have committed adultery.

I found myself the victim of a contest between that part of me which was demanding to leave the soap-boiler and his stink before I had eaten, and that which deemed it wiser to stay, as the source of future meals was as yet undetermined. In the event, I strayed through the kitchen to the door of the yard and stared intently at the hens as though I had never seen such creatures before, praying the while that the wind would continue to blow the smoke to the other side of the house.

Surely London was not entirely a cauldron, with all its trees drooping under the weight of industry's oily residue; it was inconceivable that the king and his nobles should be content to live in such a miasma.

'Perhaps, Wheatcroft, you would be willing to labour for me for a while—I'll give you a wage and your food. You can bed down in the straw belowstairs.'

Jenkins eyed me in the way of a priest who has just granted a minor penance and expects to witness gratitude shining through the grille of the confessional; he himself represents God as he sits there and in so doing becomes for a moment God himself, and even God appreciates thanks for His omnipotence.

'You are very kind, sir,' I answered, watching the expectant smile dimple Jenkins' full lips, that overlapped his mean pointed chin, 'but I cannot stay.'

'Why then, if you cannot stay you had better go at once.'

My stomach rumbled emptily and Jenkins laughed.

'I thought you were offering me hospitality, sir,' I said.

'It's none the less hospitable for being earned, is it?' and now he looked less like a man offering a starveling a meal and more like a butcher confronting his sacrifice.

'There, it's ready now,' put in Mrs. Jenkins, smirking under her grimy bonnet and prodding the supine and crisp porker with a finger. 'For payment he can help me scour the pots.'

'So that you reap the harvest of my kindness,' grumbled Jenkins. He shrugged, led the way into the parlour, a small room with a heavy oak table that was gouged and marked as if it had been used as a shield, and took up his knife. He heaped our platters generously, and forgetting him and the smell of his house I attended upon my meal voraciously and ate my fill.

After I had scoured her pots and bidden Mrs. Jenkins farewell, I shouldered my few belongings and went out into the street.

'Are you sure you won't stay, boy?' Jenkins asked, lightly gripping my arm.

'Thank you, but I must be on my way.'

'Even though you don't know where your way lies?'

'I may not know exactly where it lies, but I know where it lies not.'

'Ah, you think you know that, but you may find things very different, boy. Very different indeed. I became a soap-boiler because my father was a soap-boiler and I admired my father. But your destiny isn't as easily set, so you aren't going to travel along as straight a road as you think.'

I smiled, disbelieving him.

'Look out for the Press Gangs then,' he called after me, having reluctantly released my arm.

I glanced back at him, waved my hand and laughed.

CHAPTER FOUR

I FOUND apprenticeship with a firm of merchants: Mendip & Hozier, of Cheapside.

Cranston Mendip was a genial man, yet a man of conflict. His arse was in conflict with his breeches, his stomach with his old yellow corded waistcoat and his complexion with his wigs.

If Mr. Mendip had one cross to bear, it was that he was bald and eyed covetously every man he saw who had natural hair, especially if curly. In order to compensate for his lack of hair he possessed a variety of wigs which would have done credit to a theatre wardrobe.

Daily Mr. Mendip would enter upon the stage of his warehouse in order to show off his newest wig. One day he would sport a great russet mane, so that he looked like a benign little lion; on another day a cascading black peruke turned my merry master into a Spanish grandee. Most in accord with his drink-veined cheeks and small nose made majestic by hogsheads of porter was his blonde selection; on Wednesday he was a Viking, except for his smiling eyes, on Thursday a Hun, on Friday perhaps his top was that of a Dresden shepherdess, but his bottom was always a ploughman's.

'You're learning fast, Wheatcroft. You have an aptitude for the work.'

'Thank you, sir.'

'The romance of trade, Wheatcroft, the romance of trade, 'tis to be desired almost as much as its profit.' He would lightly tap my shoulder with the stick he used to clean his teeth—arise, Sir Wheatcroft, and tell me of the British Colonies whence we import so much. 'That grain, Wheatcroft, has travelled by sailing ship across the great Atlantic from Amerikey, from the Middle Colonies. So has that flour, while the tobacco in those sacks yonder was grown in the fields of Virginia and Maryland. But I smell trouble for those who enjoy a pipe of an evening, Wheatcroft; the news from Amerikey is bad.'

'I have read something of it, sir.'

'It is my own personal, though highly treasonable view,' in a low voice, this morning's silver wig that framed his sallow face giving him the look of an elderly Lebanese conspirator, 'that George the Third is mad. And his government also. What a collection of draggle-arsed ninnyhammers, none of whom ever bothered to go to Amerikey. Probably wouldn't have been allowed to land by any colonist or Indian in his right mind. Lord Bute, Lord Grenville, Lord Rockingham, Lord Grafton—they sound like a group of idlers and felons in a miscreants' nursery. Bute plays the flute, Rockingham rides a rocking horse, Grafton grafts—now we have Lord North, who never deigns to look west and try to understand it.

'Some of these colonials, Wheatcroft, live better than most of us. When I visited my friend and supplier James Farquharson in Richmond he astonished me with his luxury, and to the manner born, Wheatcroft, not as though it fitted him as ill as some of these perukes of mine,' taking off his silver one and standing thoughtfully, a small bald canary that had fallen from its perch.

'War means smuggling, Wheatcroft, and smuggling means danger. Prices go up, but so does the cost. Smuggling doesn't mean just financial cost, finance is something that can always be paid, because that's the reason for it. But to pay with your life—much subtler, my boy, much dearer.'

He walked away, absently putting his wig on askew, and I continued to work at my ledger until looking up I saw the other partner in the firm, Clive Hosier, standing with a frown on his face as he prodded a sack of Georgian flour.

Hozier was basically a small man who had been stretched. Evidently designed by nature to be of medium height, he had been drawn by some Procrustean imp to a height of six feet three. His face was geological, cavitied and crannied, pock-marks winding like footsteps up the craggy slopes and down the steep ravines of his cheeks to cease abruptly under his elongated black eyes. These were complemented by the perpendicular reflection of his nostrils, which swooped under flared eaves as though striving to outdistance the nose of which they were part.

Thin as a heron, cheerful as a gibbet, Hozier frowned and sighed. 'My boy, I sense war with the Thirteen Colonies. Do you know what that means?'

'It means that trade will become difficult, sir, and that means smuggling and danger.'

'You are remarkably swift on the uptake, Wheatcroft.'

'I have just been talking with Mr. Mendip, sir, who is exactly of your opinion.'

'He talks too freely. However, the Boston Tea Party is no secret, and in fact the rule of law is presently collapsing in Massachusetts, which is why General Gage has been appointed Governor there. He won't be able to do much. If the colonists themselves think that the East India Company should be reimbursed for the loss of its tea they don't need General Gage to teach them justice. If they believe that the East India Company and George the Third deserved to lose profit and taxes it will, in my estimation, take more than a military governor to make them change their minds.'

'What do you think will happen, sir?'

'I've ventured the opinion already that war will happen. I think it, Mr. Mendip thinks it, everyone I have encountered in the taverns and coffee-houses thinks it. And it's damnably unnecessary. We need statesmen, not poltroons,' indulging in a little well-merited treason himself.

'Perhaps they may come to their senses, sir.'

'Most unlikely. They have no senses to come to. Even Pitt—he has admitted to sympathizing with the colonists, but still he says they must be subordinate. They will hardly take kindly to being told that in all laws relating to trade and navigation this is the mother country and they the children.'

'If there is war, sir, shall I have to leave you?'

'You are legally bound to serve your apprenticeship here, Wheatcroft, and we are legally bound to instruct you. Furthermore, my partner and I are pleased with your progress—I feel that I can tell you that without encouragement of your vanity—and as Mr. Mendip has sired only daughters, and I have lost my three male issue to plague, there may eventually, in the fullness of time, be a singular opportunity for your promotion here.'

'Thank you, sir.'

'Reciprocity—a high-minded notion, worth remembering. You serve us well, so shall we serve you.' A brief smile, a fissuring of his craggy cheeks and Hozier went out.

Two months later England and the Thirteen Colonies were at war.

CHAPTER FIVE

'DAMNABLE, damnable, damnable.' Wearing a white wig which seem like an urn of fermented cream, a vast cheesy cascade of ripples and curls, my master Mendip stood chewing on the stem of an empty pipe.

' 'Tis a war of attrition,' he told me angrily. 'Here we are two years since war was declared, and what have we? No victory, vast profits for some and little for others, and Sir James Wright begging like a one-legged mendicant for provision. "No troops, no money, nor orders or instructions, and a wild multitude gathering fast. Not so much as a ship of war—these things, My Lord, are too much." And whence comes that plea to Lord Dartmouth? Virginia. A loyal colony, Wheatcroft, a pleasant and delightful place, as I have told you many times past.

'Is my friend Farquharson to become my enemy? It would be less costly for me to choose my enemy here, for to have Lords Dartmouth or Bute or Rockingham as enemies could, judging from their success against the Americans, bring only benefit.' He started to perform a little dance, singing his treasonous refrain about their noble lordships whom he so detested, breaking off every so often to utter vigorous abuse.

'After the war, Wheatcroft, what sort of trade then? Shall America be able to absorb all her own produce? If that be so, we are finished. We are ruined. And if America needs still to sell her trade abroad, shall we be invited to smoke the pipe of peace with her? To inhale her fine Virginian tobacco? More likely it will be the French who will prance about at full puff, farting in their commodes and covering the unfragrant perfumes of their digestive excesses with the weed.'

'Do you not think that your friendship with Mr. Farquharson will survive the war, sir?'

'Possibly, boy, provided that he be on the winning side. If he be on the losing, I doubt he will ever forgive us. But then,' he added, 'there will not be a winning side—we shall both be the losers. Only the French are likely to gain, prowling round the carcass of our colonies and seizing what they may.' His wig lurched downwards, so that very little of him seemed left outside it.

'When feeling is enraged there is but one sovereign remedy, Wheatcroft. A bottle of sack and a good dinner. You are invited to partake of both at my establishment.'

'Thank you, sir.' I roomed in Maiden Lane and although not starving found myself frequently hungry, in spite of my masters' giving me board at my place of work. My country boyhood had endowed me with a good appetite which was seldom satisfied by the victuals I enjoyed in London. Also, I spent such money as I had on the theatre, for I much enjoyed going there and transmuting myself, with the actors, into different individuals and their lives. In fact, I felt often tempted to tread the boards myself, but was bound by my apprenticeship as firmly as by my self-esteem, for I knew I had little talent for the theatre but much for trade.

My master Mendip lived hard by the fields of Soho, whither we went on horseback, Mr. Mendip riding with exaggerated rising and falling in the manner of a skiff in rough water, while his horse, a surly knave called Elphrick, looked often over his shoulder with teeth bared as though to bite my poor master in half, and then raised his tail in anal salute before dunging in the least attractive places, such as the doorways of houses and on top of market stalls, which incurred my master much odium. In fact, on more than one occasion it was his sumptuous wig which saved his life, for a seller of oranges shitten on by Elphrick was so enraged that he hurled after his rider a tankard, which scoured my master's pate but did not crack it.

Arrived at the Mendip house we found a fine roast on the spit and Mistress Mendip merry in a new gown. My master embraced her as passionately as his tailor allowed, for his clothes were so tight that they imposed on him a severe measure of decorum.

The Mendip daughters came into the pleasant drawing-room and embraced their father, after which they greeted me with less of rapture but, in the case of Kate, the eldest, more of intimacy; she had a glance whose authority quenched expectation but yet inspired hope. In face of it I lowered my eyes modestly, yet hoped they were not subservient, for if a man balance his modesty subtly, a maid may be tempted to tease him by raising her shift, but will not do so if modesty seem so deep-seated that naught but embarrassment will come of such a jape.

'A glass of sack, Wheatcroft?'

'Thank you, sir.' I took the glass, red-veined as the nose which my master at once dipped into its fellow, and drank. The fire threw its glow on the ceiling and cast swift-moving shadows across the raised embroidery of the chairs. We sat down, I giving silent thanks to God that my master was a kindly man.

Kate and her sisters left the room, and something of myself went with them. The firelight coaxed lustful thoughts into my brain; the sack had gone straight to my loins.

Mr. Mendip was squinting into his glass, silent in thought or perhaps relishing the comfort of contemplating nothing.

A tall clock ticked in the corner, a cat purred and Pepton Harbinger and its pond were far away.

After several more glasses, we went into dinner. In the centre of the table reposed the roast, a hog with a smile on its face and the round, shining gag of an apple in its mouth lest it squeal against its fate.

Kate sat opposite me; were I to sink on to the base of my spine and extend my foot at full stretch, I could touch her foot with mine. I doubted she would welcome such impertinence.

The sack murmured a question in my brain, wrought a fantasy of longing. Might not Kate later in the evening, when the household was abed, come to me? Vain thought, said the pig, rump assailed by Mr. Mendip's knife. Perhaps, argued my manhood, safely concealed in its rising vigour by the cloth upon the table, perhaps she feels as you do, perhaps she will indeed come to your chamber, and indulge in tender and joyous display.

Darling Kate, I thought, regarding her, and fell lustily upon my meal.

CHAPTER SIX

THOUGHTS of Kate forced my virginity to press ever more hardly on me during agitated nights; I dreamed of her smiling face, and her long dark hair framed both it and my dreams. I longed to toy with Kate, and with her to shed the heavy cloak of innocence; I desired to know how she was made, the scent and the taste of her.

I had heard how there were certain women who possessed a natural perfume that quite sent men mad, so that they went on all fours like dogs, begging for a kerchief that such ladies had worn. Was there similar magic below my Kate's bodice, would the raising of her skirts reveal to me several sorts of Paradise?

As I slipped into the depths of evening contemplation, my Kate thus sweetly imposed her torment on me, and so much did I desire her that my longing fanned out to encompass woman as a whole. Love no doubt sweetened the dish, but any comely damsel would be able to relieve me of the desire that had become too much to bear.

It was during an autumn evening that I finally flung away my restraint, for restraint had been chained to pride, that forbade me to pay for my indulgence. I was resolved to take a young harlot, and transmute her into Kate, to lie in her arms and pretend they were those of my love.

Perhaps the intention so to do had come upon me some time since, for I had husbanded as much money as I could, and had written to my father for further bounty which he duly sent, though not without protest.

My masters had been kind enough to purchase for me some clothes that had been little used; I donned the finest of them, put on my red suede openwork gloves and set out for Covent Garden, whence I expected to find my portion of lascivious frivolity.

Entering the White Cock tavern, which had an enticing reputation, I ordered a tankard of mulled ale and leant grandly against a post, conscious of my appearance, which owed such handsomeness as it possessed to one of Mr.

Mendip's wigs, only mildly used, a chestnut confection which might have owed some of its body to Elphrick's tail, for it was tough of fibre and slightly smelly.

I sipped my ale and warily eyed an elderly harlot whose black teeth were exposed in smiling at me; as she began to move towards me I turned away my gaze, as though unconsciously, and inspected my cuff. The woman passed close to me, but did not speak; doubtless she had supped full and often on rebuff.

The tavern was full of noise, of bawdy jest and laughter, and ripe with the odour of my fellow wassailers—it was a happy sty, and I tried not to diminish its gaiety by being too moral in my feelings, but in London, even after two years, my country boy's nostrils were still prone to suffer offence.

Amidst the stink I caught a fragrance, something of violets. I looked about me, and saw near by a maid who had just come in. She wore a demure expression, but to my delight and, I must confess, apprehension, knowing that I was now set upon an irrevocable course, there was no doubting her occupation. Her bonnet was of an outstanding red, her cheeks were lightly roughed, her lips dyed a faint carmine. I rejoiced at her subtle harlotry.

'Will you take a drink with me?'

'I will, sir. A glass of porter.'

I gave the order to the host, who returned with porter and a further tankard of ale.

'Are you a gentleman of much experience?' her eyes mocking.

I forbore to lie. 'I am a virgin, and exceeding desirous of ridding myself of such a burden.'

'I was a virgin once, before I met the whoremaster. Billy Black was his name, who started me on this career of charity.'

'Of charity?'

'Of charity and reward, let us say. For separating a man from his passion is surely a charity beyond mere price?'

'I suppose it is. I—I would not long delay.'

She laughed. 'What is your name, young man?'

'Wheat——' I hesitated. I wanted Kate to call me by my name. This harlot, though I longed for her ardently, would possess a part of me if she knew how I was called; I wanted her body but not her intimacy.

'Wheat?'

'That is my nickname, for I come from the country. My real name is Dick.'

'And mine is Maud. Will you come with me now?'

'I am ready.'

'Shall I come to your house, or you to mine? I have a room above a fruiterer's shop across the market.'

'Then let us repair to yours, for I live further afield.'

'And cannot wait,' with a saucy grin. I was pleased to see that she had all her teeth, and that they were white.

'And cannot wait.'

She took me by the hand, there was a drunken cheer from a market porter at the sight, and shouts of encouragement from his colleagues. 'Ravish the wench well, young master. And do not forget to remove your wig!'

'They seek only to jest,' said Maud, 'and not to mortify. Come.' We were outside the tavern door in the cool evening. I became oblivious of the spectacle before me, the horses and carriages, the great theatre, the passers-by hurrying towards the joys of tavern or coffee house; I was hastening to a deeper joy, provided that I could acquit myself as a young man should, and was about to bid farewell to my burden.

'Do you know how a woman is made, Dick?'

'I am fairly certain.'

'Let me then make you fully certain. A woman's body should be more than a guess.'

Off came her red silk stockings; her white chemise was quickly the sole garment left to her. She turned slowly towards me, smiling. 'Am I beautiful?'

Her beauty was peerless, but my lust choked me, so that I was unable to tell her so. I no longer saw a woman but a goddess, earthy and marvellously attainable. Dear Maud, how consumed I am by you, even before you help me to remove my clothes, so swiftly, with such sweet skill, the fragrance of you in my nostrils, violets accompanying the passion of my undoing, my blood beating in my body. uniting the throbbing of brain, pulse and loins.

Her touch. Her hand was soft and unhurried, an explorer of no mean stature. Her hand coaxed me to magnificence, yet she was soothing, murmuring endearments, pausing so that I could save myself from exhausting my delight prematurely.

When I left her I loved her. I loved her and I loved Kate, but this time my love for Kate was as my love of God, a thing ethereal, of the heart but not of the stomach. I was in a daze of wonderment.

I walked through the market, my pockets empty but my heart full, my wig stuffed into a pocket of my coat that the clear air might get to my head.

I had made a good start in London, I would serve my masters well and strive, that one day Kate and the business would be mine. I was a man of ambition because I was now a man.

A hand fell on my shoulder, spun me round. A face was grinning at me, as were other faces round it. A lanthorn was help up to my face, causing me to screw up my eyes.

'A bonny lad for the King's Navy,' the lanthorn holder said.

'I am an apprentice. I may not be impressed.' I could not believe that I would be the victim of a press gang; it was forbidden to take an apprentice and thus violate his contract with his master.

'You may not be impressed? Not if you have money in your pockets, lad. Sufficient money not to need the King's shilling.'

'I have no money, but I am an apprentice.'

'I thought apprentices always wore a leather apron, to keep us away,' one of the sailors said.

'Yes, like a crucifix against a vampire,' rejoined one of the others.

'The King has great need of sailors in his war against the Colonies. Surely that stirs your sense of patriotism, lad?'

'I love my country, yet am I still an apprentice.'

'Enough of talking. Will you come with us peaceably, or shall we hit you on the head?'

I lashed out at the lanthorn, which fell to the ground and went out. I turned and ran as fast as I could, hearing heavy footsteps behind me. A hand lighted again on my shoulder, I shook it clear. There was a whistling through the air, a loud crack, a burst of stars, and I plummeted like a soul to hell, into a void.

CHAPTER SEVEN

MY Aunt Brennan came to me and eyed me intently. Save that it was not my Aunt Brennan but her familiar, the mouse Bergamoy. A big mouse, a vast mouse, not a mouse at all, but a rat.

I came to consciousness. My head ached and my mouth was like the inside of the Fleet Ditch. Somebody laughed, the rat retreated into shadow.

About me, woodwork creaked to the rhythm of men retching. I was in a small hole heavily peopled, the sky a dream. The sky no longer existed, it was something clean and clear far beyond the confines of the hole.

'Where am I?' I asked a pair of fangs glistening in the dark a foot away from me.

'In the King's Navy, bullyboyo. Aboard the receiving ship *Fervent*, anchored off Tower Hill. You'll be out of here in a minute, to see the doctor and make sure you've enough life in you to gain a slow death. I know, I've served in the Navy before, first as a regular sailor, and now as one of the Lord Mayor's Men.'

'What are you fleeing from?' for the Lord Mayor's Men were those who sought redemption from public disgrace through service aboard, to which they were committed by the city magistrates.

'Newgate or the Fleet, that's what I flee from. Two nights ago, I embarked on a street frolic, relieving of his wallet a gentleman who had drunk too much. I was apprehended, having had somewhat much to drink myself, and here I am. It's not so bad when you get used to it—at least as a sailor you can earn pride in yourself. But be warned, bullyboyo—the punishment in the Navy don't often fit the crime. There's nothing I can think of deserves a whipping through the fleet, f'r instance, with every fresh man jack of a bosun or bosun's mate laying into you with the cat. From ship to ship you're rowed, chained to a mast, and the bosun of each ship is permitted to swing at you until you've suffered your sentence.'

I found myself trembling. 'How many lashes?'

'Sometimes five hundred. Often a man can only take a small portion of his punishment, and is then nursed back to health to receive the next portion. I knew a sailor once, Rennison was his monniker, who spent three years serving the same punishment. He died just after the five hundredth stroke and was buried at sea with honours. He was a man of endurance if you like.'

'What had he done?'

'He was impressed, just like you, bullyboyo, and tried to escape.'

I was shivering more, striving to conquer the ague of my fear but with little success. 'What is your name?' I asked my companion.

'Joe Robinson. And yours?'

'Wheatcroft Hazell.'

'A country sounding name.'

'My family are tied farmers.'

'And now you've bondage of a different nature. But steady, Wheatcroft, keep your hatch shut unless you're spoken to, and pray we've a good captain and not one of your idle well-born nincompoops whose cruelty is his plaything, to vent on another life to despoil it without cause. Hush!' he whispered, although it was himself who had been talking, 'you're about to be called.'

I might have been forgiven for mistaking his meaning, thinking momentarily that he meant that I was to appear before my Maker, but was disabused of this fancy by a seaman holding a lanthorn.

'Get you aloft, boy. The doctor will examine you.'

The doctor had a white face soft as a woman's, and a gentle voice. He glanced at me and said quietly: 'You look a strong man. Is there any reason why you should not serve your King?'

'I serve him by helping to victual his ships, sir. I am apprenticed to a firm of merchants.'

'A sailor's life will become you better than trade in these troublous times, boy. Trade is for those too old to fight. Your name?'

'Hazell, sir.'

My name was written by an officer in a ledger, after which he glared at me as though we had been old foes and informed me that the admiral's tender would convey me and my companions to the *Nore*, where we would be called to our ships.

Accordingly, a while later, we were placed aboard the tender and ordered down into the hold, so that the sky, in whose existence I had come again to believe, became once more an illusion.

Above us, round the rim of the hatchway, a guard of marines was placed, their muskets loaded and bayonets fixed, and as it had been with the officer who had attended my examination by the doctor I marvelled at the impression of enmity which seemed such a necessary part of the enlistment of a sailor who, either of his own will or the villainous practice of impressment, was ready to fight for his country.

Fortunately, we were not kept long below, for the officer on deck soon understood that many of us were overcome by foul air. As we mounted to daylight it was difficult to understand how we might best perform our martial duties, for scarcely a man of us but was not filthy, the vermin jumping from his shoulders and his scalp popping with fleas.

On our arrival at the *Nore*, boats from the receiving ships came alongside to fetch us aboard the vessels of our destiny, among which we were distributed.

Here an evil was perpetrated against us by the old hands, for our clothes, shoes, socks and other belongings were taken by mysterious means. One moment a man would have his socks and blankets hard by him, the next he was deprived of these commodities and left in sorry plight, it being hard to retain dignity and pugnacity when wearing only one shoe.

I later found out that a hook cast on a line from above, and difficult to discern in the darkness between decks, was the method used to accomplish this saucy plunder.

As I had been taken with only the clothes I wore and my master's wig stuffed into my pocket, I had little to lose, and ever afterwards, when I came to be well endowed with possessions, taught myself to reflect that were I compelled by circumstance to give up all I had to follow the Lord, either to Heaven or the bankruptcy courts, I could do so with equanimity.

Having been supplied with slops, whose price was deducted from our pay, we spent a day or two aboard our ships while orders came in from line-of-battle vessels for men and boys to complete their complements. Joe Robinson, several others and I were drafted to the *Pride*, then fitting out to join Admiral Howe, who we soon learned was to proceed against the Virginian George Washington, now come to eminence on the Colonist side.

We were to blockade New York in support of the admiral's brother, General Howe, who had recently suffered a grievous defeat at Bunker Hill, before the War of Independence was properly under way.

The captain of the *Pride* was a Member of Parliament, Captain Raymond Swerve, whose main recreation was to play cards in his cabin during the day and wassail with his friends to the music of a group of musicians at night. This captain was one of those who believed that cruel punishments were the same thing as discipline, and rewarded the slightest offence, or for that matter no offence, with a flogging at the gangway or at the least an order to start the victim.

Every boatswain's mate carried a rope's end in his pocket, and when ordered to start a man commanded him to pull off his jacket, and sometimes his waistcoat, and beat him until ordered to stop. The beating was well applied, owing to the captain's promise to start the boatswain's mate if it were not, and occasionally, if the mate's arm became tired, another boatswain's mate would take over. Being not tied up, the victim would attempt to run, or ward off the blows, which occasioned bad cuts to his face or head.

I discovered subsequently that starting was so common aboard His Majesty's ships that no minute was made of it in the log book; the two consolations granted us where Captain Swerve was concerned were, firstly, that he reserved the order to start a man to himself, instead of sharing it with his junior officers, and secondly, that he did not relish battle.

When we were ordered down to Portsmouth, whence we were to sail for America, Captain Swerve remembered that he had an even more pressing duty than to fight for his country, namely to represent a part of it in parliament, and took horse for London.

Our battle captain, Captain Gaunt, was a different manner of man altogether, who believed that a seaman who has nothing to fear from his own side will fight the better against the other.

Untainted by dread of unfair punishment, we speedily

became a happy ship, although when we were anchored at evening off the Downs one of our number tried to escape. Jumping overboard, he landed up to his waist in mud and had to choose whether to drown or face a more dramatic form of extinction; his portion was to be verbally reprimanded, which did much for his loyalty and for ours.

In fact, I had considered trying to escape myself, for I despaired of my kind masters' thinking I had deserted them, and that Kate might marry and become a dowager before I returned from the war. Joe Robinson had cautioned me: 'I know it's your last chance, bullyboyo, and take it if you've a mind to, but don't forget the rope. You're only a lad, you've got twenty or thirty years ahead of you, bullyboyo; you may survive the shot but not the noose, if they catch you.'

So I stayed; four weeks after my impressment I and my comrades set sail for New York.

CHAPTER EIGHT

THE first broadside initiating me into war was preceded by the fifer's rendering my favourite tune, the lively 'Nancy Dawson'. It was not so much the melody which appealed to me as the fact that it heralded the splicing of the mainbrace at the sounding of one bell, a gill of rum and three of water laced with sugar and acid of lemon being the portion of every man and boy aboard.

On this occasion, scarcely had the grog been ladled out than the lookout shouted from above that he spied a sail on the horizon to larboard; the fifer ceased his jig and blew the call to action stations; we gulped our grog and rushed to the guns.

The sail turned out to be attached to a French ship. As the French seemed unable to cease being our enemies for more than a few years at a time, and were presently causing us severe aggravation through the machinations of Louis XVI and his Foreign Minister the Comte de Vergennes, who supported the rebel Colonists, we were eager to loose a broadside in the Frenchman's direction.

Not only would we be thus venting our patriotic wrath but might be on our way to taking as prize some hogsheads of wine and cognac brandy. However, we first had to undergo some punishment ourselves, for the enemy, a ship of forty-four guns, fired first and did us no good with a well-aimed burst of canister and grape-shot. One of these, a double-headed thunderer termed by us a slaughtering one, came in at one of the deck ports and removed poor Joe Robinson's head from his shoulders; looking itself like a cannon-ball, the head ricocheted with vigour off the breast of a young lieutenant, who sagged at the knees, deeming himself to be severely wounded. It was only when the doctor down in the cockpit had stripped off the officer's blooded uniform and the parson standing by was beginning to intone a prayer that it was discovered the officer bore no wound, at which he rallied straight away, realizing that the blood was not his own.

We retaliated to the Frenchman's blast with a shattering volley of our carronades, and saw his topsail pucker, crumple and topple, a slow, inexorable collapse of canvas dying.

We cheered and forced more powder down the throats of our ordinance and fired again; in reply to our efforts came an explosion, seemingly slow as the falling of the topsail and rising to meet it. Up went the Frenchman's deck, breaking and splintering as planks fractured and balanced momentarily on a fulcrum of flame before being finally sundered.

Even as we rejoiced at the Frenchman's extinction we lamented that our hit on his magazine must have deprived us of his liquid cargo, but were reassured by the sight of barrels falling out of the sky to float on the surface of the waves.

That afternoon we rescued two score of barrels of cognac and twelve Frenchmen; the rest of the crew had perished.

We fought two more engagements during our voyage across the Atlantic, one inconclusive, against a vessel that vanished into mist but was thought to be an American frigate, the other another Frenchman, which tacked fast across our bows at nightfall and was not seen thereafter.

Ten weeks after we had left Portsmouth, we approached the coastline of New York, and hove to in the port of Lower Manhattan, which had been vacated by Washington and partially set ablaze.

No sooner had we moored than we were surrounded by bomb-boats, which were in fact for the most part innocent of ammunition. Some belonged to chandlers, but the most interesting to us were those freighted with the ladies of the town. Most of these were of reasonable aspect, having been carefully selected by their boatmen, who received commission on their activities and were not likely to waste their time plying us with ancient harridans.

In spite of a sailor's diet of burgoo, a coarse oatmeal mixed with water, cheese and salted provisions and none of those in too great a quantity, I felt my loins move in harmony with those of my six hundred shipmates, most of whom were also young; I was prepared to waive discrimination in favour of satisfaction.

Amidst the humid wave of lust that washed over the ship we hasted one after the other down the gangways, picked our prize and brought her aboard, so that soon the ship was fairly pulsing in every quarter with frenetic fornication.

My lady, with whom I swiftly repaired to the gloom of the lower deck, was young but already calloused and hardened by ill usage and degradation; however, I was insensible to this until afterwards and submerged myself in her with immense and repeated vigour, bracing myself, for we were on foot, by gripping a stanchion.

When I had finally done I asked her name, not that I wished to recall the experience by putting a label on it, but she answered that there were sailors about whose hunger had not been yet satisfied and took herself off to find more custom, while I contentedly threw myself into my hammock and slept.

A decision had been building up in me during the voyage, slowly and deliberately. The Bible instructed a man in one part to smite his enemy, and in another to love his enemy. It also required that a man should love his neighbour. I intended to turn my enemies into neighbours I could love and thereafter indulge in that most profitable form of diplomacy, commerce.

For the sake of my masters, for the sake of my ambitions, for the love of Kate, whose voice often cast its echo through my dreams, I would desert.

CHAPTER NINE

MY first impressions of London had come from my nose as much as my eyes, and so it was with New York. Where London, however, had exuded the ripe smell of dung brought to full maturity by the summer sun, and wrapped its fair phases in a cloak of smoke greasy with leather being tanned and soap boiled, Manhattan threw out the smoke of destruction, for the city had been well scorched.

Some of the houses were smouldering, as though there were a small portion of life still left them after a near mortal fever, others resembled hearths which had been consumed with the logs burnt in them, eyeless empty frameworks peering malevolently at the passer-by. Kites like bats whirled through the artificial dark and sank to the ground to feast in unseen corners.

New York was chill, for it was October, and the landing party of which I was one marched briskly towards the commissary. We were in the charge of a boatswain called Johnny Dann, who, although like most of his fellows was addicted to using a rope's end preferred, as he occasionally confided, to listen to the harpsichord, and could differentiate between the music of Purcell and Bach, an attainment unmatched among his shipmates.

Dann would, I knew, be severely punished as a result of my defection; I weighed in my mind his virtues and vices and tried to concentrate on the latter to help convince myself that he deserved what was coming to him, but at the same time knew that I would take my chance on an unofficial exit from the King's service even if Dann had been the second son of God.

The broad space over which we were marching divided into a number of narrow streets filled with soldiers; we were ordered to halt so that Dann could talk with a sergeant of cavalry who told him that General Howe was to march north in order to engage and defeat Washington by the banks of the Harlem River. In view of the activities of the Patriots however, Howe had deemed it prudent to delay awhile until the arrival of reinforcements.

The throng grew denser about us; gun carriages tried to make their way past in a haze of cursing and cracking of whips while redcoats hurled themselves into doorways to avoid the flashing hooves of horses driven near to insanity by the bedlam. Boadicea would have revelled in the peril caused by the wagon wheels as their spokes clutched at our garments and tried to drag us under.

Scenes of enforced intimacy took place also as terrified maids found themselves forced against male breasts eager to offer them comfort and more; many a kiss directed at a maid's mouth landed on target, while others were thwarted by her tossing her head and offering only the top of her bonnet to a soldier's passion.

In the confusion, I became separated from my comrades. I could seek to rejoin them, or by refraining from doing so offer my neck to the hangman.

Ahead, I descried the mouth of a narrow alley. To run down it would be to run away from all with which I was familiar, including myself. As a fugitive I would cease to be Wheatcroft Hazell, sailor, and become Wheatcroft Hazell, deserter, who would be very differently regarded, and must therefore behave and feel differently.

I began to run, not sure of where I was taking myself, unless freedom were a clear enough destination. If only freedom did not require such a sombre companion, treason.

A thrashing of wings as I stumbled over something; two kites thrust upwards almost knocking me down and peered malignantly at me from a ring of cold sunlight. I looked down into shadow, and saw that I had nearly fallen over a corpse. Its face had been damaged, by the kites and by a bullet, which had penetrated the centre of the forehead. The face was fresh, as were the body's clothes; perhaps only a few hours ago this young man had laughed or danced that was now dead. How long hence would I, who was perhaps the same age as the corpse, be dead? I knelt to touch its cheek.

Try to pretend that the chill of the cheek is merely the chill of October, and that neither has anything to do with the chill at your heart. I touched my own cheek, in order to try to convince myself that the cold of it and the corpse's were similar, due to the season.

With distaste, I began to try to remove the body's clothes. I undid the breeches and did my best to pull them over the rigid, brittle legs.

'Have you no respect?'

So vigorously did I jump that I nearly joined the kites, still circling with an air of angry deprivation. On landing I swung to face a girl of about sixteen. She had a dark, wild beauty, although her eyes were heavy with scorn.

'Respect for whom?'

'For the dead, of course.'

'I shall soon be dead myself if I do not put on these clothes,' hearing in my ears the drums rolling as the executioner placed the rope round my neck and prepared to drop me from the yardarm.

'Are you joining us, then?'

'You are a rebel?' knowing that no matter how she answered she was a rebel in part if not in whole; her eye would never be submissive, nor her expression entirely demure. Her neck was supple but stiffly carried, her chin was firm and her whole aspect reminded me of a light, fast frigate.

'I, sir, am a patriot.'

'Some call you rebels. King George would scarcely regard you as being otherwise.'

'And you?' she asked, as I started again to try to remove the corpse's breeches.

'I believe that there are rights and wrongs on both sides.'

'With such balanced opinions you must go through life sideways, like a crab.'

'I would delight to stay and spar with you,' wondering as I have done so often since why her sex regards an opinion fairly held to be heresy. 'Unfortunately I have no time. At any moment Johnny Dann, my boatswain, may discover me or some officious officer happen by, when I shall be lost.'

The maid stood biting her lip. 'If I hold this fellow so,' I said, taking his cracking arms and placing my toe in the small of his back to support him, 'perhaps you would not mind pulling at the legs of his breeches.' She hesitated still, I wondered if from political doubt or modesty; the corpse's modesty might also have been in question, although I hoped that I would not need to don its underwear, my own being reasonably robust.

'If you put on these clothes you might easily be killed

by redcoats. You would be safer to arrive in the presence of General Washington as you are.'

'General Washington?'

'Certainly. Or do you not wish to join him?'

'Of course I wish to join him,' as yet again she hesitated to help me, her hands reaching out to take the bottom of the breeches and pausing, while I felt myself growing purple in the face with my effort at maintaining the corpse clear of the ground. 'But I must change my clothes,' I added swiftly, 'for if I do not the redcoats will shoot me on seeing me head northward, or at least severely question me as to why a sailor should be galloping ahead of the cavalry.'

'The cavalry is still unsure whether to advance or not—such a sailor would put it to further shame,' said the girl, bending at last to her distasteful task and skilfully removing first the shoes and the breeches and then the jacket and coat of furs.

Thankfully I removed my own clothes, the girl turning her back modestly; when I was done I touched her arm.

'They don't fit you as well as they did Clay,' she told me, looking me up and down.

'Clay? You knew—him?'

'I knew him.' I hurried beside her as she walked swiftly down the alley, towards a road partially bathed in gusts of smoke. 'Clay Redfearne was a patriot. He stayed behind to fire the city and deny the redcoats shelter, in spite of Congress not wanting it burnt,' she added with some bitterness.

As we were about to turn into the road I cast over my shoulder a last glance at the corpse. I knew his name now, tried to imagine his voice. In a way I was become his other self, had slipped on his life with his clothes.

The kites had swiftly settled, doubtless regarding me as their benefactor, for the clothes I was wearing would perhaps have proved indigestible.

The kites buried their beaks in Clay's body.

CHAPTER TEN

PAST fires, through smoke, we hurried our way into evening. Gradually, the city became caparisoned in twilight, tucked itself into the dusk, it seemed, leaving us at its outskirts to stare across the fields at the glow of Washington's distant bivouacs.

An empty farmhouse stood nearby; we entered it, to find it fairly furnished with comfortable chairs and a harpsichord leaning confidingly in an alcove.

'We will rest here awhile,' said my companion, 'and continue towards the patriot lines when night has properly fallen.' The time seemed appropriate to ask her name.

'Emma Forbes.' She showed no great interest in asking how I was called, so I volunteered the information gratuitously.

'My name is Wheatcroft Hazell.'

She sat in one of the deep chairs and eyed me through the gloaming. 'You have not yet answered my question concerning your intention. Perhaps General Washington himself will be able to convince you of the total rightness of our cause.'

'I think you are jesting. After all, I am only an ordinary seaman——'

'You were a seaman, although perhaps not such an ordinary one as you claim. You have had the will to desert, and a bold will is a useful quality. Although,' she added, 'your late captain might take issue with me.' Her voice was as even as ever, but I saw, I fancied, a glimmer of teeth across the room; my hopeful loins assured me that she was not all wildcat and hostility.

I had deserted because I was more attracted by commerce than by conquest, but in the case of Miss Forbes conquest began to seem not only attractive but possible. Yet I was still naïve and clumsy in my approach, my qualifications as a lover being as yet scarcely inspiring, consisting as they did of two speedy tumbles in exchange for money.

'I would feel ungracious,' I told her, 'to espouse any

other cause but yours.' I longed to unfurl for her my pennant.

'To espouse a cause out of charity is not enough; one must wholeheartedly believe in it.'

How should I best proceed? Acquiesce, leaving nothing decided, argue instead that causes were not invariably religious, demanding bias holy in the eyes of the believer? Or should I remain silent, myself an enigma, mute in a darkened room and seeking to arouse another enigma's curiosity?

'Must I continue to call you Miss Forbes? Or may I call you Emma?' praying that I would not, being out of depth with her, at the same time go aground.

The quiet was intense, but not strained. Again the glimmer of teeth. 'If you wish, you may call me Emma.'

'Emma.' I listened to myself pronounce her name, heard the distant crack of a musket, the neighing of a troubled horse.

Apart from those sounds, we were becalmed in our world of night.

'I think we are sufficiently rested,' Emma said. 'If we leave now, we should be within the patriot lines by midnight.'

'Supposing they think we are enemies and shoot without challenge?'

'Why,' said Emma, 'surely you do not feel apprehensive, sir?'

'It has been known for a sentry to find it easier to kill than call.'

'Not a patriot sentry. George Washington is a man of discipline.'

'General Washington, unlike night, cannot be everywhere at once, to give a man orders and soothe a man's fears. Night is a fearsome general, wherein the breaking of a stick under a man's foot as he leaves the jakes can be an order for his execution.'

'I am certain that you will survive this night,' standing close to me, her hand on the latch of the door. Her scent was musky but sweet, and it seemed to me that she was not over eager to open the door and admit the cool, unintimate air.

'Can we not bide here till morning, Emma?'

'We cannot, sir.' I strove to detect annoyance in her, but there was none. Only, perhaps, amusement.

'As our predicament has seen fit to land us here together,' I began, 'could we not——'

'As our situation is of our own making,' she interrupted, 'I would scarcely term it a predicament, at least so far as I am concerned. The difference between us is, I believe, that I have a purpose while you have yet to find one. Thus I am able to lead and you need to follow.' She opened the door and went out.

'I shall stay here,' I called after her, anger rising in me at her mockery of my being adrift.

'I would not advise you to. The redcoats may be up with you in the morning, if they have an ounce of military sense and dash.'

'General Howe——' I paused.

Emma came slowly back, and shut the door.

'General Howe?' softly as a cat stalking a mouse.

'General Howe will no doubt be here in the morning. You are right.'

'Ah,' very low, a whisper of disbelief, her lips as close as her spirit was distant. My only interest to her was as an inferior oracle; ask of him what you will and if he speaks without thinking you will partake of the truth as he sees it. Pounce on his pauses, for they betray him, and coax a little till with his insistence on the opposite of what he was going to say you will espy his lie and act on it. 'General Howe will be here in the morning?'

'Exactly. So let us go.'

'If General Howe were advancing, we should have heard him, should we not? The clatter of hooves and harness, the orders bellowed across the landscape, the beat of drums. Yet, sir, we have heard nothing but the hum of the silence.' How husky her voice, how deadly, as now she played the Jesuit, seeking confession, putting forth her arguments to enable me to betray my country and myself and feel the holier for it.

'Surely General Howe is stationary. He has not pursued the patriots, and I cannot believe he is refraining out of kindness, to enable them to regroup?'

She moved nearer still, as though to imply that should I surrender what I knew I might take her as reward.

My anger with her rose, but so did another passion, blending with it, I longed to seize her and fling her to the ground, leap astride her and ride her as though I were Paul

Revere and she my gasping mare.

'If you tell me what you know, I shall be able to trust you. If you deny me, I shall not trust you, to the point of thinking you a spy. And spies,' she added, 'are shot.'

'Is that what you wish, to have me shot?'

'I do not wish it, but if my cause demanded it——'

'Causes feed on blood. Surely mine could be of more delight to you held within my body, instead of being spilled on the ground in the name of your cause?' I was shuddering now, my whole being stained with lust.

'Are you a spy?' but I knew that she spoke for want of something to say, not from patriotic curiosity; she wished to deflect my desire and doubtless to quench her own before it too ignited.

Face to face we stood in the contagion of our passion.

'Are you a rebel?' I murmured. 'Or do you countenance all the conventions?'

'I countenance those I choose,' without any great conviction.

'To rebel against puritanism is a greater thing than to rebel against the King.'

'You are original, sir. Men who have tried to woo me before have merely told me that they loved me.'

'I am not wooing you. I am demanding you.'

Emma began to tremble. I removed her bonnet and began to do likewise with her coat.

'Wheatcroft, I am cold.'

I took her hand and led her back inside the house.

With the removal of each garment her scent became more potent, its musky cloud stirring me to incandescence. I sat her naked in a chair and knelt before her, advanced my lips to her thighs and kissed her while her hand ran over my head and stayed at my ear, about which her fingers lightly played.

I removed Clay's garments—poor dead Clay, doomed to spend eternity without pleasuring a woman again—and moved closer to my lady, that her caresses might be more ambitious. My kisses rose slowly and thoroughly from her thighs, encompassing all that was most secret in her, and she likewise responded, her inspiration feeding on mine as mine on hers.

I drew her out of her chair and held her afoot, grateful for a skill acquired only the previous day yet at the same time oblivious of any memory of my sea-going doxy. Emma placed her hands on my cheeks and gave a great cry.

'Clay! My darling Clay!' and the room was full of his name, echoing from every corner and cornice; she impaled herself upon me even as I withered, empty without being emptied, hollow although yet full, the hair on end at the base of my neck, my pride a ruin.

Again Emma cried out, this time pronouncing no name but proclaiming she was done. Afterwards, she stood back shivering, with cold, with regret, and with despair as the knowledge suddenly came to her that the fabric of a man may be repeated, but his essence never.

CHAPTER ELEVEN

I LAY cramped and crooked, at odds with the chair into which I had sunk after Emma's rejection of me for her dead lover. My mouth was dry and foul, as though itself were the centre of the wretched being moulded round it. I must go to fetch a stick to rub across my teeth; if only there were some sort of fragrance I could imbibe, some sort of comfit to render my breath less unwholesome.

Across the room Emma lay on the floor, back supported against a chair, on whose seat rested her elbow. Her head was turned from me, reposing in her hand; the lines of her body bespoke her sorrow. I rose, and like a cripple made my way over to the window.

Outside, dawn had draped the world in a freezing shroud. Snow fell in alternate flurries and casual descents, as though an invisible god were scattering white seed wherewith to reap a melting harvest. There was not another dwelling in sight; I looked out only at the white of the snow and the grey of the sky; white and grey, the colours of solitude.

I went to the front door and stepped outside, opening my mouth to breathe in the cold air and freshen my jaded gums. I found a stick and plied it vigorously between and across my molars, tasting the woodiness of it. I felt a little revived.

Walking away from the house a few yards, I looked south and saw smudges of smoke against the sky; to the north of me I thought I could descry streamers of smoke from cooking pots, and at the sight my belly called to tell me that it was sure that I was right. Bread and bacon it signalled for, and a glass of mulled ale; I was loathe to disappoint it.

I returned to Emma, who stirred, stretching her arms, looked at me without recognition. I returned her gaze, waiting for her eyes to turn dark with hatred at the memory of her submission to me; as Zeus took Venus in the guise of a bull I had taken Emma in the guise of Clay, and for such a passionate deception there would be no forgiveness, especially as it was she who had deceived herself.

'You!' regarding me with loathing.

'We had better proceed,' trying to quell her wrath by ignoring it. 'The redcoats may soon be on their way.'

'Let them come. No doubt they will execute you with all due dispatch!'

'Then when I am dead too, maybe you will shed a tear for the pleasure we shared, even though briefly and as far as you were concerned, unreally.'

A minute longer she glared at me, before thrusting her hands to her eyes and exploding in a torrent of weeping. I went cautiously to her, being as yet uncertain of the exact cause of grief—was it because of Clay's death or the fact that I had taken her?—and lightly stroked her hair. She did not rebuff me.

'Emma.' I went to my knees beside her and gentled her further, thinking the while of horses tramping towards us through the snow, the dim glow of red uniforms sodden in the slush, the silent but lethal march across the muffled countryside. 'Emma, we must go.' Each red shoulder bore a dull black musket, inert tube pointing at the sky, dead metal; so little time would be needed to charge each tube with powder and bullet, invest it with the power to administer death.

I handed Emma my tooth stick; absently she used it. 'I will see if there may be boots here,' I said, leaving the room. I peered into several closets but none contained any footwear whatever; we should have to be soaked.

The front door closed with a snap and we stood momentarily like two rejected by Paradise, rooted unbelievably outside the heavenly gates before spinning downwards on our long descent to hell.

Wherein had we sinned, to be thus doomed to such discomfort of a winter's morning? I thought of the other discomforts I had weathered, and of the difference between discomfort and pain unendurable, of which there was much in the world, but said nothing of my melancholy reflections to Emma. Instead, I took her hand, although it might have been a stone, for all the warmth it was able to give or receive, and did my best to support her through the engulfing drifts which sucked at our feet.

Once Emma turned to me, and I thought I saw in her eyes forgiveness for my being who I was, or rather for not being another, and that swift glance warmed me and encouraged me to such an extent that I strode out, as though the snow to me would be no more than the waters of Galilee to Our Lord as He walked across them.

Late in the afternoon, as hungry and thirsty as we were spent, we approached a cluster of trees, from whose shadow a man sprang, musket levelled at us. 'Halt! Approach and be recognized!'

Cautiously, we made our way towards him. 'We are friends,' Emma told him. 'We would speak with General Washington.'

'Would you now?' The sentry grinned, lowered his musket, reached into his pocket and withdrew a wad of tobacco. He thrust it into his mouth, chewed awhile, ejected a stream of juice the colour of a sick man's stool.

'I am his niece,' Emma said.

'His niece?' I had heard that rebel discipline was not all that it ought to have been, but this fellow's casual effrontery was more than I could bear. Aiming at the bulge of tobacco in his cheek, I hit him. A broadside of tobacco juice just missed Emma; the sentry gave a gasp as his mouth's sickening cargo flew south and lodged in his throat.

'Take us at once to General Washington or you shall answer further for your insolence!' Emma commanded him. For a while, half choked, he was unable to comply. When at last he had recovered, I braced myself for his assault, for the look in his eye was not in the least companionable, but instead of flinging himself on to me he shrugged. Turning, he led us into the trees, droplets of blood from his injured mouth glistening on the ground like fragments of stained glass.

As we walked we heard the resonance of metal on wood, and saw nearby groups of men building defence works, steam floating from their mouths as though each were afire. I must disdain any more incendiary fancies, I told myself; my mind was too full of images of fire, of burning buildings and, aboard ship, burning men, twisted and scorched by cannonballs, lying in the scuppers screaming.

In a clearing we came to a tent, fringed with red tassels, above which flew a flag of a design new to me, barred with red and white and invested with thirteen stars. In front of it stood a tall and brawny man, musket to his shoulder. He lowered it, grinning. 'Miss Emma.'

'It is good to see you, Darby.'

'And you, Miss Emma,' hurrying towards us. 'But you look in sore plight.' Indeed, Emma seemed as chilled and fragile as any beggarwoman rooted in the frost of a winter's day, the warmth in her eyes dowsed by the tears created by the frozen air.

'Darby came with my uncle from Virginia,' Emma told me, as he came nigh, 'he has known me for most of my life.'

'Indeed I have,' taking off his cloak and wrapping it round her as we walked towards the tent. 'The General will be dismayed at the sight of you looking so damp, but I've taken care to see to it that he has a good supply of cognac wine. That will give you cheer.'

I was about to offer a silent prayer of thanks for his consideration when a man appeared in the doorway of the tent. He wore a black uniform with white leggings and white wig curled like spun thread above each ear.

'Emma! My dear child, you are drenched. Inside with you at once and divest yourself of those sodden garments. Darby, hasten you to one of the women and ask her to come instantly hither with dry clothes for Miss Emma. Meanwhile, don one of my shirts and a pair of dry stockings.'

'Thank you, uncle.' Emma turned to smile at me. 'This gentleman, uncle, is Mr. Wheatcroft Hazell, an Englishman who has decided to join us. Mr. Wheatcroft was in the King's Navy,' Emma continued.

'I shall elicit his circumstances from Mr. Wheatcroft himself,' said General Washington, looking at me with some distaste. It was evident that he held turncoats in little esteem, but I have not heard to this day of a man who reverenced them.

Emma disappeared within the tent, and I resigned myself to interrogation instead of refreshment.

'You also look uncommonly damp,' said the general. 'When Darby returns he will seek out some dry clothing for you—I take it that you will not mind wearing a Patriot uniform, if he can do no better for you?'

'I have no objection, sir,' I assured him. 'However, I would like at once to disabuse you of the notion that I am a turncoat.'

'Forgive my impulsiveness, then, in so regarding you, but those who desert their own side for another are often thus regarded,' sarcastically.

'I deserted in order to resume that peaceful occupation

which I was forced to desert by the press gang. I believe, sir, that a man has as much right to choose his enemies as to choose his friends.'

'And you do not regard Americans as your enemies?'

Not unless they continue to keep me standing in wet clothes without food or drink; I would shortly become fever's prisoner if no one else's.

'No, sir, I do not. Nor do many of the people of England, not least among them Mr. Burke and Lord Chatham, who have tried to assuage the king's wrath at your activities. People, sir, are fortunately not always representative of their government.'

General Washington's grimness seemed a mite to evaporate; Darby returning at that moment, to my immense relief, with a woman holding a bundle of clothing for Emma, was thereupon directed to take me to a small tent where I was able at last to exchange my wet garments for dry ones.

A short while later, newly clad in the uniform of my king's enemies, I was conducted back to the general's tent, where with Emma I set to to do damage to a flagon or two of wine and a keen roast.

'You wish to travel to Virginia?' asked the general when I had finished my repast. The time was near evening; the snow had ceased, the trees about us were etched against the pallid twilight sky.

'Yes, sir. I wish to aid my masters in London by providing them with the means of trade, and to work for the comfort of those people in England who set great store by American tobacco—and no other kind is allowed in by the Excise—and American flour and other goods. It is my intention to ask my masters' friends in Richmond for help to maintain trade, sir.'

The general remained silent for a while, his brow taut in thought. 'Indeed there would be benefit to both sides in such trade,' he said at length, 'provided of course that payment could be made to us. We would profit, but more importantly, our markets would be assured against that time when we have achieved our independence and shall need as much help in the world as it may furnish.'

'All I need, sir, is a horse, a supply of provisions, and a safe conduct.'

'A safe conduct? Were I to give you one and you were taken by the redcoats it would be but a conduct to your doom. I dare not give you even a letter to my friends in Virginia; instead I shall give you names to commit to memory.' He took a map, unrolled it on the table, and regarded me sombrely.

'Here you see how little of America is yours, or ours. From the Ohio valley to the west is largely Indian country, and God help you if you be taken by Indians. Their use by the British is something I cannot bring myself to forgive; evil breeds evil and we have tried to use the Indians ourselves, as have the French.

'So we have added the taking of men's scalps to war's other torments.'

'Have you ever encountered Indians, sir?'

'Yes, when I embarked on my career as surveyor. Indians, settlers and trappers were my companions when I was exploring the border regions of the Blue Ridge Mountains.' His eyes looked past the walls of the tent deep into his personal history.

'Those were the harshest conditions I ever endured, yet somehow they bestowed a certain magnificence upon the soul. To go there was to realize something of the immensity of this country—to match it one's spirit had to expand. It was as though the urban world were a small and insignificant shelter, and that by leaving it for the wild mountains and the forests one were exposing oneself to the full and majestic regard of one's God. In that regard lay comfort rather than fear, and it is that regard which sustains me now. Do you think General Howe will have to await long for reinforcements?' he asked abruptly.

'I have no idea, sir.'

'And would not betray it if you had,' reading my thoughts.

'No, sir, I would not. Bearing in mind your feeling towards turncoats and my own inclinations.' I looked into his eyes. 'Neither, sir, would I betray yourself.'

Washington smiled. 'I believe you. Did I believe you to be so inclined, I would hold you as my prisoner, in spite of the service rendered by you to my niece, in escorting her from south Manhattan.'

'Nay, sir. I——'

'I may surprise General Howe,' Washington continued as though I had not spoken. 'The redcoats are ill-disposed to fight during the winter; should my position prove untenable I shall retire across the Harlem River and continue the battle regardless of the season.' He tapped the map with a quill.

'To return to your journey,' he went on. 'The ownership of the colonies south-west of here is ill defined. To avoid reimpressment,' at which thought I involuntarily quivered, 'you would do well to ride through Pennsylvania, which although a wilderness for the most part is at least more our land than King George's, although no doubt he will try to take Philadelphia in due course.

'Your route will lie here, through Philadelphia to Wilmington, and from Wilmington to Alexandre. From Alexandre you ride to Fredericksburg, thence to Charlottesville, where the Morgan family are known to me and will help you.'

'I am deeply in your debt, sir.'

'And may at once repay it.'

'Sir?'

'The perils which you face are, I think, less than those which could afflict the Patriot army in case of adversity.

'You have shown yourself able to care for my niece; I wish you therefore to continue to extend your protection to her. This is no place for her; I have no wish to confide her to Howe's men, should they perchance overcome me.'

'I shall stay here.' Emma spoke from a small doorway leading presumably to the general's sleeping quarters. 'Other women are helping to nurse the sick and wounded and to load the guns. I can also cook; I can, like them, be of use to the army.'

The general stood up and, autocratic as King George himself, gainsaid her.

'You shall do as you are bid, child. Your mother has one score to settle with me, in that I did not return you to her from your visit, before the war had properly started; she will be even less likely to forgive me if I permit you to become a soldier.'

'I shall stay here,' not one whit in awe of him.

'You shall obey me.'

Protest Emma might, but I knew well that she was destined to become my companion and, in case of danger, my delightful encumbrance.

CHAPTER TWELVE

THE snow had ceased falling when we rode off in the early morning. My seat was uncertain, for I had done little riding since leaving my Gloucestershire home, save for accompanying my master Mendip to his house; Emma rode with grace, her mount a lean black beast called Pomfroy, while mine was a piebald gelding who responded, on occasion, to the name of Franklin.

I understood, as I looked about me, General Washington's comments on the immensity of America and its effect upon him; it was as though nature had thrust her hand deep into a vat of dye, brown and green, orange and grey, and flung it at the horizon so that it streamed out on all sides in undulating grandeur, a landscape bright and sombre, intimate and magnificent, all invested with the fine wash of eternity.

Behind us the tracks of our horses stretched into infinite perspective with ourselves at their apex, as though they had produced us rather than we them. Those trees that were not stark in winter undress bore a glowing garment of red and golden leaves, honey-rich in the sunlight.

Looking at Emma, her pale cheeks suffused with colour, her elegant poise, I could scarce believe that I had possessed her, in another's right admittedly, and might again possess her, in my own. Kate seemed further away than she had been since I had left England, further than she had been in the slaughter shed of the Pride's gundeck in the midst of battle, I was aware that Katie was in temporary exile while I was with Emma, and that the compliment might be duly returned to Emma should the day arrive that I were once more with Kate.

London, however, and England itself, seemed now unreal, to the point that I doubted their existence. This vast and rolling land across which Emma and I were travelling in the intimacy of solitude, was in the Garden of Eden. We were the first man and woman, and none of the evils of mankind had been committed. Man as yet had a virgin soul, innocent of wickedness; there had been no war, no cruelty, no torment, no persecution; the countless numbers of those who had been extinguished in so many dreadful ways were as yet unborn, and when born would live their full span.

So it appeared in the rich pure wilderness in whose centre we rode, and this grand isolation bestowed a great peace and a fulfilling hope. I would succeed in my ambition, I was sure, even though at this moment my ambition seemed as puny and unreal as everything else outside my immediate surroundings.

'Can you hear the choir?' asked Emma softly.

'The choir?'

'I fancied I heard a singing. It was only a fancy, of course, yet it seemed to me that a rich melody echoed across the sky. It was the song of the wilderness.'

Listening, I now heard the song also, though there was no way of knowing if it were identical with that heard by Emma. I listened to its strange and inaudible cadences, born of the echo of emptiness and knew that never again would I hear such music; never again know such tranquillity.

CHAPTER THIRTEEN

THE Indians appeared on the third morning of our journey. We were awakened by an unearthly howl; I lay asleep for a while after hearing it, so that it appeared as a great hound in my early morning dream, a black hound, silent, save when it opened its mouth wide, purposefully moving, baleful. The hound bayed in my sleep, but when I awoke I perceived that it was no dog that had voiced its anger, but a human being, if one might so describe the tall, long-haired figure, axe above his head, who rushed into a small clapboard house not a quarter mile from the place where we had passed the night in a small wood.

There was a fearful scream from the house, followed by others; a small child ran out, to be instantly captured and held by another redskin, who like the first held a small hatchet above his head. Securing the child with one hand, he swung the axe with the other, and as the child fell held something aloft.

As Emma and I watched, frozen with far more than the chill of dawn, we felt the ground shake and dropped to our faces; when we looked up we beheld a band of soldiers accompanied by a regiment of redskins surge from our copse; to my horrified disgust I saw that the soldiers wore red coats.

The redcoats made no attempt to stop the butchery taking place before them; as women appeared, reeling and clutching at her head, and was promptly eliminated by a downward swing from an axe, they halted in front of the dwelling and watched as the Indians put it to the torch, afterwards picking up their victims and hurling them into the flames.

'Dear God,' murmured Emma, 'dear God,' and vomited, fortunately with decorum, for the sound of loud retching might well have betrayed us. When she was done she stared again at the flames and I could see that the innocence of spirit which I had discerned in her and in me was, like the dwelling, burnt out. In its place emerged a hard resolve to combat cruelty wherever it might be found, to try in some fashion to light up men's minds and hearts. Even as these noble feelings invaded me I was aware that they were subject to another, stronger and more primitive, to avenge those whom we had just seen butchered.

I would aid the American cause where I could; if I were condemned in the sight of others as a turncoat, that was their affair; for myself, I considered only that the British by their behaviour, and not my own weakness, had done the turning.

'We shall be safe now,' I told Emma, as the motley regiment of butchers disappeared into the distance. I made to rise, but Emma pulled me back.

'No, let us wait. I do not wish to run the risk of meeting—them.'

'They are gone.'

'No. They are waiting for us to show ourselves. We shall perish also,' she cried out, 'did you see what was done to that child, and that poor woman? Did you see what was done, and shall be done to us!' I did what was counter to my instincts, and slapped her face. She closed her mouth and stared at me with a sort of wonderment, afterwards allowing me to help her mount Pomfret, whose eyes widened with fear as he smelled the smoke and reek of flesh.

Franklin liked the reek no more than his companion, and pawed the air, nearly throwing me, but as one braced on a tilting deck I clung on; we passed the ashes circumspectly, lest we glimpse a further horror which at present we were equally helpless to aid, a mutilation that would shame the scaffold of a traitor.

A short distance, perhaps two miles, beyond the scene of the massacre, we came upon another. In a clearing, surrounded by tall trees, we found the bodies of a platoon of redcoats, the cloth of their uniforms double-dyed with blood. Their faces without exception bore the marks of hatchets, their cheekbones protruding through maggoty gashes, while their scalps had been peeled off, to leave them raw and bald.

'Maybe what we saw earlier was revenge for this,' I said slowly. On whom could I seek to avenge the murdered now, against whom turn? We members of mankind were it seemed of equal culpability; we had been created cruel and only our feebleness as babes prevented us, at the moment of our birth, from taking up knife or hatchet to do damage to another.

From the cradle leapt the soldier, and whatever the colour of his skin and however deep his innocence within the womb, he would not long be exposed to terrestrial influences, and to the world's four elements, before he absorbed them; air in his lungs, earth in his soul, water to leaven the earth that the seeds of wickedness might be the more easily implanted, and fire, whose contagion overrode sensibility and flung itself lustily on to life, wherewith to extinguish it, for itself was too strong to be extinguished.

After leaving the clearing, we rode for the rest of that day without speaking, our revulsion a bond between us as strong as love; that evening, although her uncle had no doubt relief upon the inclement weather, as well as on his trust in her character, to protect Emma's virtue, she embraced me as though we two still retained our purity amidst such evil as we beheld, but had little time before we too were either slain or corrupted.

'Wheatcroft,' she murmured, and my joy in her was sweet; in the fragrant darkness of a pine tree's shadow I gently took her, in passion and in love.

CHAPTER FOURTEEN

My desire was for a real four-poster, richly endowed with thick mattress and silken curtains, behind which to cavort and tumble in fashion leisurely and profound. Instead, our bed was the ground and leaves or creepers our curtains. As for love-making, we took each other like hares, ears always alert for danger, aware that the snuffle of our horses might bring extinction upon us as quickly as an unrestrained shout of passion.

We slept uneasily, forcing ourselves to mount of a morning with our eyes half-closed. When we lay down at night after mumbling our simple victuals, we took each other for warmth as much as for love, and such love as we practised was imbued with desperation, as though we were determined to show that, if we must die soon, we would take from life our small portion of that which man is put into life to give, namely affection.

It was difficult to believe, as we rode into Philadelphia, that we had reached it unscathed; after the rural emptiness in which we had for so many days been immersed the city was as much the seat of civilization as old Athens.

The Quakers were kind to us, we replenished our supplies and rested a brief while before continuing on our way, through Delaware to the small town of Baltimore.

The next metropolis on our route was Alexandre, on the Potomac River; three weeks or so after setting out from General Washington's position we arrived at Charlottesville.

We had given some thought to the manner in which we should conduct ourselves where the Morgans and others known to Emma were concerned, and had decided that we would treat each other with that impersonal courtesy that would best keep tongues and speculation silent. We must practise not looking into each other's eyes, save in the normal manner of one person conversing with another, must exert ourselves not to bestow the slightest caress.

Thus for the last day of our journey, before reaching

Charlottesville, we rode some way apart, talking about unimportant matters and staring ahead, although through our consciousness of it our impersonal pose was often wrecked by outbursts of laughter.

At that time I fancied myself in love with Emma, and she with me; however, although a romantic at heart I was also, like herself, capable of being practical. I was able to realize that our mating had been nurtured by the circumstances of war, than which there are none more peculiar, love being distorted by death or the threat of death. The radiance of passion is undimmed, but out of focus.

Emma had been my solace; I was a sufficient man, but the wilderness was greedy for my sufficiency, and without Emma I do not think that I would have been entirely adequate to face it.

As we approached the Morgan plantation I felt a twinge of unease, for here was the end of our journey together, and what happened beyond it would encompass myself alone; I drew close to Emma as our horses paused, themselves reluctant to separate.

Discarding our rehearsal in formality, Emma and I embraced, our kisses this time being infused, not with the desperation of poised danger, but the more subtle menace of imminent loss.

CHAPTER FIFTEEN

JUNIUS MORGAN was a jovial man who kept three hundred slaves. 'I have heard about you from your masters, Master Hazell. They spoke well of you, and thus I am prepared to consider your suggestion, especially as it accords with my own inclination.' He screwed up his eyes, so that his face looked momentarily oriental and sinister. 'The Navy must have matured you, sir.'

'It is, sir, something of a forcing-house for manhood.'

Junius Morgan chuckled. 'So your experience in it will benefit that which is commonly considered the obverse, the dark side, of nautical achievement. Smuggling is a trade, sir, that a man may not put aside entirely in time of war, certainly it may not be ignored by a man intent upon profit. There are many here who would be happy not to deny to the English the pleasures of American tobacco and American flour, for apart from the lucre to be gained by trading without the benefit of customs scrutiny they still bear a portion of goodwill towards the English. This in spite of the wonderful obtuseness of the British government and that remarkable Hanoverian who dominates it; let me put it gently, George suffers from Teutonic subtlety. That is to say, sir, that he handles men and their affairs with the delicacy of a troop of horse.' He laughed, fanning himself with a large hat whose like I had not seen before.

'You admire my hat? It is known, erroneously, as a Panama, but comes from lands much further south than that. It is in fact made of fibres from the South American screwpine. I would bestow this one upon you, were it not of some sentimental value and, further, were it not at least two sizes too large for you. One may not confront the world with one's headgear about one's ears, if one wishes to retain the respect of one's fellow man.' Again he chuckled, and reaching out, lightly tapped the buttocks of a passing female slave.

'Hattie, we would be obliged if you would bring us some cool cordial, child.'

'At once, Massa Morgan.' She smiled and hurried away.

'No doubt the sight of my plantation would bring Wilberforce to the point of bursting asunder, but I treat my slaves well. Had they been left in Africa they might well have enjoyed a lot more wretched than is theirs here, assailed as Africans are by their own fellows. In the forest, sir, they are barbarians, but when brought to the plantation are gentle and, I believe, loyal. That is because I do not treat them with the whip, sir, for the whip is not a universal cure for all afflictions of the mind and body.'

'I have had some experience of the whip myself, sir. It is one of the principle motive forces employed by the Navy.'

'The world needs a sight more imagination and a sight less unkindness in it. We have too many martial folk and too few poets. Smuggling, now, smuggling is as it were poetry, which is to say that it has an element of poetry in it, and cocks a pretty snook at authority.

'Poetry, or, if you like, romance; I am not afraid of boudoir words, sir. Smuggling is after all, a form of rebellion, and we here in America are not entirely insensible of the poetry of rebellion. Or, as it might be, justice. There is a mite of poetry in that too, is there not? An element of elegiac majesty, as the goddess of justice strides across the land wearing her blindfold—a pretty conceit. There is poetry in that sort of conceit too. One could hardly have as the symbol of justice a judge, do you not agree? Who would wish to see justice as a sere and frowning male, instead of as a gentle goddess, poised forever in the midst of decision?

'And now, sir, having vented my loquacity on you, I shall remain silent and attend upon your ideas for making England a better place through the continued introduction to her shores of American tobacco, American rice and such other products as she may need of us.'

'I would need a fast and nimble ship, sir. Not too heavy, and slippy before the wind. A vessel able to challenge deep waters but suited also to waters where a small draught would be an advantage, for she might need to anchor in streams. I envisage a ship of some two hundred tons burthen, lightly armed, dependent for her business upon speed and response to her helm rather than on armament.'

'I have a pair of brigs, well found but not eminently suited to our purpose.' The word 'our' was of great cheer to me, signalling as it did his commitment to my enterprise. 'However, as you are aware we have been building many of England's ships for her in our dockyards.

'There is a graceful and light schooner fitting out in Newport; she is intended for their lordships of the Admiralty, but as we are here and their lordships are not—although one of their nautical representatives may arrive in Chesapeake Bay in order to carry out some mischief—I suggest that we indent for her.'

'Indent for her?'

'Why, steal her, sir, appropriate her in the name of our just cause. There is, do you not think, sir, an element of poetry in theft, when larceny is allied to principle? As a man of honour I would in normal times consider the picking of a flower from my neighbour's property an act unthinkable, but to steal the Admiralty's schooner for the noble purpose for which we intend her—why, sir, that is heroic.'

'And there is poetry in heroism,' I said boldly; Junius Morgan laughed.

'Indeed, sir,' raising his goblet, for Hattie had returned with two well filled, 'let us pledge each other to the task.'

We drank. 'I shall,' continued Morgan, 'arrange a meeting with my friends, owners of other plantations about and merchants; such as Farquharson; we shall establish our strategy and when we have the bones of that clad it with the flesh of tactics.'

'I am delighted that you have received my idea so readily.'

'It is an excellent idea. I have found in this world that there are far too many reasons given for not accepting good ideas; the human spirit is often tainted with sloth, so that a man prefers inaction to action, compromise to boldness, and in general weakness to strength. Those of us who are blessed in not suffering from this form of moral debilitation, may rejoice in our initiative, for we shall triumph over the rest. Now, sir, what part do you see for yourself in our affair?'

I paused, reflecting momentarily on Kate's face. The imminent acquisition of the schooner had brought her visage suddenly near; it was as though the shores of England had reached out to me, so that in that instant of time I was back in London within touching distance of those who were deep in my affection. I could smell the very air of Billingsgate and hear the oaths of the fishmongers, could reach out and pat the flank of the rogue Elphrick as he bore my master Mendip homeward in a mist of farts.

'Sir, are you dreaming?' asked Morgan kindly, his broad face creased in a smile, his broad nose wrinkled—there was something of the ship about this man, a powerful vessel broad in her major parts, overriding every wave with the weight of her hull and sending fathoms down the weight of her displacement.

'Forgive me; I saw, for a moment, England.'

'I have been there. I have cut mutton with your masters—who shall, mayhap, at some time in the future be no longer your masters but your partners.'

'Such is my hope, sir.'

'Therefore, sir, may I repeat my question: what part do you see——'

I interrupted him, though not I hope brusquely. 'I wish to sail in command of our vessel, sir. I shall superintend the unloading of her merchandise at a safe place, and thence make arrangements for it to be transported to London.'

'You have been a sailor in the King's Navy, but you are still, sir, if I may make bold to say so, not as experienced in the ways of the sea as you might be. May I suggest that you have authority over all doings on land relating to the cargo, but that we appoint a master mariner to captain the ship and recruit her crew?'

'Have you such a person in mind, sir?' disappointed, yet realizing the truth of his words.

'I have, sir. There is a most notable fellow who lives in Richmond; he has sailed the oceans for many years, traded with Cuba, whence he has brought me many a keg of fine rum, and made me the gift of this hat, sir, which he brought back from Brazil, where he was in fact held for some months in a Portuguese gaol, whence I was able to disinter him.'

'How did that come about, sir?'

'He had sailed far up the Guanabara River in order to bring back a shipload of amethysts and other stones not so precious as diamonds but nevertheless not without their acceptance by the ladies. Being, as I understand it, remarkably drunk, he ran his ship aground and remained marooned in mid-river on a sandback for three months.

'His owners having thought at first that he was sunk, diligently mourned him and cargo and hull. Later, being apprised that he was very much alive, although in a heavy state of insobriety owing to there being little navigation to carry out and much to drink, his owners commanded that he should on arrival in Rio, be arrested.

'It was I, admiring the villain, who secured his release after much bargaining in a high moral tone.'

'But is a mariner so addicted to drink entirely suited to our enterprise?'

'He is, sir. He now touches not a drop when at sea, although compensating for his abstinence when ashore. Indeed, although I have heard him boast, to the dismay of an eavesdropping priest, that abstinence is the only thing he renounces in Lent, he has acquired a highly developed sense of right and wrong. He is cunning and he is alert, can pilot a vessel in shallow waters that would appear to most sailors unnavigable, and has a sense of right that attends his loyalty as powerfully as his sense of wrong his views of imposed authority.

'In short, sir, he is a damn good captain and to boot an exceeding worthwhile rebel.'

'And his name, sir?'

'Elkan. Captain Elkan, as fine a man to steal a ship as one could hope for.'

'Excellent, sir.' I added reflectively: 'and we are not so much stealing her as confiscating her.'

'Do not diminish the enterprise, sir. There is no poetry in confiscation. The snuffy-nosed legality of confiscation quite extinguishes any poetry. Confiscation is a matter of legal endorsement, dry as the parchment on which nibs scratch the orders of dry minds charging men of sap to do their dry bidding.

'I am informed, sir, that Admiral Howe may well sail here with two hundred or more ships in order to land an army with the purpose of marching across country to take Philadelphia—should he come, the schooner will be one vessel denied him.'

At the thought of Admiral Howe and an encounter with my former shipmates, I shivered. I had no desire to come under the lash wielded by Johnny Dann, always supposing that he had not been hanged for permitting my defection, nor see, with the last moments of vision left me, a hawk's eye view of the *Pride* as I dangled from her yardarm.

'We had best get under way as quickly as we can, sir.'

'Aye,' agreed Morgan, his cheeks folded with mirth to

his lower eyelids. 'We'll keep you clear of your erstwhile masters; tomorrow we shall travel to Richmond and meet Allan and others I have in mind, after which we shall load the *Joyous James*, my own brig, sir, with her cargo.

'We shall transfer it to the schooner at Newport and you shall at once thereafter be away, sir.'

I was about to express my thanks, but he stopped me. The smile was gone, the cheeks became smooth hemispheres framing the broad nose and straight mouth.

'Have you given thought to Miss Emma?'

He eyed me shrewdly, as though he could see back through the recent nights in whose dark shadows Emma and I had loved; we cherished each other, but I knew that affection and esteem were not that irresistible sort of combustion that ignited me when I thought of Kate, or had warmed Emma when Clay was alive.

I therefore answered Morgan's question without any prick of conscience. 'My feelings for Miss Emma are most amiable, sir.'

'Ah, most amiable.' Disappointment momentarily infected him, before he smiled and was again jovial Junius, host and not inquisitor.

The latter occupation ill became him, for there was no poetry in it.

CHAPTER SIXTEEN

My masters' friend John Farquharson, out of Scotland thirty years before, had hove to in Richmond after divers adventures and circumambulations on the way; he was a small man whose eyes were briny owing to long hours spent poring over his ledgers and whose clothes were impregnated with the smell of his goods, for he was, it appeared, exceedingly fond of prodding every bundle and sack he had in stock, in order to make sure of its reality and presence.

I liked him well, or doubtless would have done had I had more time to make his acquaintance, for he was a man who throve on avarice and instead of withering away for love of it, found much good humour in its cherishing. He did not gloat over it only, nor let himself be so bewitched by it that he rested upon the value of his gains; he was a man who liked to increase his wealth and regarded such increments as a game, and when a man combines love with entertainment in such a fashion he has a good chance of being jolly.

Farquharson's enthusiasm for our venture was considerable; he, Junius Morgan and several other planters and merchants were gathered round the table in Farquharson's Richmond home, discussing our intent and how to carry it out, when the arrival was announced of Captain Elkan.

The captain resembled an owl sitting on top of a pelican. He had great round eyes close on each side of a severe beak of a nose; a large sagging belly made its way towards his knees, which it overhung, peering down at feet that were large, flat, and for all I knew, webbed.

'I endorse your plans, I endorse them, gentlemen,' he said, comfortably apprised of the matter a while later, a corncob pipe in his mouth, a glass of cordial by his side.

'We can fair skip among the enemy, taunt him a little then lose him, in that fine new schooner you speak of. I have had occasion to study her, gentlemen, while sailing past her about my lawful occasions. Hull of Honduran mahogany, decks of spruce. Twelve guns firing from her main deck, save that they shan't, not having been fitted before we make off with her.' His laughter was like the crackle of rockets.

'We shall rely upon speed, rather than armament,' the captain went on. 'As you are aware, gentlemen, Lord Dunsmore, having been cast out as Governor of Virginia in our little skirmish with him at Great Bridge, now lurks miserably in the vicinity of Chesapeake Bay hoping for aid to restore his collapsed grandeur.

'However, I think that once we are cast off from Newport he will be unable to hinder us, having in his service naught significant in the way of a sea-going whippet. A few sloops, ungainly vessels alongside our schooner; some of them, so far as I could espy through my glass, were in process of being devoured by weed and wore their load of barnacles as an ugly woman does her trinkets, being not so much adornment as distraction. Such a fleet will avail Dunsmore little.'

'And how do you suggest we lay hands on the vessel, Captain?' asked Farquharson.

'Why, sir, through a morsal of gentle piracy. I shall take my ship, the *Acorn*, down river, until we are nearly at Newport, hand over my command to Lieutenant Grippe, a capable officer though so witless as to marry my daughter, who has something of the shrew in her, and with my crew shall row in our boats with muffled oars abaft the schooner and take her by surprise, always supposing that there is anybody to surprise, aboard her.

'By the following dawn, gentlemen, we shall have her ready to take her place as a scourge of the British in the American cause.'

'What do you say, Mr. Hazell?' asked Junius Morgan.

'Why, sir, that the captain's plan has about it those elements of enterprise and initiative which you had so rightly led me to expect of him.'

'A fair answer, sir, I confess myself satisfied with it,' Captain Elkan told me with a black-toothed smile; I hoped that his molars were not a reflection of his soul. 'We shall, after appropriating the schooner, provision her at once from the *Acorn*, and with our exceeding valuable cargo, which will rejoice the British people as much as its unauthorized arrival will disconcert their government, do our dance through such blockade as they may have awaiting us.'

'My intelligence is, that the First Lord of the Admiralty,

the Earl of Sandwich, is more concerned about the French than about us, considering them the real enemy of his country,' Junius Morgan told us. 'Therefore the Royal Navy is in large part kept at home in order to guard the Channel, so that Howe does not have as many ships against us as he would like. He has in fact been singularly teased by one or two of our mariners; Captain John Paul Jones has already led the British fleet a jig, and has as his ambition the capture of a British ship with his new armed merchantman the *Bonhomme Richard*.'

'Commodore Esek Hopkins is also a merry tease,' Captain Elkan said. He chuckled. 'We are dancers who lightly lead, our partners being too heavy to follow us skilfully, for they cannot foretell our steps. We are doing a roundelay before they have properly been able to disengage from the minuet.'

'An overall advantage that we possess is that we do not have to win the war at all,' a tall, skinny man with a copper wig said; I believe his name was Fane and that he was a member of the Virginian House of Burgesses. 'All that is vital to our cause is that we should not be defeated. The British may take as much of our territory as they have soldiers to administer it, but they cannot conquer our hearts and our hearts are in the Declaration of Independence. That no man shall be able to conquer; it is the drawstring that has united the thirteen colonies and is in process of erasing our several disparities.'

Captain Elkan I could see was more at home in the brusque waters of the sea than in the cloudier waters of political philosophy. 'Fine words, sir, fine words,' he said rapidly, 'and they shall be matched by a fine ship doing fine deeds. Her deeds shall be subtler than shot and shell may accomplish, for she shall strike at the revenues of King George, that thought to take us so heavily and so unjustly. It rejoices me to think of the sovereigns that shall be denied him in duty.' He sucked at his pipe, his great round eyes peering at me.

'And you, Mr. Hazell sir, I am informed that it is to you that we shall confide our cargo at the end of the voyage?'

'That is so, captain.'

'You have comrades in some distant inlet who will help? You know of a bay remote from the activity of King

George's customs men in their cutters, that quarry every vessel to make sure she pays her due and reside quaquaversal in mid-channel, so I've heard, like a cluster of bloodhounds strung together sniffing the wind from every quarter?'

'The only comrade I am able to muster in that regard, captain, is experience, and the experience of others at that. I learned much of other men's tricks during my time as a sailor in the Navy; principally it was our officers who were able to smuggle without hazard and their men upon whom the full rigour of the customs was directed.

'Much smuggling was done at Portsmouth, because that port is so heavily used; I had thought of parts farther away from London, such as the coves of Devonshire and Cornwall, where I have heard often that a man may engage in smuggling to his heart's content and run his greatest risks not from the law but from his fellows, whose greed may outdistance loyalty.'

'Greed,' Farquharson said mournfully, 'is an evil fuel. It drives us all, save we keep constant watch upon it and take its measure.'

'A large measure, James,' said Junius Morgan, laughing.

'Do not mock me, Junius. I do, I confess it, enjoy what I have, just as I delight in acquiring more of it, but greed—that is not, I think, quite the same thing as material ambition?'

'There's certainly more poetry in ambition than in greed,' Junius answered. 'On the other hand, Cupid, that sweet god of love, has given his name to desires less ethereal than love. Cupidity, James, now would you say that perhaps cupidity was more your fuel than greed?'

'Aye, it is possible, albeit a man cannot desire inordinately that which he already has.'

'Unless,' put in Junius, 'she be his lovely wife,' and laughed.

'A man can better desire that which he has not,' Farquharson went on as though he had not heard.

'Ah!' Captain Elkan interrupted with an explosion of mirth, cut swiftly off as though it had run into something hard. Evidently he did not believe in his laughter, for he once more navigated us back to the quarter which we had left.

'What we need most is wind, a good breeze to blow us east, for there is nothing worse, gentlemen, for a sailor than to beat about before the wind, seeking a way through its implacability.

'What I would suggest,' he continued, 'is that we forget the careful and elliptical approach to our task, that we eschew for instance the safer berths of Devonshire and Cornwall, which may be more private than those which I have in mind but are at the same time a paradise for wreckers. Alas they are a separate dominion from London, which city I understand it is to be the ultimate destination of our cargo.'

'True, captain,' I said. 'What is your suggestion?'

'Why, that we seize King George by the cod-piece. That we stare into his eyes while heartily kicking his arse. In other and softer words, gentlemen,' he went on, his eyes subdued as though the candle-snuffer of conscience had allayed their glow, 'I would like to put before you the idea that we sail as far up the Thames as we may, and discharge our goods into the vicinity of Greenwich. The marshes will be an eager recipient for our offerings to that beleagured and tobaccoless isle which so contradicts our interests, and although it has been made plain to me that ours is a political as much as a commercial venture, nevertheless such proximity to London for the delivery of our cargo will serve our trade as well as our politics.'

'Freight from further quarters would certainly cost dear,' Junius said.

'Indeed it would, sir. And our wagons would be too conspicuous for too great a time on their voyage from, say, the west of England, Also the people there are I believe a mite clannish, and might not hold together so well in discretion for a stranger as they would for their own.

'By going into London's outskirts, gentlemen, we would both reduce our risk and our costs.'

'Surely our risks would be increased, captain?' from James Farquharson.

'I think not, sir. Apart from the river mists and fogs which lurk in that region, ready and willing to enshroud a vessel, there is naturally the universal phenomenon of darkness.

'I suggest that we so adjust our speed and navigation that we arrive off that part of the Thames after dark, after which we can proceed upriver as we deem sensible and necessary to discharge our cargo before daylight. We shall be in a British ship under the British flag, sirs, our scuppers fair drooling patriotism,' he told us, leering and drawing on his evil pipe. 'If we are challenged, we can comfortably respond, and if suspicion is so unkind as to precipitate a boarding, why then we shall have naught but our innocence to show. We may land again with our return cargo at night, and be on our way thereafter soft as a poultice on a bruised buttock.'

'My dear captain, although not a man of great imagination, but a little sensibility, I can envisage your enterprise without having to close an eye,' said Junius Morgan. 'What is more, captain, I can smell the odorous breeze off the marshes and sense its dankness. Darkness and dankness shall be privy to our venture, then,' laughing.

'Precisely, sir.'

'And after the cargo is landed?'

'Why then we stow it in a safe place until we are ready to transport it to London, to the warehouse of Messrs. Mendip and Hozier.'

Raising his glass, the captain went on enthusiastically: 'I need no prophet's eye to see into the future, I need no seer's crystal to foretell our success and our expansion. With sugar approaching 5 shillings a pound on the London market, we shall be able to bring in rich cargoes from Cuba and the Indies also, if we've a mind; it takes restrictions to make men rich, it takes laws and decrees and imposts to light up the way round, which can be so much more profitable than the way direct.

'Think, gentlemen, how were it not for King George's customs and excise men, we should not tonight be gathered here in cheer and expectation. We would not be able to contemplate wealth and the opportunity to do patriotic deeds in the name of smuggling and such sublime felony. Were the world open and aboveboard it would lose much of its spice.'

'That it will not do, until each man can govern himself,' Junius Morgan assured him. 'And when the day comes that each man may govern himself, when each man has drafted his particular, personal declaration of independence, why then I doubt not that a faction will arise composed of men who would rather govern others than themselves. So shall history repeat itself, and with history, profit.'

' 'Tis a warming thought, a hot glass of grog of a thought,' said Captain Elkan, pouring more cordial into his own. 'So let us drink to it, gentlemen, let us drink to all that shall come to us, consequent on our seizing the schooner.'

The captain's eyes were narrowed now, his shoulders braced forward as though he were about to fly out of his chair with a rustle of pinions; the owl is indeed, I bethought me, a bird of prey.

CHAPTER SEVENTEEN

THE *Acorn* was risen upon with canvas, her anchor kissed the bows, and we were cast off. I had a last embrace of Emma, the previous evening, a kiss and a mite of fondling in the Farquharson warehouse amidst sacks of flour which made phantoms of our garments; surely I was not condemned for ever to tumble her on her feet, but might hope at some distant time to sail into her on the horizontal?

Junius Morgan, Farquharson and other good fellows were on the quay to bid us farewell, cabbage nets full of eggs were loaded aboard, cattle and sheep hauled in with expectation.

So we made our way down the James River towards Newport and our prize. A good breeze brought us down swiftly; we hove to at nightfall off Williamsburg and proceeded again at first tide the following day. When we dropped anchor we were only a mile from our destination.

Twenty of us were lowered into boats and with muffled oars proceeded ahead of the *Acorn*, which with only her foresail rigged sailed behind us. My instinct was that there was nobody aboard the schooner, which lay beside the docks.

Newport was no man's land at present; we were as uncertain of Dunsmore's position as he of ours, did he even knew that we existed, and I did not see how he could, although Virginia was far from being free of spies.

The wind off the river was chill; although the latitude of Newport saved us from the savagery of the New York winter, yet we were far from warm and the stars were obscured by heavy clouds that boded snow.

The darkness contained a deeper dark; we were under the lee of the schooner.

Six men swarmed aboard her, silent in stockinged feet. We strained our ears for the sound of an oath, for some intimation that we were discovered, but heard nothing, else we should have been at once aboard in support.

The good fellows grappled our prize with ropes, casting

their other ends down to us, that we might secure them. In the time it takes to turn an hourglass our comrades rejoined us; nay, should I think of them still as my comrades, or as those whom I commanded?

I thought upon the past and received from it nerve and sinew; sailors had been my comrades, and even though I were distanced from them by new-found authority, my comrades I would always consider them.

We hove to in midstream, the vessel which we saw was called the *Sprite*, was boarded by her complement from the *Acorn* and jury-rigged in the light of lanthorns, for her own sails were not quite ready; when all was secured we resumed our way through the night, aboard our prize.

I went to join Captain Elkan on the poop; he had a glass of rum in his hand and in a sliver of fitful moonlight breaking through the clouds I perceived the blissful look on his face.

'A pretty piece of booty,' he said, tapping the deck with his foot. 'The British may have named her *Sprite* but I have a fancy to call her something else, something that contains in it a hint of her purpose. Shall you join me in a glass, to give you inspiration?'

I wondered at his drinking after Junius Morgan had assured me that he did not drink at sea, but reflected that after all we were still not fully away from land.

'How about the *Commerce*?' suggested Captain Elkan. 'Not,' he continued before I could discourage him from thus naming the vessel, 'that there's a deal of romance in such a name, nor of religion either. If a ship may be called by some name both merry and devout, her crew may rest easy.

'Now I've been as far as Lisbon, to the east, as far as you like southward—I mind a Portuguee I came across, the *Vento e Espirito Sancto*. Now to mingle the wind with the Holy Ghost—that is the sort of appellation I enjoy, but it don't translate well enough. The Portuguees are lucky—they combine almost anything with the Holy Ghost. There's even a bank in Lisbon called the Bank of Commerce and the Holy Ghost—a man could no doubt draw a truly celestial draft on that.'

I laughed. 'How do you fancy something with Neptune in it?' I asked.

'Aha, something, as our friend Junius Morgan would say, of poetry in that. Ahoy there!' he yelled at a vessel lying almost athwart us and showing no lights.

'Ahoy!' we were answered. 'Where are you bound?'

'Outward,' answered Captain Elkan, fingering his pistol.

'That is apparent, since you sail downriver and not up. But whence are you outward bound?'

'To whom should I be giving the information?' asked Captain Elkan, as we approached the vessel until nearly touching her.

'His Majesty's sloop *Bertha.* Heave to!'

'We are in haste. We sail to New York with supplies for General Howe.'

'Then you had best change course for Trenton, for that is where you are most likely to find him.'

'Grateful for that information I'm sure,' responded the captain. 'I shall drink a toast to you, sir. And so, I am sure, will the general.'

'Your servant, sir.'

'Yours, sir,' replied Captain Elkan, stifling his mirth with his glass.

'So we are endowed with the sense that we have been first roughly greeted, and afterwards courteously passed on, by a vessel called *Bertha,*' he said when he had a little calmed himself. 'Now Bertha is not a name that I would conjure with, sir, for in my view there's a damn sight too much girth about it. Bertha's a fine name for a barge; it has a heavy tramp about it which might be becoming painted on the stem of a line-of-battle ship, but it's not a name I relish.' Under his breath he added: 'Trenton, eh? So General Washington has been forced to retreat to New Jersey.'

At the mention of Washington's name my mind flew to Emma, but even as I was about to suggest that our ship might be named for her I paused. A name more likely to appeal to Captain Elkan had occurred to me.

'Why should we not call this vessel Neptune's Trader?'

'Why, sir, that's a fine name, that will satisfy the gods of the sea, no doubt, that we bear them in mind. Boatswain!' he called, 'have the painters inscribe the name *Neptune Trader* at stem and stern.'

'Aye aye, sir.'

'Neptune, sir, rather than Neptune's. An apostrophe's a difficult thing to paint for a man who's near illiterate. Shall you turn in now, sir? Methinks a little sleep will be beneficial, for there's much to do shortly.'

'I shall turn in soon, captain.'

'Very good, sir. Good night to you.'

'Good night.' I stayed awhile, and saw the clouds break up and the stars appear. I savoured my circumstances, for there was much to be said for the stride I had taken from lower deck to quarter deck, from the terrors of discipline to the administration of it; I vowed that here I would err always on the side of gentleness, for gentleness becomes any man more than cruelty. I drew a deep breath, bringing into my body the chill vigour of the sea air, and before making my way to my quarters looked once more skyward, and wondered which of the bright clear stars I saw, was mine.

CHAPTER EIGHTEEN

We saw the English line-of-battle ships before they saw us, and at once Captain Elkan ordered that every item of seaman's bedding that could be found was to be lashed to the shrouds in order to protect the rigging and sails from being cut to pieces by shot.

I made it my business to go below to the cockpit and instruct Dr. Clegg and the Reverend Simon Bream, our parson, that they were to tend the wounded in order of the gravity of their wounds, and not in the order in which they arrived in the cockpit, for I had seen too many men die who might otherwise have lived, on account of the Royal Navy rule that every man must have his wounds dressed in rotation as he is brought down.

Dr. Clegg was a bedraggled man who did not like the sea and who was with us principally at my insistence, for Captain Elkan would have been happy to sail without any doctor at all, he having as much use for doctors as for clergymen. Indeed our parson was comparable with the doctor in that he was a poor representative of the species, who had confessed to us on being engaged that he loathed the sight of blood as much as he loved God, but had conquered his aversion by contemplating for many hours Our Lord's body on a crucifix.

We were telegraphed by the nearest ship to identify ourselves, which we did, running up our pennants and at the same time moving skilfully with full sail so that we showed our adversaries our stern.

It was extraordinary to me to think of Englishmen as my enemies, but I knew well that so long as we were at sea and I a refugee from the Navy they were surely not my friends.

The leading line-of-battle ship ordered us to heave to; at our refusal to obey she opened fire and a bunch of grapeshot sizzled by. She tacked about in order to let us have the benefit of a broadside, but we presented her with a mighty small target. A salvo however came close, and one ball carried away the legs of a seaman on the deck not far from me.

Hastily he was taken down to the cockpit and administered to by the doctor, who sawed away at the ragged ends of his bones and tidied him somewhat, while the parson turned his head away so that he should not witness the sight and said his prayers at the top of his voice, that his words might drown the noise of the saw.

I poured rum down the poor seaman's throat and made him as comfortable as I could, which gained me his thanks and a brave jest, for he managed to cry out: 'Now sir, to the Devil with the shoemaker!' after which he died.

The *Neptune Trader* swiftly outdistanced the ships-of-battle, to my great relief, and as we crested the waves under a full head of sail I became excited at the thought that Katie, as the saying was, had hold of our tow-rope, and that I would in the space of a few weeks be seeing her, and my masters. These, I was convinced, would not be masters long, but my partners, and I felt myself riding on a full swell of ambition and reflected that life was doing me proud.

CHAPTER NINETEEN

THE smell of England. The deep fragrance of green fields, the clammy hand of the twilight mist, an odour compounded of the varying fragrances of distant smoke. Smoke that came from boiling, smoke that came from frying, smoke that gushed along the industrious arteries of London, hull-down over the horizon.

'The albatross is lying off the puffin's nest,' said Captain Elkan. 'Two turns of the hour-glass, sir, and we shall have hove to and started to shift our merchandise.' He squinted at me. 'You look, if I may say so, a mite waterlogged, a trifle sunk in your emotions. Emotion is not a sea to founder in, sir, when there's business afoot.'

I looked at his black teeth, revealed as he smiled, and at his mariner's eye glinting in the cold evening. He sat down, hitching up the the overhang of his belly as though it were the hem of a garment.

'You'll be back to see us shortly,' he murmured confidently. 'Miss Emma's a prize no man wants to leave adrift for long. Who knows but that when I've turned the *Neptune Trader* about and started to take her down towards the sea I shall hear a shout, and turning see you in a wherry rowed by a frantic boatman, panting less you miss your passage back to America and joy.'

'I shall go back, captain, but there's much to do here. And joy in the doing of it.' I said nothing of Kate, mistrusting the captain's complete discretion and in no case wishing to afford him ammunition for unseemly mirth, for he was hardly a man of sensibility. Calloused by nature and rough by inclination, he held no woman better than a whore, upon whom he might cast himself for his usage as he cast himself at mealtimes upon his victuals.

At thought of Kate I wished that I could dash across the marshes swift as a bird of the region, scattering the shallow sucking waters like a moorhen or plover.

In grallatorial splendour I would run through the icy grasses and span the frozen streams until before long I would float past the Tower and up through the Poultry to Cheapside, past the establishment of Mendip and Hozier with its windows fettered against the night, until having left Newgate and Holborn Bars behind me I would at last halt before the house of Cranston Mendip in the newly built-upon acres of Soho.

A knock at the door, and the warmth of greeting. The face of her whom I loved.

This was the strange beauty of that moment: that engaged as I was upon a larcenous enterprise nothing of its criminality touched me. All that I was aware of was that my accomplishment of it had brought me back to England.

I bethought me of what might have been my lot had I not managed to hoist myself from naval bondage but instead remained in the king's service; would I now be coursing enemy vessels up and down the American coast, or blockading an American port? Or would I perhaps be dead, these past months having happened to others in the world but not to me?

I could not imagine myself with juices stilled and all swiftness of mind and heart abolished, as Clay's had been: sweet had been his unintentioned legacy to me.

Death was a wall over which there was no seeing, death was the axe that severed all the ropes that anchored us to feeling, sense and thought. In death was neither sight nor sound nor hearing nor scent, and whether death came after life or was there to usher it in, the black firmament on the other side of the womb, I knew not and wanted no part of it.

As we sailed, scarcely moving through the deep evening, alert for challenge of customs and excise men, I was vividly aware of living. Every man should have the right to sniff the crisp air awhile, to revel and to love without his span suffering curtailment, every man should be able to dwell briefly within the fragile golden canopy of majesty and strength that is young manhood. For soon enough will a young man leave his bright clothes beside the river of his youth, and emerge from it to discover instead apparel that is creased and grey.

Wishing to relish to the full these moments of returning I cast my mind back to try to encompass all those pleasures I had known: the smell of polished oak in the Dames School, the severe expressions of the Misses Howlett who had, thanks to my father's being able to afford his fourpence a week for my education, taught me to read and write and been diligent for my further learning. They had not taught me anything so great as how to learn, and my curiosity had been a switch with which I had often flicked my father and elder brother, whose minds like their bodies resided mainly in their fields.

My poor Aunt Brennan had taught me something of the radiance of thinking, for she was wont to project her mind far from our village and spoke much of what she had imagined.

'We'll heave to here.' Captain Elkan's voice broke the spell of my thoughts. The anchor fell into the water and nudged its way into the icy riverbed, the *Neptune Trader* wagged her stern like a dog its tail until the sea-anchor went out; quietly and efficiently our cargo was broken out of the hold and unloaded into the ship's boat.

'We'll take one of our boats and reconnoitre,' said Captain Elkan. 'Fortune may have guided us to a spot firm enough underfoot to bear a wagon, and with a wagon to hand,' waving at the distant lights of a house.

The skiff slid across the water, myself sitting with teeth clenched, that the captain might not find amusement in their chattering. It was exceeding cold, and the lights were obscured by the mist, which swirled about us with rare malignance.

'Now there's a pretty sight,' muttered the captain, as the mist lifted sufficiently for us to see a deserted chapel on a small mound to our right. 'That reminds me of the church of Nossa Senhora de Dores, up the Guanabara River, to which I was taken when rescued after many days stranded on a sandbank surrounded by reptiles. Great long beasts they were, called alligators, and their teeth could part a man's leg from his trunk better and more swiftly than the saw of the finest surgeon.

'They were almost on to me before I managed to leap ashore with my crew, the beasts being distracted by a priest throwing into the river a quarter mile from where we lay the carcass of a dog.'

I refrained from mentioning the knowledge I had had from Junius Morgan of the captain's stranding.

'That church spelt refuge and so does yonder building, which in the nature of religious edifices has a spire in exaltation of God and at the same time a basement to placate him who dwells below. We shall put that crypt to good use, Mr. Hazell, until we have arranged transport for our cargo.'

When the boat grounded we stepped ashore and found ourselves on solid ground, although about us there seemed to be much quaking.

We returned to the ship, the captain gave his orders, and ere long the pinnace nosed her way inshore and was unloaded, each sailor looking like a hunchback beneath his burden.

The chapel was locked, but the captain swiftly broke open the door. 'God has long since deserted this place,' he told us, sniffing, 'and his worshippers with him.' A bat sighed past our heads; the captain held up his lanthorn and the chapel poured the breath of its decay upon us. The statues of Christ and the Virgin still peered from their alcoves but as we approached we saw that they had suffered the fate of us all, for they were devoured by worms and thus had an aspect that was not loving but hateful.

'Perfect,' said the captain. 'When the bat leaves the belfry for the nave 'tis an excellent indication of privacy. Unload, boys, and stow our treasure below,' leading the way into as dank a crypt as ever made a corpse welcome.

'Meanwhile, sir,' climbing upstairs again at some speed, for he was as little enamoured of the crypt as I, 'you and I, I suggest, shall explore further.' He opened the chapel door and I followed him into the churchyard.

'As a literate man, sir, that can scan a bill of lading and on occasion read a journal, I confess myself baffled that a largely unread population sets such store by its epitaphs. Messages on headstones, carefully carved in Latin text or in English, but alike destined to remain a mystery to the bereaved. Aye, our habits are romantic with lack of logic.'

Had I been warmer I might have laughed at his observation and at the sight of him standing there among the dead, with his owl's face and the great descending gradient of his stomach, but the night was too chill and the presence of all those who had found lustre in their unlettered lives too manifest, for me to do aught but smile, and hasten as gently as I could away from that place, towards the distant lights.

CHAPTER TWENTY

THE tavern that Captain Elkan and I entered was a low place. Tallow candles guttered dismally over pock-marked faces, and the eyes that regarded us were empty of goodwill, as though they were mirrors on to no ordinary souls but spirits composed of the sulphurous mist off the marshes.

'Welcome to the Jolly Fisherman,' said the wizened tap wench.

'And well does it live up to its name,' replied the captain jovially, affecting to blow his nose, for the place smelled like a bear-pit. 'Tell me,' he went on, after we had eaten plates of half-cooked mutton and bread so coarse it nearly stripped the palate, 'which one of you excellent fellows would like to be of service to us?' He stared profoundly into the black patch over the eye of a rascal nearby. 'We would hire wagons for our enterprise, and return here within three days.'

'Is it something delectable you're carrying?' asked the tap wench, who was of divided nature; she had a strongly cleft chin, breasts that drooped like frost-bitten marrows on either side of a grubby valley, and a forehead cleft above the nose where ill temper had left its imprint. Doubtless there were further clefts beneath her apron, but these I would fain not contemplate.

'Aye, in a manner of speaking,' the captain answered her. 'As one delectable item encountering another, madam, you'd no doubt be diverted by a portion of our cargo. I would be delighted to stuff that clay pipe of yours with good Virginia tobacco,' taking his pouch and offering it to her while the men about remained taut in seeming anticipation of a kill.

The crone took a taper as the captain began to fill his corncob and inhaled a mass of smoke, holding it inside her until her eyes swelled like a frog's. Pursing her lips, she emitted it in a great gust, and I pitied it for where it had been.

'That's fine baccy—I'll take a pound of it in payment of your supper, my dearie.'

'But of course, madam,' said the captain gallantly.' And there will be another pound distributed to those who will help us take it to London.'

'Happen I've a cart,' said a tall thin man. 'Seven pound it will cost you to London and back.'

'That seems a mite heavy,' the captain told him quietly.

'You need a cart, though, do you not? You need it, and I've got it. Not many carts hereabouts, nor men to handle them. Sadie owns one,' nodding at the crone, 'and Jersey Fry the blacksmith yonder, and several others I know of. All charge the same, I wouldn't be surprised.'

'But we'll save you turnpike tolls, dearie, by taking the ways we knows across the marshes,' the crone put in, 'and we'll transport your baccy and whatever else you've a mind to take, and carry any return load you might want to bring, and we'll carry it lovingly, eh boys?'

One or two grunts answered her; Captain Elkan tilted his pot and swallowed a draught of porter.

'Very well, madam, gentlemen, delighted with your understanding. What may I offer you?'

They each took a tankard of ale, and swiftly downed it. 'Now,' the crone told a group of men playing shove ha'penny at a table, 'do you go and help load the carts, boys.'

'We're busy, Sadie,' grumbled one of them, a passing big fellow that put me in mind of a mastiff, so heavy was he.

'Load the carts now and play later, if you don't want my head in your belly.' She cackled with laughter. 'They don't call me Sadie the Goat for nothing,' she told us, embracing the captain and myself with her confidence. Her breath would have melted a sword. 'See that jar yonder, on the shelf? That contains a mighty special cargo.'

'Indeed, madam?'

'Them's ears.'

'Ears?' I echoed.

'A man comes in here and misbehaves, I butts him in the belly and bits off his ears. There's more than a dozen of my trophies in there, but the chaps 'as have lost 'em was drunk at the time, so my surgery's no more painful than anyone else's.'

She cackled again, but stopped short. 'Half the cost of your transport now, my darlings, and the other half when you gets back,' she demanded.

'Very well,' I agreed, bringing out my purse of sovereigns

with reluctance; had it not been that our crew was nearby and that we ourselves were armed I would have given little for our chances of not being robbed and murdered.

We went out to supervise the loading by the light of lanthorns and a gibbous moon; I could still scarce believe that we were seeing the cargo brought out of the chapel so soon after we had laid it there, for I had anticipated some delay before transport could be found.

Dawn was still some way off when, thanks to vigorous effort on the part of our men, we were ready to move off.

'I shall have the ship careened while you are gone,' said the captain, 'that it may look to any passer-by that she is being subjected to cleansing. An innocent and necessary pursuit, unlikely to arouse official curiosity, should there be any customs men about. As the Thames, sir, is a large river, and the forces of authority light in proportion, I do not despair of our being completely untroubled.' He grinned, putting up his hand in salute.

'I wish you good fortune, and hope to see you back within three days with my outbound cargo, sir.' He placed his small mouth close to my ear. 'And do not let your hand stray too far from your pistol, sir.'

'I shall certainly heed your advice, Captain.' I fondled the butt to reassure myself and swung on to the rear of one of the carts which, with a surly cry of its large ironshod wheels bounced a short way up the road before it dipped and lurched on to soft ground.

Through the night vapour my squadron of contraband chariots set off towards London.

CHAPTER TWENTY-ONE

THE dawn was bloodless and pale as the frost underfoot as we crossed Poplar High Street near the ancient Roman road leading to Old Ford; by mid-morning we were all parcelled up in the acrid fumes of the kilns which had given their name to Limehouse.

Distantly I could see the Tower, and shivered as I thought of the beginnings that had taken place there of my naval bondage. As we proceeded towards Cheapside my apprehension was dispelled by excitement, so that I longed to rush before the cart like a full-blooded stallion striving for the winning-post.

I deemed it prudent to pause at a nearby pump and wash my face before embracing my masters, one of whom was standing at his ledger. I stood in the warehouse doorway, savouring the past. Cranston Mendip wore a ruffled cambric shirt set off by a yellow silk neck-cloth. For wig he had chosen a grizzled bob speckled with blue powder, so that he resembled a fine plump sponge on a stick.

'Mister Mendip, sir.'

His head flew up from the ledger. 'I do not believe it, sir! I do not believe it! My lost apprentice, my vanished young friend—Wheatcroft, I confess myself astounded! Astounded and delighted, my dear boy.'

After we had flung our arms round each other: 'You have much to tell me, I am sure,' he said stepping back, 'for you are something changed. You have acquired girth and strength of body, and also I am convinced of mind. But before you utter a word of what has befallen you, sir, I shall carry you home for dinner.'

'I long, sir, to have dinner with you and enjoy again the exquisite pleasure of seeing your family, but first I have something to show you.' I led the way into the yard in which our caravan was being unloaded; all about us was a great mess of barrels and bales and strong men sweating.

Cranston Mendip skipped over to some of the merchandise, smiled up into the eyes of a horse that looked somewhat moodily back at him, and turned to me. 'What sort of stuff is this, my boy?' but I could tell by his pleasure that he knew.

'Tobacco, sir, of the best Virginian kind, and rice and flour from the same quarter. Also, sir, I bring you compliments and expressions of esteem from your friends Junius Morgan, John Farquharson and many others, that desire me to say that in spite of the war they are still your friends, with affection untarnished.'

'The rogues,' chuckled Cranston, his eyes moist. 'They are endearing fellows, are they not, and you have by some magical means that I cannot contain myself to hear about, encountered them.

'You have been trusted by them, trusted and liked, and to be trusted and liked are two of the essential ingredients of successful trade; without them, a man may not endure.'

'I have a vessel beyond the Isle of Dogs, sir, awaiting a return cargo. I am informed that a consignment of wool would be most welcome in America.'

'Wool? Of course they shall have wool, and were I to have my way I would send also the tailors to cut it. They are a pesky crowd, always banding together to demand higher wages, as if two shillings a day in winter and sixpence a day more in summer were not enough.

Also,' he continued, preceding me back into the warehouse and adjusting his neck-cloth before a mirror, 'they do have too much conceit of themselves, posturing as gentlemen and claiming that they must be ever clad in finery in order to show their artistry and encourage high fashion.' He turned to me, his face glowing.

'But come, Wheatcroft my dear boy, I shall not this day venture reproof even against a tailor, for you are wonderfully returned and I am in no mood to cavil. As for my family, they will be beside themselves for joy; it may be of moment to you that for the past seven or so months my Katie has scarce smiled for worrying about your disappearance.'

At these words my spirits ignited like dry bracken; shortly Kate would not only smile, but laugh, to see me back.

My other master, Clive Hozier, came in. 'Behold who is here!' cried Cranston Mendip.

Mr. Hozier managed a melancholy smile, for he was as always pitched in gloom. 'I thought you had deserted us,

Wheatcroft. I thought that you had, as so often happens in this life, rewarded kindness with inconsideration. I had resigned myself to your desertion.'

'I have indeed deserted, sir, not to leave you but to return. I was taken by the press gang, and found myself as a result in America. I have this instant arrived back.'

'And not alone,' put in Cranston, 'for he is come plentifully endowed with merchandise, as you may see yonder,' waving at the fellow with the black eye-patch, and directing him where to set down his bale.

'I am as happy to have my faith in human nature restored as I am to have sight of profit,' said Hozier, his emotion evidently deeply felt, for it made its way up the fitted planes of his face, softening them and even stretching his thin mouth in a smile. 'Pray, sir, recount your adventures.'

'Nay, Hozier, not until I have borne him to the barber to be shaved and to buy him a new wig.' Mendip patted Hozier's shoulder. 'Pray give orders for the carts outside to be loaded with wool, and bring yourself and your wife to my house this evening for supper, when together we shall toast our young friend's return and listen to his story.'

'Gracious of you. Pleased to accept,' said Hozier, inclining himself in a small bow and managing another smile. He went into the yard; Cranston and I set off for the barber.

To my impatience, the barber's was filled with city men come there for a sip of ale and a gossip while being attended; I strove to fight down thoughts of Kate but found that I could barely sit still in the chair from longing to fly to her.

At the same time, I was interested to hear the latest troubles and afflictions outraging my companions, particularly those of an immense man that seemed to have the dropsy, for his stomach far outsagged that of Captain Elkan while even the brothers Chippendale could have done little for the shape of his legs.

' 'Tis monstrous,' the fellow roared, 'that because Nature has so fashioned me that I am something heavier than my fellow man I cannot hire a sedan chair. At sight of me the rascals that should carry me flee, and on those occasions that I have managed to catch one, and have taxed him with his offence in declining to serve me, he has barely tried to apologize, but in expiation has pleaded lack of strength.

'Now is it not a matter of logic, my friends,' looking at us all with a round blue despairing eye, 'that a man should not set up to carry sedan chairs on the principle that his customers shall be Queen Mab's people, all gossamer and silk, and weighing lightly as feathers? Where is the merit in that, where the responsibility? We all have to accept our share of hardship—shall a sedan chair carrier be exempt? "Oh no, sir,"' he mimicked dreadfully, "I can't take you, you're too heavy. One glance at you and I'm bound to scuttle into a dark corner." So I am condemned to walk.'

' 'Tis sure no horse would gallop to you for the privilege of bearing you,' said someone else; the fat man's plaints were submerged in thinner men's laughter.

At last I was done; my razor-bared pate bore a blue skullcap of silk, on which had been delicately adjusted a toupée of merry blonde curls in the latest fashion.

'Why, my boy, the mariner is become quite the macaroni,' Cranston said with a smile, for the macaronis were young dandies notorious for their foppery yet much followed in their fashion. I had heard of their favourite dish, which one of them had discovered on his Grand Tour and ever after promoted as though he were selling the South Sea Bubble, but had not tasted it, nor did I think that it would much appeal to me.

We mounted. I longed to put my horse to the gallop but my master proceeded quite sedately, or at least as sedately as Elphrick would allow, for he was a captious beast and had his rider in some awe of him.

We passed a fish-seller and stopped to buy a pike for Mistress Mendip to jelly, but as Cranston Mendip was bargaining the villainous Elphrick disgraced himself by scorching the fish-seller with as potent a fart as ever I heard, afterwards letting fly cobbles of dung all over his wares, burying them and steaming them, including the pike.

'I think perhaps we shall forego the delicacies of the river today,' murmured Cranston apologetically, and dug his heels into Elphrick's sides; behind us was much confusion but we were fortunately not touched by it.

To my delight, we arrived at the Mendip house in good order not much later, though the powder was all blown off Cranston's wig and my own tonsorial folly was askew.

'Dinner! I am home for dinner with a guest!'

'Who may that be, Father?' asked a voice. 'Wheatcroft!' A moment later Kate, her father's blessing in his smile, was in my arms.

CHAPTER TWENTY-TWO

KATE, Kate, and am I really betrothed to you? The world is indeed a lust'rous place, with a beauty to wed and a father-in-law as kind as Cranston Mendip.

Even though I had accepted the loan of Elphrick with some alarm, on whom to escort the wool back to Captain Elkan, I was now over my fears, and as I rode ahead over the fields I hummed a little ditty and smiled at its folly, for its author, a raconteur and scribe called James Boswell, had evidently not known a Kate like mine, and nor had Master Garrick, who had set the words to music:

In the blithe days of honeymoon,
With Kate's allurements smitten
I lov'd her late, I lov'd her soon
And call'd her dearest kitten.
But now my kitten's grown a cat,
And cross like other wives,
O! by my soul, my honest Mat,
I fear she has nine lives!

Never would I bewail it if my Kate had twenty lives, provided that I could share them all with her; how well I remember myself that crisp February morning, poised on the threshold of the springtime of the year and of my life, steeped in joyousness and regarding no man as beyond salvation.

I continued to chant and smile to myself like the leader of a group of minstrels until dusk fell; with the dying of light from the sky came, slowly but inexorably, a sense of unease.

The landscape assumed a biblical quality; I felt myself surrounded by the hosts of Midian, bent on my destruction. I held my pistol, its barrel almost touching Elphrick's neck, but it was heavy, and by and by I returned it to my saddle holster.

The lights of the Jolly Fisherman were now in view, but afforded me little assurance, for I was sure that my caravan was to be ambushed. To alert those members of my crew who were escorting it would also alert the villains I suspected were only biding their time before pouncing, trying to take us by surprise that we might be disarmed or slaughtered before fully awake to our peril.

Against the distant and sombre flicker of the tavern's candles I saw a man's silhouette close in front of me. Elphrick saw it too, and reared up, nearly throwing me; I reached for my pistol as soon as I could but had the man been a foe I should have been too late. To my great relief, I heard the quiet greeting of the redoubtable Captain Elkan.

'I smell something of danger,' he murmured. 'My crew is on the qui-vive, but is ordered to behave as though without suspicion. My guess is that we shall be lured into the Jolly Fisherman and there plied with hospitality until the ship is loaded, when an attempt will be made to remove you and me, sir, and capture her complete with cargo. Our betrayers will then be able to claim reward from the Excisemen for both.'

'What then do you advise, Captain?' slowing Elphrick so that the captain was able comfortly to roll along beside us, the bowl of his cob pipe as red as Mars in the dark.

'Why, we conduct ourselves in our customary friendly fashion, but we are highly attentive, sir, we are extremely alert, and station ourselves so that we shall not be taken unawares. That is to say that we do not stand with our backs to an open door, but comfortably arrange ourselves with a wall behind us and an angle of fire that will benefit us rather than them.'

'Would it not be better to attack first?'

'I think not, sir. We don't know for certain that we are going to be attacked, we can but surmise. Also in such a situation attack can be mistaken owing to our not being sure at whom to aim our sally: success is difficult to achieve without concentration, and we cannot usefully concentrate till we know our target.

'Then, sir, if they are hesitating as to whether to fall upon us or not, and we take the initiative in destruction, we may ourselves be destroyed whereas such destruction was not definitely intended. Hostility is like love, Sir, in that it can be aroused and made to blossom by reciprocity. If we remain gentle and passive'—and I could imagine his grin as he spoke—'we shall not so easily force hostility to bloom. Instead, who knows, that sweet tap wench may feel herself conceiving a mighty affection for us.'

'Which may be beneficial for our ears.'

The captain laughed. 'Now here we are almost within the shelter of yonder inviting tavern. I shall command that the wagons be unloaded.' Before giving his commands he took a lighted lanthorn from a cart and signalled with it in the direction of the river; at once I heard orders shouted and from the darkness sailors appeared, apparently innocent of any suspicion of Sadie's men yet successfully mingling with them so that a concerted attack on their part was forestalled.

The door of the Jolly Fisherman opened to reveal Sadie and behind her, enormous across the wall, her shadow, as though she was wearing a cloak of evil.

'Welcome, good sirs. We must celebrate. Celebrate and count,' she said, turning back into the room.

'And pray that the ale be not poisoned,' murmured the captain. 'Dear mistress, your hospitality is well conceived,' he called, following her inside.

'Why, sir, we have something to celebrate, have we not?' in a voice like a chain rattling round a capstan.

'Indeed we have, dear madam, indeed we have,' replied Captain Elkan at his most effusive, accepting a large tankard and raising it to his lips, although I remarked that his gullet did not move.

'Now let us to business, sirs,' said Sadie the Goat, seating herself at our table. 'For the hire of a half dozen of carts at seven pounds a cart——'

'Half of that sum paid, madam.'

'Of course, my dear, I would not likely have forgotten that,' with a leer. 'That leaves owing twenty-one pounds and ten shillings, does it not?'

'Certainly,' I answered her, taking out my purse. I counted the money into her shrivelled palm.

'Then there's danger money on top of that, of course,' eyes narrow and flinty as a rat's.

'Now, madam,' said the captain, hero of maroonings on South American sandbanks and not a man to seek flight from argument with a woman, 'such was not discussed between us. Indeed, the great size of the sum we agreed naturally took danger into account.'

'Not so, dear Captain, and not only danger but convenience. Supposing you had found here only righteous citizens as never had a thought in their heads not to break the law of the land, what then? You'd have been scuppered, would you not? You'd have had to abandon your enterprise or go downriver, whence it would have cost you much more to transport your goods, and far more inconvenience. Or,' she continued, taking the captain's tankard as though to refill it and frowning when she saw that it was still nigh full to the brim, 'you could have proceeded on your way upriver, and as like as not run foul of the Customs men, and had both yourself and your cargo put in jeopardy. Thus I think my request only reasonable and right, for a further twenty pound.'

'Twenty pounds, madam? That would turn our profit into loss,' said the captain benignly.

'Indeed, captain? Oh well, forget it then, for that would never do.' She smiled at him, rose, and went over to a door, the captain stood up also, a small smile under his beak of a nose, and ran his hand over the front of his breeches as if to convey his innocent intention of going outside for a piss.

The Goat opened one door, and at the same moment two men ran in by another, knives in their hands. I leaped up, dragging my pistol from my sash, but the captain's was already in his fist. As the woman stood back to let in more men, the captain fired with as much accuracy as aplomb, and following hard on the roar of his weapon came the cries of two of our assailants who fell pumping blood, which irrigated the earth floor as though to nourish the roots of some venomous flower.

I fired next, and the squalid room was filled with noise and smoke and the reek of torn flesh; as the captain strove to reload, Sadie the Goat lowered her head and charged at his large and rotund midriff. Skilfully the captain stepped aside, so that her head struck the wall.

She stepped back, shaking her noddle, and being of roughly the same height as the captain stood in front of and level with him. She grinned, and quick as a fighting cock tried to spring the heavy trap of her mouth over his ear, but he was ready for her, so that her teeth merely grazed his neck.

I raised my pistol butt to club her, but the captain was quicker. His knife swept upward, laying the Goat open from stem to stern so swiftly that she had no time even to shriek but spilled her steaming guts in a heap at his feet.

The little captain waited for the woman to follow them, smiled down as she collapsed. First to her knees she fell, a pierrot at prayer, thence keeled on to her back, presenting to us the wide and empty chasm of her abdomen. The captain's face as he stood there had lost its usually cheerful expression; the owl eyes were narrow, the mouth concealed, to reappear slowly, full and smiling.

At that moment, I knew my friendship with him bonded; he shifted his knife to the other hand and I took the one that had wielded it, and as I held it was aware that I was shaking hands with death.

'And now, Mr. Hazell, I think we may safely quaff a draught,' and in amused salute at the carcass on the floor, Captain Elkan drained his tankard.

CHAPTER TWENTY-THREE

HAVING ransacked the Jolly Fisherman and imbibed part of their loot on the spot, the crew of the *Neptune Trader* went aboard and made her ready for sailing at sunrise.

'So it is farewell, sir,' Captain Elkan said, holding out his hand. His eyes were a trifle cloudy with liquor but even so he was no man of whom to try to take advantage; a sailor similarly encumbered with alcohol ventured a jocular comment and was sent sprawling by the captain's fist.

'I hope that we shall meet again before too many months are passed.'

'Say three back to America and a rest and refit, then the return—who knows, we shall perhaps be drinking to the Infant Jesus together come next Michaelmas. And to our further profit.'

I smiled at him, seeing him multiplied; hosts of Elkans and a fleet of merchantmen would ply their contraband wares between the shores of Britain and America, and shorter, swifter turns-round too, between Britain and Europe, wool for wine, cotton for cognac. The firm of Mendip, Hozier and Hazell would thrive on these affairs.

I watched in solitude as the *Neptune Trader* cast off; Captain Elkan waved from her quarter deck as she tacked slowly about into mid-river and began her long voyage. I had thought of giving the captain a letter to Emma, to deliver alongside those to Junius Morgan and John Farquharson, from Cranston Mendip and myself, but what could I say to her that would not have been either untrue or inadequate? It were better to have sipped the sugar in the cup and then to have left in unstirred, for there was nothing now for it to sweeten, all my affections being centred on Kate.

Touching Elphrick's glossy black flanks with my heels I began with the sheer joy of the morning to gallop across the fields, to my love.

CHAPTER TWENTY-FOUR

KATE and I set up home in the pleasant parish of Islington, where I felt much at home owing to its preponderance of dairy farms and fine fresh air. Here the cattle paused after their walk from the farms of Yorkshire and Lancashire, and fattened on the sweet grass before ending their journey a few miles further on, at Smithfield Market.

To my great joy it was not long before my household was blessed with a son, who was delivered by the midwife on June the twelfth 1778. We named him Hannibal, for Kate liked the classical ring of it.

Our second son, Garth, was born to us in 1779 and our third, Gavin, a year later. These were pleasant years for me, for as grew my family so did my fortunes, built on commerce legal and illicit, so that as it were the firm of Mendip, Hozier and Hazell held the drawstrings to a purse filled with adventure.

Our fleet, to which we constantly added, plied all over the world, and thanks to the things I learned while gossiping of a morning in Jonathan's coffee-house, in Lloyds and in divers other places where a carefully cocked ear could yield much profit, I became exceeding rich.

I acquired several thousand shares in the East India Company, described in the British Directory, I recall, as the most formidable commercial republic since Carthage; as my first son bore the name of that republic's most illustrious child, so I decided that my fourth son should be called Warren, in honour of the Company and India's first Viceroy, but no more sons were given me.

Instead Kate gave me a daughter, Elizabeth, who did not survive beyond a week, and later two more, Anne and Isobel, who likewise perished.

In 1780 we suffered a grievous loss in the death of Cranston Mendip. He and I had been taking coffee in Old Man's, in Scotland Yard, a place where the coffee was good but the noise great, for every man that used it seemed to own a snuff-box, and to seek to converse with it, with much opening and shutting of its metal jaws so that the air was filled with minor explosions.

Ourselves preferred Jonathan's, which was quieter, and had we gone there that morning my father-in-law might have lived out his full span.

As it was, we emerged from Scotland Yard into Whitehall to find ourselves carried up by rioters, inflamed by the rhetoric of the reprehensible Protestant fanatic, Lord George Gordon.

We tried to escape but were engulfed in the tide; I was whirled about as though in a maelstrom at sea, and spared, as the mob thought that I was one of themselves, but my dear Cranston was felled by a brick hurled at his head, and died.

The militia descended upon us and, refusing any explanations, hurled me into prison together with my father-in-law's assassins.

One of my fellow-prisoners, who had however in some measure deserved his fate thanks to his having smashed several windows in the ecstasy of his rebellion, was called William Addis, and through him I attained a measure of physical comfort. For my mouth tasting foul and not a stick to scrape my teeth to be had, I was resigned never again to feeling fresh when this fellow Addis took pity upon me. Scratching about, he found a few strands of horse-hair, and dextrously threaded them through a piece of bone in which he bored holes; afterwards he drew the hair taut with wire.

Thus I was able to brush my teeth and so held Addis in a measure of esteem, not deeming him savage but merely high-spirited and so easily led astray by others informed by malice.

When I was released, with many apologies from the smirking turnkey, who I am sure enjoyed seeing his betters in such a predicament, I arranged for Addis' freedom also, and encouraged him to set up shop as a brush-maker, which he did with much success.

Upon at last arriving home, where I had nigh been given up for dead, I was greeted with incredulous joy, which soon dissolved in sorrow upon my relating the sad news of Cranston's death.

My Kate began to go into a savage decline, becoming shrewish and disheartened, so that I often did not know either my latitude or longitude with her, and for my pleasure consorted with lascivious doxies. On afternoons when I was ostensibly exploring new ways to increase my profit, I would instead explore a beautiful young wench; one I knew, an ink-seller called Louise, had consecrated herself to pleasure as a church to worship, and with her I would pass frivolous and tempestuous hours in rooms off Covent Garden.

While drifting into sleep there when our first wave of passion was done, I would sometimes think of the first woman whom I had enjoyed nearby, and whose name I would always associate with innocence, though it were mine, not hers. Maud, the smiling, violet-scented harlot, was no doubt now dead, diseased or prematurely and terribly aged.

At other times my thoughts would turn to Emma; I wondered whom she had married and sometimes allowed myself to yearn for her, though at the same time aware that a woman who is yearned for years after one has known her, is a rhapsody most muted.

In order to amuse myself and give Kate a new interest I decided to build the house at Pepton Harbinger which I had long ago promised myself as a means of vengeance on those who had put my Aunt Brennan to death.

I would dominate them, own them, become a cruel master of the manor, appoint an overseer to make certain that the lot of the Pepton Harbinger unemployed was excessively harsh. Yet in truth my bosom could remember my longing for vengeance little more than could my eyes the visage of Aunt Brennan, so swiftly does the tapestry of life fade.

Pepton Harbinger was not only the place where my aunt had cruelly died but the site of my happy youth; I had worked in its fields, studied in its school, leaned against its walls of an evening and climbed its stiles.

'Must I endure the discomfort of a post chaise, then?' demanded Kate, when I spoke to her of my intention. 'And where shall we stay while your house is a-building—in some villainous inn, with vile food and a landlord poised to rob us as we sleep?'

'We can stay with members of my family. There are many who would be pleased to offer us the shelter of a roof.'

'What sort of roof? Thatch, filled with the scurrying of birds and the squeaking of rats? And beneath the roof a small room, with no glass in the window and the smell and feel of damp rising from the floor? Is that what you wish upon me?'

'No, my sweet. My family do not live in such dismal circumstances. We have cottages of good Cotswold stone, and——'

'I shall die of boredom in the country. What would I have in common with peasants, or a drink-sodden squire and his fowling-piece?'

'Would you not like a handsome country residence, my sweet?'

'Not if I cannot enjoy your company here while you are building it. I should go mad alone.'

I did not comment on Kate's exaggeration of her fate, but was instead patient, as a man can afford to be who has not the slightest intention of giving way.

'You have the company of your friends and the children.'

'I want your company, Wheatcroft.'

I refrained from pointing out that she was doing her best to deprive herself of it; I was not a man to thrive on his wife's petulance and beg her for more of it in order the better to love her. On the contrary, petulance is a disease of the tongue which stimulates its victim into loving another, can he but find her.

'I am with you every minute of the day, my love, whether physically present or not,' I told Kate, bending over her hand and kissing it. I was not wont to play the Whited Sepulchure, although I would have put Garrick to shame in my interpretation of it.

'I am sorry, Wheatcroft, I am sometimes a trifle shrewish,' said Kate, in her caprice bussing me on the lips. My anger with her at once dissolved, although I knew that it would bloom again the moment she decided once more to exasperate me. 'Build your house in the country, then, but on one condition.'

'Any condition, my angel.' I said the words with feeling, for my old love for her overcame me as I looked into her eyes, brilliant now with affection instead of anger. 'What is it?'

'That you later build a fine house in London, for me.'

'Do we not have a fine house?'

'Yes, but not so fine as the one I envisage. Also the house we live in was another person's dream, not ours. Ours,' she continued, illuminated by the wild beauty and gay enthusiasm for which I had first loved her, 'shall be in the fields near Lord Grosvenor's estates, and you shall have Robert and James Adam design and furnish it, for I do admire their work exceedingly.'

'I can see it clearly,' I told her. 'A house to live in but also a house that will endure and inspire. A house of the centuries.'

To create such a house would be not only a joy but a duty, for unless a rich man creates beauty he and his wealth have no significance.

Kate's conception of a magnificent mansion had about it a renaissance grandeur, a cultural perspective that would enable her and myself to live on long after we were dead.

I was seized with a desire to start building it at once, forgetting for the present my desire for a country seat, but assured myself that my relish for it would only be increased by postponement, and that it were better to proceed as planned.

My inspired Kate looked at me as she had not done for weeks, her eyes and extended arms inviting; I swept her into our chamber and bedded her, needing thoughts of no other woman to arouse me as I took her.

Sweet Kate, joyous Kate, Kate of the vivid and luminous moment; tomorrow she might again be turned into a shrew by the malign wand waved by her own spirit, but tonight she was my glory.

CHAPTER TWENTY-FIVE

I ARRIVED in Pepton Harbinger after a journey which contrasted greatly with that to London less than a decade before. Instead of tramping across fields and along rutted roads with my bundle on a stick dangling like the ensign of a foundering ship, I travelled in comfort in a post-chaise.

My life was in danger only once, when the coachman having enjoyed overmuch hospitality at an inn began to sing loudly and off-key, beating time with his whip against the flanks of our unfortunate horses; I instructed him to desist but he merely laughed. As I prepared to climb outside to assault him, the coach began a Gadarene descent of a steep hill; the coachman was flung off and I was bruised and dazed by a tempest of parcels and boxes as we bounced along with prodigious rapidity.

At last the horses came to rest and stood looking ashamed, swishing their tails and pouting. Half shaken to death, I limped back up the hill to find the coachman mumbling to himself in a clump of fern.

Seeing that he was in no state to resume command of the conveyance I thrust him into the coach and mounted outside myself, being soon put into good humour by the warm sunshine and my view over the vales of my dear Gloucestershire.

On the last night of my journey I stayed at the Talbot at Stowe-in-the-Wolde, whose innkeeper was very civil and whose furniture was of mahogany. I was not charged for the chintz curtains and extra candles allotted to me, and dined comfortably on pigeon pie, cutlets, lamb and asparagus, with an excellent cheese, the whole costing only sixpence, which I deemed good value.

There was a warming-pan in my bed and the sheets were clean; I knew not if I would have fared similarly had I travelled by ordinary stage, but doubted it. For it was not only money, but the dignity it created, that caused even the most superior landlord to crouch in genuflection, when normally, as coach-owner or even local magistrate, he considered himself to be above the ruck of those he entertained, and offered them little solace for the rigours of their journey.

The following afternoon, I bade the coachman, now recovered and afflicted with a remorse as profound as his headache, halt at the crest of the hill leading down into Pepton.

I descended from the coach and stood awhile, remembering. I regarded the pond in which Aunt Brennan had been ducked to death; from it my eyes, and I have to confess my heart, contemplated my home standing in its four acres of fields. There was the Dame School in which I had learned to read and write, and gleaned something of history and the world outside Pepton Harbinger, and not far away the gaol and the workhouse, where I intended to recruit my labour, in exchange for a small hire fee.

Thinking of it and its inhabitants, I allowed myself a stab of pity, for although their lot was wretched, yet I could not help reflecting that every man has at least some say in his own destiny, even the most miserable. A man coddled is a man weakened; I remembered Defoe's words, that a pauper given employment was a vagabond given a favour.

At the same time I thought of my children, and how I wished them to know the childishness of childhood, instead of having to dismiss it as an aberration of nature, a hindrance to the new arrival in this world to earn a living at once. If most of England had had its way, we should all have been born adults, and emerged from the womb bearing our hoes and shears, ready to labour.

I returned to the chaise and went on down the hill. Outside the workhouse I stopped the chaise once more, and found myself drawn from it towards the wretched building before me. Inside it a child was crying and a voice shouting; there was the sound of a slap.

Granted that these wretches were a burden on the rest of the community and that they were far better looked after, as I knew, than those in other countries, yet there were some, not able-bodied, whose fault it was not that they were forced to rot and freeze and languish in tumble-down buildings that had been described as Houses of Terror, and for them I felt pity.

I went inside. The smell was as bad as that of Newgate, perhaps worse, a devil's smell like that of ferrets and faeces, dysentery and death, that cast itself into the nostrils and churned the stomach.

A small child stared at me; filthy-faced, trembling, she put her finger into her mouth and I marvelled that any child could do anything so childlike, having known no love since birth, no care, and probably not a moment's play.

'Yes, sir?' A man came towards me; the child rustled rodent-like into the shadows.

'I shall need some labour to construct a house,' I said. 'I thought I would look in to see if you had anybody available.'

'A few children to go up your chimneys,' he answered laughing, 'and a few demented crones and broken-hearted widows a-dying. Nothing what you could really call useful.'

I looked into the shadows after the little girl. 'I shall be able to employ your children,' I told him. 'And any fit men you know of. Later perhaps I shall have work for your unfortunate women, too.'

'Scrub them, polish them, place a new wig upon each one's head and a new gown on her body, and none of them would show sufficient improvement to tempt a monk what had been marooned on a rock for twenty years,' the man sneered.

'I do not seek to be attracted by them, but to employ them,' I said coldly, tempted to bring my gold headed cane across his face.

'Quite, sir, I did but jest, I did but jest,' ingratiatingly.

'People who are weak through thirst and hunger will be little more use to me than they are to the parish. Give everyone in this place food and drink and see that it is charged correctly to me. If I find that you have tried to cheat me you shall answer for it.'

'Oh, I am an honest man, sir, an honest and a conscientious man, sir.' He came closer to me, studying me in the ray of sunlight that struck through the ravaged roof. 'May I ask, sir, whom I have the honour to address?' staring down at the silver buckles on my shoes and raising his gaze slowly to take in my black velvet breeches and cut velvet coat.

'I am Wheatcroft Hazell, and I shall be staying with my father.'

'Wheatcroft Hazell?' he said slowly, his white pointed face in the sun's ray like the figurehead of a hellship. 'We played together before you went to London after the death of the wi— of Brennan Daly.'

'The murder of Mistress Daly.'

'Quite, sir, quite,' looking now into my eyes, now at my feet. 'May I make so bold as to welcome you then, sir, to tell you how delighted I am to set eyes on you again after so long, and to see you in such fine condition.'

'And who are you? Is it Spence, Timothy Spence?' His father had been one of the leaders of the mob which had borne my aunt to the stool.

'Ah, your memory is as sharp as your sword,' glancing at its hilt.

'How clever of you to have guessed that it is sharp.' I flashed it from its scabbard so that it flickered past the tip of Spence's nose. He leaped back, and the spurt of fear in his eyes delighted me.

'I would like to see your father again,' I told him. 'Where can I find him?'

'Where the Reverend Mr. Herrick buried him, in the churchyard,' still quivering from the wind of my blade. 'The Reverend followed him two years afterwards. There's many as was involved in your aunt's death as has joined her since in Paradise.'

'On the contrary, I doubt much that they have joined her there,' I said, sheathing my sword. 'Murder is no qualification to enter Heaven.' I turned to go. 'See to it that you obey my orders regarding nourishment for these people.'

'Of course. Without question.' I sensed his vaporous presence behind me as I went out into the fresh air.

'Wheat—Mr. Hazell,' he said, 'do you remember that we played together?'

'I remember much.'

'I was six year's old before my father could afford to buy us a chair. He tried to make one before that, but it collapsed.'

I laughed.

'What I am trying to say,' he continued, 'is that I have had little luck. My life has, as you might say, been a life without chairs. Whereas yours——'

'Is none of your concern whatsoever,' I said sharply, ready again to strike him with my cane or with my sword remove the tip of his nose. I saw his father at the head of the mob, heard his own fist on the child's face.

I climbed back into the chaise, and commanded the driver to take me to my father's.

CHAPTER TWENTY-SIX

'MY son—is it my own dear Wheatcroft?' My mother stared at me with the intensity, and something of the alarm of an unbeliever vouchsafed a vision.

'Indeed it is, mother.' I took her in my arms and kissed her cheek, and sniffed for perfume that was not there. I held her and looked at her, small, slightly bent now, work-worn yet a woman of sinew still, and smiled.

'It is good to be home, mother.'

'The value of your clothes is greater than that of our land. You must be used to a palace—from the descriptions in your letters you and your Kate do live in little short of one. And now you stand here in your finery, and are still able'—she began to weep—'still able to call this your home.'

The ceiling of our room pressed gently against my head, and I felt boxed in yet not oppressed, for although I was used now to size and something of majesty, yet I was rooted here.

'Your father will be in shortly, and your Uncle Sebastian.'

'How is father?'

'Grown a mite feeble, but otherwise in good health. Your uncle on the other hand is in appearance as strong as an ox but complains constantly of a pain in his side, so that your father has to do a portion of his work in addition to his own.'

'I see.' I remembered Uncle Sebastian, Brennan's younger brother, as a lazy man about whom there was an indefinable quality, an aura of dankness, a refusal to be completely born. When he had been ejected into the world from the womb some part of him had remained behind, unseen and unguessed at, perhaps alive, possibly dead. Had my Uncle Sebastian been accused of consorting with Satan and causing murrains, I could have understood it.

I inquired then after Sebastian's young son Meridian, whose mother had died in childbirth.

'Poor little orphan that he is—Sebastian's not much of a father to him. A gentle child, but a mite slow. Not an idiot, mark you,' she said hastily, 'but it takes him a little time to understand what he's to do.' We looked at each other, and said nothing for a while, merely holding hands to give us all the communication we needed.

'How long will you be staying, my son?' eventually.

'I shall be returning to London in a fortnight, but I shall be coming here often thereafter. I am going to build a house here. A fine house which I would like you to live in.'

'I've lived in this house as long as I can remember, and should not know how to go about my business in a palace. But I would try,' she said urgently, fearing that I would change my mind about building and vanish again from her life.

'Do you continue to live here if you will, but allow me to see to it that you and father no longer work so hard. I can place a fine plump cushion between you and your labours, if you will give me the chance.'

'We have worked always from dawn till dusk, and slept from dusk till dawn. 'Tis not hardship, but habit, my son. 'Tis our way of doing things here, as I am sure you remember.'

'Aye, but I want to help you, mother. I have a right to help you.'

'Of course you have, my love, and don't think me ungrateful because you claim that right. We shall see if your mother and father can bear to abide at home in their old age, instead of working about barn and field.' We heard voices, and the door of the cottage opened.

My father entered first. He was a small man, wizened and carrying a scythe over his shoulder. He saw me and stood still. Behind him, my Uncle Sebastian, who had to stoop as he entered, managed to avoid a collision but could not know its cause until he was able to sit down and look up. He had a thatch of furze eye-brow resting above a great nose which played the referee in keeping apart small black eyes.

'Wheatcroft—a fine young coxcomb, a dandy indeed, a fop! Nay, I jest—look at his eyes, Thomas, there's something of steel there.'

My father had not spoken; he stared at me awhile before coming forward to clasp me to him. I kissed the rough fabric of his cheek, grazed over the years by abrasive seasons, and felt in his hold of me his forgiveness for my leaving him.

'Tell us all,' my father said later, after we had supped hungrily on salt beef, carrots and pudding, and drunk a few flagons of ale, 'tell us everything that has befallen you since you left here. What you wrote in your letters was doubtless incomplete, and in any case how should one rely on those who read them to one not to leave out something here and there?

'Besides,' he went on, 'I have not heard your voice these past several years, and would therefore like to hear much of it now.'

He, my mother and Uncle Sebastian settled themselves in their chairs and, gesturing by the dim light of a pair of small candles in iron candlesticks, I told them of my adventures, and concluded by illustrating the manner in which their future and mine might, through the building of my house here, be drawn closer together.

CHAPTER TWENTY-SEVEN

In the autumn of 1783, my house at Pepton Harbinger and the American war were both completed. Their termination gave me great satisfaction, for the most momentous events have their intimate and personal aspect; I would now be able to develop my business with America without fear of interruption by the British Navy or Customs. As for Pepton Grange, it would be a haven for my parents as well as a pleasant berth for me in the country.

I had at first intended my estate to be a formal affair, inspired by the skills of Capability Brown or Le Nôtre, but I decided against such splendour, for it would have seemed ostentatious and unseemly. Therefore I settled for a typical country residence, something of a farm and something of a manor, with its major emphasis on being a home.

The one thing upon which I did insist, and sated any malice that I still felt, was to have the pond in which the mob had drowned Aunt Brennan moved three feet, a prolonged and difficult enterprise necessitating much hard work—I would have abolished the pond altogether, were it not beautiful, and in any case it was hardly the fault of the water that it had been made my aunt's assassin.

As it was, I wished it to lie exactly in perspective with my house and its relation to a copse cresting a distant hill-top, and during my visits from London watched with interest the efforts of my workers to carry out their orders, draining and filling, pumping and digging, until the work was done and the balance I desired achieved.

The approach to my house was through a vale, flanked by soft-swelling slopes; there was a long driveway, rolled flat that the occupants of carriages might not be shaken to pieces, which thrust at a broad oak front door.

The door opened on to a hall paved with black and white marble, which at one side cast up a noble staircase, and at the other gave on to a drawing-room directed more towards comfort than elegance. Here stout upholstered settees and deep chairs were presided over by a mantle-full of figurines and a chime clock.

My mother and father felt most at home in the kitchen, and would share their food and happily converse with anyone who stopped by. Tinkers, rat-catchers, gardeners and farriers, were all recipients of their bounty, so that the atmosphere was by and large one of warmth and contentment.

In an adjoining scullery farm men stood eyeing the female servants, who chattered and laughed at their own side table, called fashionably a bouter, and bantered with them.

The only lack of geniality was at the table of Uncle Sebastian, which was set aside from the others. Here my uncle frowned to himself as he tore at his meat, or rebuked Meridian for some unimportant failing; at other times Uncle Sebastian would parade through the house like a captain on his quarter-deck, administering and commanding, so that he rather than my father seemed the place's chief occupant.

Never did my uncle behave thus overtly when I was there, but it was certain that when I was not present the tyrant in him held sway.

My mother I saw was restless, and did her best to banish the idleness I had imposed upon her by polishing and cleaning and tending as she had always done. She had been all her life a woman of industry in a narrow world, having I believe left Pepton Harbinger only once in her life to go to a fair at Stow, which was but ten miles distant. Me she regarded with wondering devotion, finding it hard to believe that I was really her child, the farm-boy who had set off for London with empty pockets but a few years before and returned weighted with sovereigns.

Kate was not often with me, disliking the journey and finding little in common with my parents and the other country folk. She remained in London with our children, of whom my son Gavin rejoiced me most. Gavin had the appearance of an enlightened child, merry but shrewd, letting little pass him without examination. I resolved that when he was older I would take him to America and introduce him to my friends there, that he might be as well and as kindly launched in matters of business as I had been.

I was therefore ill pleased at the purpose of the visit

made one autumn afternoon by our squire, Sir Joshua Frayle.

The squire was a round man who rode a round horse, a pale chestnut without vigour, had it possessed a spark of equine spirit its master would have spent his life being flung to the winds, for he seldom sat his seat sober.

I was reading when, glancing through the drawing-room window, I beheld Sir Joshua far down the drive, ambling towards me, leaning first to the left of his horse, then to the right; each time I glanced up he was a mite nearer, so that he seemed like a series of engravings, each larger than the last. Beside him, fragile as the Virgin on an illuminated scroll, rode his son Brereton, his chinless face and thin body in ridiculous contrast to the inflamed visage and robust frame of his father.

'Ho there, Hazell, we are come for refreshment!' was his boorish greeting, as he slid from his thankful steed. Brereton tumbled untidily to the ground and tottered on spindly shanks behind him.

'Good afternoon, Squire.'

He came into the hall, and stood blinking at the floor. 'Damme if I could ever learn chess,' he said, 'and now here I am destined it seems to be one of the pieces.' He swung round and demanded of Brereton what he should be, pawn, bishop or king; Brereton hesitated, one foot on a white square, the other on a black.

'Bah, can't make up your mind in which direction to move, as usual. Can't move, can't speak—he's the despair of me, this poor pale evaporated seed of mine!' His voice had the volume of one who lives in a house of the deaf, and fails to recognize when consorting with ordinary folk that he is not entirely surrounded by ear trumpets.

The two came into the drawing-room; the squire threw himself on to a settle and sprawled there with legs akimbo; Brereton carefully sat down on the edg of a chair. The clock struck four, and Sir Joshua turned to it and raised his hat. 'I thank ye for your reminder,' he told it, 'four o'clock is me favourite hour. Me belly hour, as I call it, for now's the time me guts rumble in expectation of me dinner.'

'I shall be delighted if you will stay, Squire,' with as little warmth as I felt.

'Of course ye'll be delighted, there's naught like entertaining a guest. And I'm delighted, for not only have I the pleasure of your imminent hospitality, sir, but the expectation that ye'll grant me a small request.'

'A request, squire? I wonder what that might be,' I said casually, for he was not a man to be committed to in advance.

'Me son here, me first-born, the sun of me eyes and the joy of me heart, this rabbit-faced buffoon, may be of service to ye. As you perceive, sir, he's hardly a rural fellow to look upon—his face is always white and he's constipated for five days out of seven! Doubt if he's ravaged a milkmaid or seen a sow spayed—if I weren't so sure of his mother's virtue I'd have me doubts as to whether Brereton had sprung from me own loins!'

I was also sure of Lady Frayle's virtue, she being exceeding plain and heavily pitted by the pox; the attractions of wealth were also denied her, her dowry having long since been invested in her husband's complexion, which shone with the product of the vine.

'So,' the squire continued, 'I bethought me how best to advance the boy, and found to me great interest that trade is become these days less frowned upon than it used to be as the occupation of a gentleman. Me friend Doddington Slab, who is as ye may know a magistrate down Worcester way, was not aghast at the notion of apprenticing his son to a merchant, and did so with some success. Young Slab will gather more coin there than he would have done in the army, which God help him was the other career his father had devised for him.' He smacked his lips hopefully, but I desisted from providing him with wine.

'Now yourself, sir,' the squire went on, displeased at being denied, 'being in a good way of business, so I believe, would no doubt accept as apprentice this fellow Brereton. His knowledge of anything but dreaming is sparse at present, but take him by the scruff and throw him into bed with a knowledgeable doxy instead of one of the poor provincial whores I sought for him in Gloucester, who were a sight too rough for him, and he ought at once to gain some stature.'

'Father——'

'Ye could teach him arithmetic,' ignoring Brereton's attempt to interrupt 'never could master it meself, but then I'm more inclined to the hunt than me son, I may not be able to add but I can take away—I've subtracted my share of maidenheads from their owners!' He laughed loudly and licked his lips.

'When Brereton's learned to do sums ye'll have a rogue of some import in your counting-house, or he may trade and voyage for ye. Would ye not like to go to Genoa?' he demanded of his son, 'or to Cathay, and do something that even your father hasn't done, namely cover a yellow wench?'

'No,' whispered Brereton.

'I don't think ye'll ever cover any wench!' roared the squire.

'I—I—I doubt I am yet ready.'

'Not ready? Fifteen years old and not ready? Why, ye sag-livered, stodge-bowelled, square-arsed simpleton, what yardstick do ye use to measure your readiness, but your own?'

Brereton, who had gone pink, blushed yet more deeply. 'I—I——'

'Ye can't sight a fouling-piece save at the peril of all about but the ducks, ye cannot drink without toppling presently like an uprooted sapling, and now ye ain't ready for an endeavour that every barnyard cock learns in the egg and practises as soon as it can gurgle at the dawn!' He turned to me with a gesture of despair.

'Pray take him, Hazell, and infuse in him some sort of craft, that he may not spend his days entirely devoid of majesty.'

'Into what sort of craft, Squire?' I placed at last a glass in his hand and a decanter within his reach, which he regarded with a glance a good deal more benevolent than that with which he had favoured Brereton.

'Why, sir,' incredulously, 'did I not make myself clear?' He gulped wine vigorously. 'I want to apprentice the boy to ye, Hazell!'

'You spoke, squire, of the counting-house and of voyaging in my behalf,' I said coldly, as the decanter grew rapidly empty, 'but your son's lack of enthusiasm for your suggestions is as apparent as his lack of ability. Or at least,' I added for the boy's sake, 'the lack of ability you have inputed to him.'

'Imputed to him? Do ye deny that he's a cack-handed idiot? I seek his salvation, Hazell! I seek it in changed circumstances, changed surroundings, I seek it in someone who will guide him for reasons soundly commercial, rather than sentimental and paternal.

'Besides, sir,' he continued, bulbous eyes wide with pretended hurt, 'I am sure that ye would not deny the request, the small request, of a fellow member of the county? Do ye not realize that ye would acquire not only me gratitude for your service, but also merit in the eyes of your Maker? So ye would, sir!'

I declined to accept his guarantee. Instead, I looked at the wretched Brereton. 'Tell me, wherein does your desire lie?' I asked him.

'I—I wish to become a player, sir.'

'A player?' barked the squire, instantly, 'a player at what? Cards, perchance? A game of hazard, with your coat worn inside out for good luck? Ten thousand sovereigns on the table and a greedy-eyed jade leaning over you to watch if you win, that she may adore you? I've seen gambling, boy, with the city fops wearing leather patches over their fine lace ruffles so that they shan't be spoiled, and the women rubbing against them more vigorously than a bow against a fiddle!' He snorted. 'Or is it the fiddle you yourself want to play, or perhaps the harpsichord?'

'I want to be an actor, father.'

The squire flung his glass into a corner of the room, to its detriment, for it exploded like a grenade. 'An actor, a strolling player?'

'Yes, father.' Brereton's eyes screwed up and unscrewed like the palpitations of a halibut in extremis. 'That—that is my ambition, father.'

The squire was swelling so much that I expected at any moment that he would float off the settle and rise like a hot-air balloon.

'Some actors are men of stature and social consequence,' I said, in support of the boy. 'David Garrick, for example, is most highly regarded by all, and has a retinue of admirers, many of them noble, who supply him and his company with their stage finery, which previously rested on their own backs.

'Then there is the opera, squire, very much loved——'

'I have been to the theatre, Hazell,' announced the squire with glazed eye. 'I have sat in a box on the stage, sir, at five shillings the seat, and felt the wind of rotten oranges whizzing from the pit towards their targets. One such, sir, hit my hat, and had I seen the thrower of it I should have cut him in two with my sword.

'So that is your ambition, is it?' he continued, turning again on, rather than to, his son. 'To be a shy for orange-throwers, like a member of Bedlam escaped to a fairground; to try to talk against the shouting and the noise of insolent vagrants banging against the side of the gallery with their sticks? To consort with whores,' quite forgetting that he had a while ago been recommending just such a course, as a way to overcoming the barriers to self-fulfilment, 'that strut before the candle footlights while futile fellows declaim their simulated passions for them? That is what you wish to be?'

'I—I——'

'Even should we make the assumption,' said the squire, helping himself to another glass from my cupboard and more wine from the decanter, 'that I was willing to allow you to make your living so—such as it might be, for I do not believe that actors are much better rewarded than ostlers—and that your appearance on stage did not kill your mother, who is not in the best of health and has not been these past ten years, more's the pity—am I not correct in another assumption, namely that you have to possess some sort of talent to be accepted among theatre folk?'

'I—I——'

'Nay, Mr. Hazell shall take you in and make a man and merchant of you. Now, sir, do ye name your fee for Brereton's acceptance, remembering that although I am squire here I am nonetheless far from being a man of riches.'

'I regret, squire, that I shall not be able to take him.'

'Not take him? Not take him?' The squire rose unsteadily to his feet. 'Sir, I regard that as an affront. Do ye hear me, Hazell? I consider meself to have been insulted!' He fumbled in the pocket of his coat for a glove, and waved it in front of my face.

'Father!' beseeched Brereton.

'Nay, my son, ye too are enveloped in the insult. I shall have satisfaction for the two of us!' I felt the flick of his glove on my cheek.

'I shall expect ye tomorrow at dawn, sir. On the lawn in front of the manor. The weapons to be pistols!'

'Father——'

'Swords,' I told him.

'Pistols, sir!'

'Swords!'

The squire's glove again flicked my face. 'Do ye add insult to insult by arguing with me, sir? Why then, I shall have to slay ye twice over. With my pistol.'

'May I propose, sir, that you use a pistol and I a sword, for I doubt that I shall suffer overmuch from such a seeming disadvantage.'

'Are you implying that I cannot shoot straight, sir? Upon my cod I have never been so insulted!'

Brereton followed at the trot across the room. 'And may I then go on the stage, father?' he asked foolishly. The squire smote him across the head, and flung wide the door. Outside stood Uncle Sebastian.

The squire glared at him, strode across the hall and out to his horse. Having propelled himself into the saddle from the mounting-stool he turned once to wave his fist, before leaving as he had arrived, an unsteady figure rolling from side to side of his beast and gradually growing diminished as he proceeded.

'I'll meet him for you tomorrow,' said Uncle Sebastian quietly.

'I shall not hear of it, uncle. However, you are very kind,' although I was vividly aware that kindness was not my uncle's motive. 'Do you know how to use a pistol?' I asked out of curiosity.

'I would not fight him with a pistol, nephew.'

'With a sword, then?'

'Nor a sword,' with soft menace.

'With what, then?'

'Why, nephew, with my bare hands, of course.'

I looked into his little black eyes, trying to read there if he were jesting, but they gave nothing away; his eyes were as deep and as still as the pond in which Aunt Brennan had perished.

Again I had the feeling, which often came upon me when I contemplated my uncle, that part of him was stillborn, and wished to inflict upon others its corruption.

CHAPTER TWENTY-EIGHT

UNCLE SEBASTIAN, whom I had accepted reluctantly as a second, walked beside me, barely visible through the dense dawn mist. He walked silently, his nose tilted to sniff the fragrant air. We emerged from a belt of trees to find ourselves confronting the ill-defined figures, dark as shadows, of the squire and Brereton.

'We don't want to disturb the womenfolk,' the squire said curtly. 'Might be the death of me wife, if she knew we were duelling. There's a glade yonder where honour may be satisfied.'

We followed him back into the trees, until we emerged in a thick pocket of mist on open ground.

'Now, Brereton, ye can learn from what ye are about to see,' the squire told him. 'Ye will learn of how impudence must be punished, and presumption quenched, as a man punishes and quenches. Are ye still certain ye will not use pistols, Hazell?' taking a deep wooden case from Brereton and opening it, to display a pair of pistols, innocuously bedded in blue velvet.

I slowly drew my sword from its scabbard. 'Quite certain, thank you.'

'I've no wish to butcher ye.'

My own honour forbade me from suggesting that, as I had no mind for butchery either, the most sensible thing to do would be to call off the duel. Instead, I confronted the squire, imbibing a quart of brandy at second hand from his reeking breath, and then, in time with him, turned with all the dignity of a crane embarking on its mating dance. I felt the back of the squire's round head against the centre of my shoulder blades as we stood back to back, and was vastly relieved that we are born with neither mouths nor nose behind us, else I should have been suffocated again.

'As we have no referee, squire, which one of us shall call?'

'Why, sir, as ye persist in matching your sword with my pistol, I suggest that we each call two paces in unison.'

'Very well.' I was tense, my stomach taut as a shield as though it would deflect the bullet should the squire aim straight. I resolved that I would not thrust to kill, for although my opponent was a bully and a boor, yet he was not entirely unlikeable, and I had seen too much futile shedding of blood not to respect conservation of it.

So we stood awhile, the squire I was sure as reluctant to call as I. Our clothes were heavy with dew, so that if we delayed much longer the chill might prove more deadly than our weapons.

'One,' called the squire at last, stepping away from me so that my back felt cold and unprotected.

'One,' I called, slightly out of rhythm with him, and: 'two!' we both shouted together. I hurled myself round, and cut down with my sword at the barrel of his pistol, which glared at me black and empty as Uncle Sebastian's eye. As I cut, I twisted my body; there was a roar from the pistol and a pain such as I had never dreamed of, in my side. I fell, half-conscious, to the ground.

'My boy,' said the squire, kneeling above me and ripping my coat away from the wound, 'didn't mean so to wound ye. There's honour enough in giving a scratch, without having to blast a man's hip from him. Brereton, quick, take off your shirt and tear it, that we may make a bandage for Mr. Hazell.'

Brereton did not hear him, having swooned.

'The puppy, the feeble piss-veined whelp!' growled the squire, tearing off his own shirt and rending it in strips. 'I'll bind ye up, 'tis nothing mortal. Oh what an idiot ye are, to have chosen a sword against a pistol!'

As I looked up at him and felt the black vapours of unconsciousness flooding into me, I beheld two great black crabs slowly make their way over his shoulder on each side of his neck, where they paused. The crabs raised their claws and pinched the squire's throat, squeezing until his eyes became ever more bulbous and his flesh blue.

I heard myself utter a thin, hoarse cry: 'No, uncle, no!' and with my last waning strength stared up at his dark figure braced behind that of his kneeling victim. ''Twas a fair fight,' I whispered, 'let the squire be.' I saw Uncle Sebastian smile; he snatched his hands away as though he were a conjuror, displaying empty palms before extracting a candle-snuffer from his ear.

The squire squatted, retching, while my uncle took over the task of tending to me.

'I am sorry, Wheatcroft,' he said softly, 'at sight of you so sore wounded my calmness left me, so that I thought only of vengeance. Pray accept my apologies, squire; I am a man of peace in all things, save those pertaining to injury of my family.'

'Ye murderer, I've a mind to shoot ye as I would any other sort of vermin,' gasped the squire, when he had a little recovered. 'I'll have ye in court, I'll send ye to the gallows, I'll have ye locked in the pillory for a year, so I will, that your bones may filter out like the rotten egg from its shell and the crows leave ye for other pickings.'

'I do ask you to believe me penitent,' said my uncle. 'I am as overcome with sorrow at my action as I was first with the rage that prompted it.'

'Aye, rage abolishes reason.' The squire slowly stood up. 'I'm aware of that, and so is poor Brereton yonder, that has swooned clean away at the sight of bloodshed.'

He walked over to his prostrate son, and stood looking down at him. 'Maybe the stage is the right place for him,' I heard him say, 'what say ye, Hazell, shall I give in to him and let him have his way?'

I tried to answer him, that I thought that by doing so he would be showing both sense and mercy, but the blackness overwhelmed me and my consciousness followed Brereton's into limbo.

CHAPTER TWENTY-NINE

My side healed quite well, but my love of the country was impaired. I seldom visited Pepton Harbinger, although corresponding occasionally with my parents. Each time that I made up my mind to visit them, Kate dissuaded me, playing upon my preference for London to keep me with her.

Nearly two years had passed since my unfortunate duel when, visiting the theatre one evening, I saw to my amazement Brereton, quite transformed, declaiming his lines with presence from the stage.

After the play we took a glass together, and he told me that his father had yielded to his desire to be a player, and having yielded had graciously given him sufficient to live on until he had become established, telling him that after all the same sum would doubtless have been spent on having him apprenticed.

I noticed during this tale that Brereton was uneasy about something, and asked him what it was. At first he denied any embarrassment, but finally confessed that his father was far from being the only one at Pepton who regretted that he had refrained from having Uncle Sebastian hanged. He had shown this mercy out of deference to me, whom he considered a courageous fool who had saved his life but a minute after trying to take it.

It appeared that my uncle was regarded with a disquiet amounting to fear in the district, and that as a result my house was almost empty of servants.

Therefore I decided that I must go to see what was afoot; my decision, however, was contrary to Kate's wishes as usual when it came to going to Gloucestershire, and in addition my side, it being now winter, was paining me considerably, for the cold seemed to enter my healed tissues and painfully unravel them.

I deferred going until the spring, when a letter arrived, dictated by my father, to inform me that my poor mother was dead.

I retired to my bedchamber and wept, reflecting that I had neglected my duty to her. I had loved her dearly, but for the most part from a distance, and now that distance was grown impossible to bridge.

Stretched upon my bed, I embarked on a voyage into my childhood, in which my mother was the principal feature of every landscape. She it was who had encouraged me and abstained from rebuke, she it was who had insisted that I go to the Dame School to be lettered.

Kate came into me, and sitting beside me began to stroke my hair. Her tenderness however could not erase the fact that she in some measure was to blame for my not going to my mother, who had without doubt needed me. I tried to be as just to Kate as I was harsh with myself, but found it difficult to conceal that I was vexed with her.

'Come, Wheatcroft my sweet, let me console you. Still you're fretting, my darling.' She placed her mouth close to my ear, so that her breath entered it and, in spite of my sorrow, began to excite me.

Kate continued so to caress me and murmur her endearments that I began to want her and thus, first to my immense surprise and later to my shame, took her and worked upon her with marvellous dexterity, as though with my cod I would cauterize my grief.

Afterwards, as I lay beside her, the shame stole upon me in step with the twilight that began to drain their colour from the hangings. Was my conduct a fitting accomplishment to the launching of my mother into the hereafter? Why had I not also hired trumpeters to bray an obscene melody, and beaters of tabors to thunder out a rattling jolly rhythm for her?

Sensing my disgust, Kate pulled my face into the hollow of her neck, and gentled and coaxed me, and stroked me and soothed me, until I gave way to her endeavours, and sank into sound and dreamless slumber.

The next morning, before I was fully awake and thought the sadness that lay upon me merely the residue of a nightmare, Kate told me that I must find something new and stimulating to occupy my mind and refresh my spirit.

'Perhaps we shall go on a voyage,' I said. 'I have long wanted to return to America, or as your father called it Amerikey, should you not like to see it?'

'Certainly, were I able to walk there; as it is, you know dearest how the very thought of the ocean makes me feel quite queasy.'

'I intend to return to America in any event, when Gavin is older.'

'That will not be for several years yet,' Kate answered amiably. 'Poor father, how I still do miss him.' We sat silent awhile, contemplating our respective bereavements; I was perhaps the more moved, the earth being yet so fresh upon my mother's grave.

'If I am to find something new to occupy me,' I said at length, 'and it is not to be a voyage, what then do you suggest? Shall I ascend in a balloon like the Montgolfiers, or build a kite large enough to take me and strive to soar above a valley?'

'Nothing that is so taxing,' Kate said, laughing. 'I was thinking that now is the time that we may start to build our town house.'

I saw in my mind a glistening mansion, which my mother would never see, and with that thought the mansion crumbled. Yet I chided myself: did I not believe in the life after death? Did I suppose that my mother would walk blindly about the vault in which she now was, unable to watch her child, unable a little to boast of him to another? Did the hereafter exorcize all echo of pride, taking even maternal pride to be a deadly sin that had no place there? I could not believe that when we died we lived on an endless, pale plateau, with no reflection of a summit.

'After all,' Kate said softly, 'you have built your folly in the country, surely now I have deserved my little London palace?'

I did not at once answer her; at her mention of my folly I recalled the words of Brereton Frayle, and remembered that my father was now alone with Uncle Sebastian and Meridian, and I had a sense of unease, that my father was menaced, which swamped my immediate desire to build Kate's house.

'My father, I must go to him.'

'Of course, my love. I did not mean that you should put the work in hand this very day.'

'When I return it shall be done,' I promised her. 'I shall cast myself into its creation with gusto, you shall be dazzled by such radiance of endeavour.'

Kate smiled and embraced me, servants were summoned, and not long afterwards I was loaded into a post chaise with my baggage, and hurrying to Pepton.

CHAPTER THIRTY

'YOUR poor father, Wheatcroft. His heart was broken by your mother's death. He survived her by only two days. Had I been able to write I would have sent you the letter so informing you direct, but as it was I had to seek out the letter-writer, an awkward and elusive villain, and only dispatched the missive this morning.'

I sat in the kitchen, once so filled with merriment, my head in my hands. I accepted my uncle's proferring of a glass of wine, and looked about me for sight of Meridian's mournful countenance, but did not see him.

'Is Meridian out in the fields?'

'I sent him to stay with neighbours,' answered Uncle Sebastian. ' 'Twas bearing him down, being in a house filled with grief. Perhaps a spell in London would do him no harm,' he added lightly, as though jesting. 'He's a mind to do what you did, setting off from here, leaving all behind, to try to find his fortune.'

'And do you believe he should?' conscious that Meridian was not altogether suited to such ambition.

'Why, I take it he'll have his cousin to help him sometimes, that he shan't be entirely overlooked.'

'I shall of course help him if I can.'

'He won't be a burden to you, Wheatcroft. He's a quiet boy,' with the satisfaction of a father who has oppressed his child till all spirit has left him. However, if Brereton had managed to accomplish his desire, once free of the squire, why should not Meridian flower when removed from the black shadow of Uncle Sebastian?

Yet I wondered why my uncle so lusted for solitude, that he would send away the sole companion left him.

'Shall you not be surprising lonely without him?'

'Aye, I'm not much loved here. Wheatcroft. Some are born to be loved and some to be unloved, and it seems that I am condemned to other folks' dislike. However, a man can get used to it; when a man's alone he can acquire a sufficiency of soul, a robustness of spirit, which fortifies him mightily.'

'What did my mother die of?' I asked him, before realizing what I asked. He looked for a fragment of time not only surprised but discomfited, before shrugging his shoulders, and to cover his discomfiture, poured me more wine.

'She had been ailing for some time, Wheatcroft. First she was chilled, then it was as though she could not breath for an invasion of phlegm, which made her chest its battlefield.

'Your father and I did what we could; we mulled wine and put a cloth over your mother's head and encouraged her to sniff the vapour of it, but to no purpose.

'One morning your father awoke to find her beside him colder even than usual, for her feet were always like hoarfrost, poor dear, and perceived directly that the life had left her. I went to the parsonage and returned with the curate, who arranged your mother's eyes and uttered his blessings over her, commending her to God.

'Your father and I dressed her then, placing upon her head her prettiest bonnet, so that she made as handsome a lych as ever I saw, and under the lychgate the parson stood with his bible and counted her in, and we saw her lowered with much care into her coffin, that was made of oak, a sturdy casket with fine handles of brass, and the coffin lowered decently into the grave.

'I was not to know, I am happy not to have guessed, that within a few days I should again be attending at the churchyard for the burial of your poor father.' He wiped his eyes on the back of his sleeve.

'Did my father die in bed also?'

'Oh yes, he had that comfort.'

'Then God be thanked,' I said, wondering what it was that forbade me believe him. It was as though there were a presence, unseen but frantic, that contradicted him.

'What shall you be doing now? he asked.

'I shall doubtless sell this house,' watching him closely.

Again he shrugged. 'If Meridian's going to London no doubt I can find a hut for myself.'

'I shall see to it that you have somewhere comfortable.'

'You're a good boy, Wheatcroft,' he said warmly. 'But will the house not be useful later perhaps, as an inheritance for your childer? Or you may yourself wish to escape London for a time, and come hither.'

'If I decide to keep it, will you stay on to take care of it, Uncle?'

'Of course, Wheatcroft. It's a big house, but I've naught else to do. And there's bound to be someone who I can prevail upon to help me—I may be alone, but it's not as though I was condemned to it, now is it?'

'Certainly not, Uncle. I shall return to London tomorrow, and on my way go to see the curate, to thank him.'

'No need to do that, nephew. He's an odd fellow who has managed to ingratiate himself with the squire, and lives at the manor with him. They say round about that the squire pays for his keep and that of his horse, though not for its corn. And he has his linen washed there too, and is paid £18 per annum.'

'No doubt he provides the squire with companionship, now that his son lives in London.'

'Maybe, and maybe too they've pistols in common,' said my uncle, confidentially touching the side of his nose.

At the mention of pistols I felt a painful twinge in my side. 'How so, Uncle?'

'Why, 'tis alleged that he fought a duel in London, and shot his opponent dead, the rascal. He was tried by jury and found guilty of manslaughter but managed to bribe his executioner so well that instead of being branded on the hand with a hot iron he was merely touched upon it with a cold like a guilty noble.' My uncle laughed, a habit he indulged in so seldom that his laughter was more like a creak, as though it were rusted. 'So the squire and he enjoy much merriment and wine together, and like most of the curates and parsons about, this reverend shows the church to be less godly than one was taught to believe.'

I looked at him, longing to ask him if my parents had really died, as he had described, or whether they had in some evil fashion been aided to their deaths, but my uncle showed me such warmth, and at any discussion of my father and mother such sorrow, that I could not broach my suspicions, which gradually wore away, seeming built upon sand.

Yet the air still felt alive with agitation, and I could not let the matter lie.

As I had suggested to my uncle, I would the next day pay a visit to the curate.

CHAPTER THIRTY-ONE

'By the sacred cod of Zeus—it's you, Hazell. Enter!' Sir Joshua Frayle stood in the doorway to his drawing-room and greeted me as though I were a dear friend who had for years been living abroad.

'This is the fellow I told you about,' he shouted across the room at a thin, white-complexioned man who looked like some fruit of the night that had sauntered forth from the stews after taking his pleasure of a doxy. His face was concave about the cheeks and full about the mouth, so that they seemed strangers, and he held a glass brimming with wine.

'Hazell,' the squire continued, 'allow me to present to ye me parson, the Reverend Silas Torve.'

'Your servant, sir,' said Torve, eyeing my finery, and no doubt hoping in the fullness of time that I might swell his stipend.

'Delighted to make your acquaintance, sir.' I accepted a glass of wine and sat down. 'I am here to make a somewhat delicate inquiry.'

'Ah,' said the curate, looking deep. 'I admire delicacy.'

'Before you inquire, permit me to offer ye me sympathies about the death of your parents. Went off rather sudden, I hear.'

'Indeed, Squire, I understand that they did.' I eyed the curate inquiringly. He did not have the appearance of one guarding any secret concerning them, but looked at me with a regard sympathetic but not in any way sinister.

'Your mother, I regret, died of cold, and your father no doubt of sorrow,' he said. 'But he was composed and peaceful,' he added hastily, 'be in no doubt of that. His brow was smooth, his expression angelic, as though it were a reflection of his state of grace.'

'Amazin', when you consider that he and your mother had for so long consorted with that murderous jackanapes your uncle!' shouted the squire. 'Ye suspect him of something, I see ye do. Never fear you'll land in court for slander in this parish! Speak your mind, man, and if there's a breeze, a gossamer hint, of suspicion, I'll have your villainous knave of a relative cast into gaol to await trial! Upon me word as a magistrate I will!'

'I do suspect, but I wonder if there is any justice in my suspicions.'

'What makes you think that there is anything amiss?' asked the curate.

I hesitated, before confiding to him my feeling about forces unseen that cried to me for help.

'Stuff, sir!' exclaimed Sir Joshua, disappointed. 'I can arrest him, but 'twill be hard to hold him, on that. Why, it seems to me that you have been seeing overmuch of that bard fellow whose words Brereton now passes his life in spouting—chap who comes from down Stratford way—Shakespeare, I think Brereton said his name was. D'ye know I wasted my entire evening at the theatre, when I could have been wenching or offering my custom to a tavern! Yet in some manner incomprehensible to me, I was happy to do so, because I felt something I did not think ever to feel in Brereton.

'Pride, sir! Rich, peacock pride! That that hare-faced boy could turn and face the hounds as he does, night after night, and not only speaks his words but is audible above the uproar—that, gentlemen, is what astounds me most. That, and the fact that I was mistaken for so long in me own offspring!'

'And was Lady Frayle with you, Squire?' I asked.

'Nay, Lady Frayle would perish in such a place as a theatre. Yet she has become reconciled to Brereton's success, and no longer expects him hourly to step crest-fallen from the stage and carry his boxes hither, asking forgiveness for his folly!'

I stayed a while longer, before leaving with the secular blessing of the squire and the religious benediction of the curate, who put down his glass while it was being charged, the better to pronounce God's name.

So far as confirmation of my feeling about Uncle Sebastian was concerned, I had discovered nothing, and in a way, was thankful for it.

CHAPTER THIRTY-TWO

KATE and I were at last bound upon the great adventure of building our new house. Swiftly we rode through the pastoral countryside south of Islington, cantered past the school and almshouses, our course set south-west.

We paused by Grays Inn Road as a torrent of cattle flowed by on its way to the pens at Smithfield. Before us lay Holborn, blocked as ever by coaches and wagons, which were compressed by the narrowness of the road at Staple Inn on the one hand, and by the turnstiles set up by the inhabitants of Lincolns Inn on the other, who did not relish stray beasts dunging in their neat squares and blasting turds at Chancery.

Leaving behind us the confusion and a thunderstorm of oaths that rolled and echoed unceasingly between the houses, we rode west to Charlotte Street, where we left our horses at a stable in order that Kate might walk at her leisure past Oxford Street's glossy shops and perchance purchase something; when she had seen her fill and bought some lace we had a few glasses of brandy at a tavern, before retrieving our horses and continuing on our way.

We had resolved to site our house on Park Lane, overlooking Hyde Park; as we approached Tyburn we were caught up in a mob on its way to enjoy an execution at Tyburn Tree.

The felon who was to be hanged was surrounded by friends with whom he jested; he was a tall fellow, and the coffin on which he leaned was small, so that he protested that he had been either given the wrong one, or was going to be curled up and restored to the womb, rather than to his Maker.

'Should we build so near the scaffold?' cried Kate, as we strove to stay together. 'If we are to be disturbed by beasts I would rather it were by the lowing of kine than the shouting of men in a frenzy as they go to a death.' She watched in fascination as the executioner and his ordinary caressed their rope and fastened it round their prisoner's neck.

I did not answer, being occupied in soothing my horse, which reared up as the crowd let out a great shout of morbid joy and exaltation; the executioner had given the nod to the cart's driver to move forward at the gallop, leaving the prisoner dangling from the rope round his neck.

He spun for a while, with a slow, mortal grace, before expiring; as he was cut down the crowd sighed, as though to empty their own lungs in sympathy.

'I have heard that there is a likelihood soon of Tyburn Tree's use as a scaffold being discontinued,' I told Kate as we rode down Park Lane. 'The congestion caused to traffic by the bringing of felons from Newgate is so great, that shortly executions will take place outside the prison, instead of here.'

'I am glad. I do not want our new home to be sullied by such affairs. To think,' Kate went on excitedly, 'that we shall have Lord Grosvenor for neighbour, and I am told that the first American Minister—what is his name? John Adams—is resident in Grosvenor Square at Number 9.'

'It was I who told you,' I said with a smile, 'after I had gone there to meet him and discuss some matters of business.'

'Of course, I remember now that it was you,' laughing gaily and in her exuberance setting her horse galloping. I followed; Kate reined in suddenly and gestured at a piece of land between Upper Grosvenor Street and Mount Street. 'Here,' she said, almost in a whisper. 'Here, sweet Wheatcroft.'

I looked at her dear radiant face, and at the site she wanted, and felt deep joy, for it exactly suited me also. Removing to this place would not remove me from the countryside I loved, for the park lay in front of us with its cargo of horses and deer, its haystacks shining in the afternoon sun. It was a great banqueting table for the beasts of London, and as I drew in a deep breath of the hay-sweet air I was grateful that my circumstances would enable me to live here.

'Let us go to buy the land now!' cried Kate, 'lest someone else be first. And when our house is built, we shall have such a party that the air shall ring with our mirth, and the King hearing it swirl in at the windows of his palace will come hurrying to join us.'

'If he does so I pray he shower us with his yellow tickets,'

I said, laughing, 'that we may use his private roads when we travel to his villages of Chelsea or Kensington yonder. The press and bustle of the traffic becomes ever worse—even without the benefit of felons being brought to the scaffold—and the West Bourn flows so near the surface at Knightsbridge that the mud can suffocate an ass.'

Kate laughed, leaned over and bussed me heartily. We looked deeply at each other, aware of a sweet sense of fulfilment.

So I began the house which has been my home for nigh two hundred years.

CHAPTER THIRTY-THREE

ROBERT ADAM was a man of convincing authority. He stood beside me on my site and drew patterns on the ground with a pointed stick.

'You may have confidence in my judgement, sir. Elegance and comfort are required, and elegance and comfort are easily come by. Until recently, they were not.' He paced the length of the land.

'Not a great deal of space for a formal garden, but a small one, laid out in a natural way—if I may quote Lord Kinnoul—is carried to greater perfection in England than in any part of Europe. So shall it be here, sir.

'The outside of your house shall be imposing, but not ostentatious. As for the interior, I have more than once uttered my convictions regarding decoration.' He jabbed with his stick at the sky. 'The massive entablature, the ponderous compartment ceiling, the tabernacle frame, almost the only species of ornament formerly known in this country, are now, sir, universally exploded.'

'What shall you put in their place, then?'

'We have introduced a great diversity of ceilings, sir, we have friezes and decorated pilasters, we have adopted a beautiful variety of light designs, delicately enriched, gracefully formed, and arranged with propriety and skill.'

He rose and fell on his toes, tapped the side of his nose with his finger.

'We shall use a mixture of grotesque stucco, sir, and combine it with painted ornaments; they, and the rainceau with its fanciful figures, are the instruments which shall give grace and beauty to the whole.'

Adam smiled. 'In order to protect what will be indubitably a work of art, sir, a residence with the warm ambience of a small house combined with the dignity and appurtenances of a palace, may I suggest that you insure it?'

'I shall indeed,' I assured him.

'I am delighted to hear it, sir. That will bestow mental ease on yourself, as the owner, and on me as the artist. I recommended the Phoenix Insurance Company,' he added 'It is my experience that, almost as soon as your application is received with draft enclosed, the Phoenix will build a reservoir nearby your house and station fire engines there, so zealous is the company to avoid the necessity of claims upon it. "To quench a flame is to quench a claim" might well be the company's motto, sir.'

I laughed. 'They shall have my draft directly the house is built,' I told him.

'Excellent. And you will find further comfort in the protection of your property from your position so near the barracks at Knightsbridge, should there be urban riots.'

'A friend of mine was killed in the riots inspired by Lord George Gordon,' I said, feeling for a moment melancholy as I remembered my beloved Cranston.

'I am grieved to hear it. I lost an uncle to a mob a few years ago. We need an increase in the number of Runners from Bow Street, and a militia that is more likely to resist the mob than to join it.'

I looked down at the patterns he had drawn in the earth. 'How long do you think the building of my house will take, Mr. Adam?'

'The completion of the structure shall not be delayed beyond eighteen months, sir. We will be helped by the diggings within the park yonder for brick-earth, which will be therefore the more swiftly available from the brick-kilns over by Knightsbridge. Your entire house, sir, should be ready for your occupation within three years.'

'They are three years that will pass slowly, Mr. Adam.'

'Age lends the years a remarkable degree of acceleration,' smiling. 'It will seem to you that you are installed presently.'

He left me then, climbing into his chaise and driving off, to leave me looking at my land and dreaming of the home that would arise there, to be a delight to my family and a shelter for my old age.

CHAPTER THIRTY-FOUR

MY life had made of me a strange mixture of the Epicurean and the Spartan; although by nature I inclined much to the former my experiences in the Navy and afterwards on my trek with Emma to Virginia showed that I was not altogether soft.

Occasionally, to keep myself hardy, I would go on a short voyage in one of my ships, perhaps taking Gavin with me, for the boy showed a great love of the sea that it was my delight to encourage.

Thus it was that I was amused to find myself perched with Kate atop a great pyramid of servants at our house in Park Lane, and it seemed to me that they had been hired by Kate not only for such skills as they had but for their appearance.

Our First Minister was called Gregory, a butler that in his previous employment by a bishop was often mistaken for his master. He was a big, unctuous fellow that knew well how to rule, belling his orders as though in the pulpit and making gestures with his fat white hands as if to invoke a cascade of hell fire on any caught in error, or who dared dispute with him.

Below Gregory were pages, gardeners, coachmen, chaisemen, postilions; there were maid-servants and kitchen maids and carpenters. Most feared of all my people, apart from Gregory, was my French chef Raton, a man of savage temperament but won'rous art, to whom I paid £60 per annum.

Altogether, as I told Kate, our servants' bill was some £750 a year, but she was unimpressed by the sum, and demanded to know what it could better be employed on, than our comfort.

One servant, however, she would fain have got rid of, a handsome, sulky wench called Patsy, that was supposed to be a personal maid to her, but spent much time in her bed. There she was not always alone, for I delighted to tumble her, she being excessively sensual, and liking to play all manner of lascivious tricks.

After I was cooled, Patsy would let me rest awhile, before with a smile beginning to coax flame from what had been a spent ember; having thus fanned me she would lie back and laugh at what she had wrought before guiding me by the pole star straight into Heaven.

'I must send Patsy away,' Kate would complain, 'she gives herself such airs that a man might be forgiven for supposing her to be the mistress of this house, and not a maid.' I forebore to comment that she was at least the mistress of the house's owner.

'It is too bad, though,' Kate told me one day, 'that this wretch of mine should now wear laced shoes instead of neat's leather ones, that she should wear fine white stockings instead of yarn ones, and of course a good silk petticoat like her mistress, instead of a linsey-wolsey one. Not only does she dress and behave like a London madam but she has the impudence to drink tea and take snuff.'

'She is high-spirited,' I said, doing my best to soothe Kate, and resolving to enjoin a little more prudence on Patsy.

'Then I shall advertise her as being high-spirited, a young horse that leaps up and down and does its best to throw its rider. I shall put a notice in Poor Robin's Intelligencer: Maidservant to be hired, either weekly, monthly or quarterly wages. One that is an incomparable slut——'

'Nay, that is I think hardly just,' I interrupted, not daring to say too much in Patsy's defence, lest I arouse suspicion.

'—and goes all the day slipshod with her stockings out at heels——'

'Kate, my love, but a moment ago you were complaining that she was as well dressed as yourself,' I put in.

'—an excellent housewife, that wastes more of everything than she spends; an egregious scold, that will always have the last word,' warming to her work of denigration; 'an everlasting gossip, that tells abroad whatsoever is done in the house——'

Now there, dear Kate, you are as wrong as in the rest of your condemnation; praise be it may continue so, for Patsy holds much of me in the power of her discretion.

'—In short,' Kate concluded, 'she is a lazy trollop!'

She glared at me, and I felt a stirring of apprehension, for although age had now rubbed a sooty finger under each eye, and dampened the passions within her breast, yet she was as likely to play dog in the manger over her husband as would any other woman.

Unable to give me the pleasure I was used to, and still needed, from the division of her thighs, Kate would deny me categorically the right to intrude between those of another.

Bringing sweet relief, Patsy was the candle-snuffer to my flame, as well as its arouser; the flame did not exist for Kate, for she had now entered the years of woman's incomprehension.

So I teased her gently about the vast number of those who waited on us, and mentioned the names of one or two whom I could fault but who were deemed by herself entirely virtuous, and we kissed and laughed and forgot.

Afterwards, I sought out Patsy, who was lying on her bed, and stepped as swiftly as I could out of my finery, and toyed with her and was toyed with, and enjoyed and was enjoyed, putting my mouth about her proud young silken globes, that were not yet quite ripe, and feeling in return her tongue sinuous about the stem of my cod. I looked down into her eyes, that were sultry yet laughing as they returned my gaze above my rigid offering, and I cried to her to let me kiss her in her most secret places, for I longed to taste her.

Still smiling, she resumed her work, denying me until I beseeched her further, when at last she squatted on her haunches above me and allowed me my desire.

So we played out our comedy, sometimes in Patsy's room, sometimes in the spacious dimity cupboard wherein Kate kept her mountains of linen; we frolicked on sheets that were clean but not laid upon the bed, we frolicked on pillowcases and bedcovers, and we laughed secretively when Kate complained they were crumpled, and that the laundresses were shirking their jobs, and were slatterns, although I interceded for them later.

I found myself ever more drawn to Patsy, and managed to resist all Kate's endeavours to discharge her, for she was become a necessity to me, a hearth in which I could still blaze and burn.

I sometimes fancied that I loved her.

CHAPTER THIRTY-FIVE

‘’TIS a pity that Cranston is not here to see it. At least, not in the flesh,’ added Clive Hozier piously, raising his eyes as though Cranston were smiling down on us from the bosom of the Holy Ghost.

We were standing, my son Gavin with us, surveying our new docks. They lay outspread before us, carved from the alluvial soil of Wapping; the dozens of spars we saw belonged in the main to our own ships, now no longer having to contest with throngs of Newcastle colliers for open water further upriver.

To each side of our fleet of sail lay hundreds of barges moored at the river bank; dozens more, laden with stone, brick and timber, moved slowly towards their distant quays by Horseferry and Parliament Stairs at Westminster. Other barges emitted a ripe smell as they passed, even from far off, for they carried the dung which had nurtured London’s vegetable gardens over the centuries, giving her citizens pleasure and a portion of good health.

‘I am old and tired,’ Clive went on, ‘but I am glad I have lived long enough to see this day. Had we not taken you in, Wheatcroft, we would have avoided much excitement,’ with his solemn smile, a brief quarrying of his eroded face, ‘and much achievement.

‘To see the river filled with East and West Indiamen, and the ships of Mendip, Hozier and Hazell so thick at anchor they look as if we had replanted the forests from which they are made. It gives an extra shine to the eye and an extra fullness to the heart,’ dabbing his eye with a silk handkerchief.

‘Only a little longer, and we shall have more ships, Uncle, and bigger docks,’ said Gavin, tall and slender, with a rugged face that had nothing of the fop about it and seemed already prepared to be beaten by the weather. ‘We are a tree that shall grow ever mightier.’

‘Bless the boy, he’s as ambitious as his father was. It’s a fine thing to have a foundation on which your heirs can build,' his eyes turning inward as though to gaze upon his own sons, dead almost as soon as they were born. He looked at me afterwards with affection, patting my arm, and I felt for a moment almost as though I owed him an apology, for having my Gavin next to me.

I tried to voice a remark of consolation, but was silent, for what can one man say to another, to solace him for the loss of a son? I put my arm about Gavin's shoulder, and was fortified by the touch of him.

'You shall live a long time yet,' I told Clive; he seemed indeed indestructible, thin and bent but in the depths of his age moving through life with an even rhythm.

'Nay, Wheatcroft, death is a great champion at winning trophies. He shall win another ere long.'

Two weeks later, I received the intelligence that Clive Hozier was mortally ill, and hastened to his house in Paddington.

He lay upon his death-bed like a long pillar of salt. His white face was taut, scalloped out and hollowed by sickness and life's seasons. He looked at me, with eyes that had retreated into deep caverns. When he closed them, shutting off the reflection of his soul, his qualities were so closely wrapped round him as to be themselves a winding-sheet of the spirit, giving out nothing of the sort of man he was; a stranger regarding him might not have known whether Clive were a good man or an evil, save by the tears of those who stood about him.

Clive's austere kindness, his gloom and carefulness, were transposed into this stretched parcel; only his Adam's apple, independently animated, bounced in his ravaged throat.

Again he opened his eyes, rested them for a brief while on his family and on me, smiled, sighed, and was gone.

I looked down and wept, not only with regret for my late friend and partner, but for myself; I was poignantly aware now of my own mortality, and saddened by the reflection that the vivid joyousness of life is matched cruelly by its brevity.

CHAPTER THIRTY-SIX

KATE continued to play the great lady, and to devote all her time to the amusement of others, seldom heeding her husband's need for gratification.

The dimity-room accordingly became my play-room, in which with Patsy I lived a sort of voluptuous childhood.

The games we played were however far from childish; so often did we laugh and sob, so frequently was the linen a witness of our gaspings and thumpings, that I felt the place to be impregnated with our pastimes, and that even when we were not there the room itself must send echoes of our passions out on to the landing and downstairs to Kate's ears.

A toll was taken of me for my pleasures, for my side, where it had been gouged by the squire's ball, pained me frequently, and furthermore I feared I had the stone, for even Patsy's body could not cushion me against the sharp and persistent ache below my belly.

I therefore repaired to St. Thomas's Hospital to be examined by William Cheselden who could, it was said, extract a stone from a bladder in less than thirty seconds.

Through a long, stifling dormitory, whose windows were shut, I was led to a bed clotted with the previous inhabitant's gore; the floor and table were likewise blood-stained, so that the place smelled like an appendage of the slaughter-houses at Smithfield.

When I remonstrated, that the windows might be opened to spare my lungs from petrifying for lack of fresh air, I was told that to do so would be to allow invasion by noxious vapours from without, certain to kill the sick with their poisons; when I persisted I was moved to a small room and allowed to breathe sweet air at, it was explained to me, my peril.

Being given much brandy, I was very drunk when Cheselden arrived; I was loaded on to a table, and lay there like deck cargo until he was ready. An assistant held up a basin to receive that part of me which was to be removed, the surgeon held his knife aloft like a Moor his dagger and swept it down into me.

The pain was awesome, being far more terrible than that made by the ball, but the brandy sat upon it and wrapped it about and muffled it.

I saw the assistant look admiringly into his bowl at the prize which Cheselden had tossed there; on catching sight of it, an obscene cobnut cocooned in my own blood, I vomited over it with some skill. The assistant looked affronted, Cheselden smiled with satisfaction and wiped his knife on the sleeve of his shirt, already stiff with the blood of others. I sank heavily into oblivion.

When I awoke I was stitched, and asked for more brandy, which was poured down my throat. Better than that, I saw Kate come into the room, for once without a retinue, on her arm a basket of fruit and on her face a look so affectionate, so thankful that she had not been widowed, that I was moved by her concern, and for a while considered renouncing Patsy and making my way alone through the comfortable but barren marital desert.

My thoughts of virtue lasted only as long as my convalescence; having returned home prematurely against Cheselden's advice, owing to the unendurable cries of the patients and the miasma of decay that swept into my chamber every time the door was opened, I longed only to mend swiftly, that I might again feel Patsy's tongue upon me, and hear her laugh of triumph.

The love I had for my house was helped to burgeon in large part by this young and naughty maid, and all its splendour, all its joy, the sight of the ornaments, furnishings and paintings that I had so come to love, lapsed in significance when I thought of that small, secluded part of my mansion, the dimity-room, and of her who awaited me there.

CHAPTER THIRTY-SEVEN

If my favourite place of recreation indoors was the dimity room, that outside was Lambeth Fields, where I delighted to go ballooning with Hannibal.

The balloon and its retinue went by cart, we following on horseback; I well remember my first voyage, my sense of sickening anticipation as the bellows played on the fire beneath our improbable conveyance, which strained as though trying to get away from the searing breath below. Hannibal and I climbed into the basket, and were cast off.

The sky was overcast, and I found it difficult to believe that were we able to penetrate the black barrier of cloud above, we would find sunshine beyond. The wind sighed in melancholy fashion through the cables, the wickerwork creaked rheumatically, and I was torn between apprehension and exaltation.

At first I reflected morbidly on the probability that the ropes from which we were suspended would break; we would fall away from the great bulk of the balloon above us to be violently extinguished against the ground. Or perhaps, the swelling, bosom-like shape bearing us up might fissure; the basket would cant while we screamed in unison with the fierce and serpentine hiss of escaping air.

Such fears ill became my pride; I must be growing old, a victim of years that had scarcely ambled, before breaking into a trot and now a gallop.

The fears vanished in the face of exaltation, of seeing the pristine wonder of London below, the teeming streets and minute people, the churches from the point of view of their spires, the houses and squares and the whole glistening green and yellow canvas of the place, some of it daubed with smoke, most of it shining and clear.

With the aid of flying and the continuing novelty of Patsy I hoped for some time yet to deflect the aim of death, the unerring marksman. Tumbling Patsy kept me well in body and preserved my wits, flying bestowed its comforting philosophy.

Where better could I ponder the ephemerality of those things to which we give so much importance, than in our basket, rocked like a cradle by the soft gyrations of the balloon, beaming down at us like a mother carrying her child, shining with benevolence? Life's tragedies and troubles became distant, insignificant; only life's joy was as vivid as ever.

Hannibal studied the sky with his sextant, the earth through his telescope, but I was content to dream. The flights we made were excursions into history, conferring on us a measure of immortality. It was as though my eyes could penetrate the ground and see beneath the city Roman burial mounds, Saxon earthworks; not only was the Thames sprinkled with modern vessels, but those of the Vikings, come to rape and ravage.

Katie did not approve my venturing into the sky, deeming it lacking in dignity, but forbore to discuss it, knowing how I relished such escape.

For my house, that I so loved, was growing alien to me; Gregory was in his unctuous fashion transforming it into a cathedral, our dining-table his high altar, before which he posed and postured in devout self-worship. He practised incantations, telling us that dinner was served in different tones of voice and varying emphasis, as though reciting the litany and expecting us to make appropriate responses, while footmen genuflected to his announcements and served braised rabbit in time to murmured benedictions.

If Gregory held sway over his coterie of footmen, Raton donned the purple in the kitchen, overseeing everything with the red and fiery eye, not so much of the perfectionist as of the fanatic.

It was as though every sauce were peppered with the spite of revolution; the infection of the Commune spiced our dishes as though the most ordinary capon were the head of poor Louis, peering blindly at us through a curtain of pale garnish.

Nevertheless, although the heavens and the dimity-room were my places of refuge, I was smitten with grief beyond believing when my Kate became ill and went into steep decline.

She had attained her ultimate ambition, of inviting the Prince Regent himself to dinner, and having her invitation accepted; I found him amusing but gross. From that time she seemed to feel that there was no further reason for surviving, no cause which could possibly transcend that of royal entertainment. Her sons were grown, her husband loved but no longer needed her; she had become a human flying buttress, decorative but not obviously essential.

Hazell House became for a time rudderless, devoid of purpose; Gregory put off the bishop and donned the undertaker, the dining-table the bier about which the footmen played the part of pall-bearers.

Katie died at seven o'clock of a Sunday morning, to the trill of festive birds. I stared at her lying so silent, smooth and blank with death's composure, and saw her alive again in my mind; I saw not this woman, inanimate, but the vital creature whose laughter echoed in my ears as it had down the years.

Were I to lift her eyelids I would see eyes sparkling with gaiety as a brook with sunshine, and the thin lines of her mouth were drawn tightly only because she was playing, and would in a moment become full and ripe with mirth.

Perhaps it was a deliberate act of consolation on the part of destiny, or merely a quirk of nature's desire for balance, but shortly after Katie had left the world, Patsy repaired to the dimity-room and there, stuffing her mouth with linen to quell her own cries, gave birth to our son.

In view of the manner of his conception and the place where he was born, we called him Dimity.

CHAPTER THIRTY-EIGHT

DIMITY was a pretty bastard. Gregory would have sent him and his mother away, but I was resolute that they should remain. There was no need for my legitimate sons to know that they were endowed with a brother suddenly emerged from the wrong side of the blanket, and upon Patsy I enjoined discretion. I intended in the fullness of time to disclose to Dimity the fact of his inheritance; in the meantime, I continued to bed Patsy, in more comfortable surroundings than our coupling had been used to, and was thankful that her giving birth had in no way impaired her sensuality.

That, and going up with Hannibal in his balloon, continued to be my principal pleasures. The running of my business was now fully entrusted to Gavin, while Garth went to sea to learn the business of our fleet at first hand and, like a huntsman after a stag, took to whaling.

I was not with Hannibal on his last voyage, but I witnessed the end of it. I was standing, discussing with a gardener the siting of a new flower bed, when Hannibal appeared ahead over the park. The balloon was as always a satisfying sight, a rich globe striped in red and yellow gleaming bravely against the clouds.

As I watched, the globe, as in my early nightmares, tore with an audible screech; I saw Hannibal clinging to the sides of the basket, which tilted and began to pirouette, faster and faster, spinning and canting and falling.

Hannibal could hold on no longer; I remember that I shouted, and put my hands over my ears as though to blot out the sound of my agony, as my son fell, as a dead eagle, lazily, lethally.

He landed but a few score paces away; I kissed his bloody face and held him and prayed that he might breathe, but he was broken beyond reviving.

In the few minutes between Hannibal's hitting the ground and my having to accept that he was dead, I withered.

Like a half-blind dog I seldom left my fireside; gout came to settle on my right foot like a scorpion. I looked at my gnarled hands and, as I so often did, now that the future was becoming ever shorter and the past more attenuated, saw them as they had been, calloused but young when I was a sailor, smooth but not soft since I had become a man of business.

Dimity solaced me; he was a child pert but not captious, with something of beguiling wickedness about him. Although I could see myself when young, I could not envisage Dimity old; it was beyond imagining to see the young body, the palace he inhabited, become, as mine had done, a hovel.

My disclosure to Gavin and Garth that they had a half-brother could no longer be delayed. As Garth was still at sea I sent for Gavin and, mustering as much courage as I could, made my confession.

'So Dimity is your bastard, father?' without either pleasure or understanding.

'He is.' Was it so serious to sire a child, albeit a bastard, and to love it? 'That in no way diminishes my love for you, my dear.'

How bleak he looked; forgiveness only comes with experience. 'Am I to understand that you wish me to—to cherish your bastard, father?'

'Would that be so difficult? He is the same child that you cherished yesterday.'

'And his mother, should I elevate her in my esteem also? Perhaps to rank with mine?' Gavin, my Gavin, I shall soon enough be far from you; a dying man wishes his children to draw close, not to thrust them from him.

'My wish is, that you should respect his mother and love him.' My bowels rumbled; I besought them to be continent, lest I were no longer beached on a vestige of dignity but forced to abandon it.

Gavin said nothing, but stood slender and taut. Silently I invoked the bond between us to help his understanding, called upon his childhood and my young parenthood, strolling together through shared rich pastures. The one thing I was determined not to invoke was his pity; I strove to prevent my hand trembling, to ignore the perpetual stinging of the gout, and I looked at him as once I had stared across the ocean at a distant headland, with eyes that were sharp and not shrouded in everlasting twilight.

'I shall do my best to respect your wishes,' Gavin answered at last, his voice stilted and artificial. I had almost rather he had flung out of the room with a valedictory oath, a roared: 'Pox on you, sir!' There was meat in that; I did not relish his anaemic compliance.

'Continue to pay Patsy her allowance and love the boy—that will be respecting my wishes!' I said brusquely. 'Damn it, my son, I may have erred in exercising my loins on a lusty wench, but you yourself may err one day, when the hearth burns low in your marriage bed. Not with lack of love, my boy, but with lack of novelty!

'Credit me with having sufficient love in me for all my children, in wedlock and outside it! Must a child be unloved because he is a bastard? England is full of Fitzes, who sit at the highest tables and have long and creditable lines going back to the straw pallets of roistering kings tumbling women who were not their queens. Does that make a Fitz less likeable? Must he be disinherited because of his father's potently sprayed sap? Love is not a matter of morals, my dear, but of feeling.'

'To listen to you, Father, one would have thought that it was I who had done wrong,' Gavin answered me, 'and was being upbraided for it.'

'I beg your pardon, my dear. I wax too emphatic in my concern that you should understand and be tolerant.' I held out my hand to him; slowly, after infinite meditation, he took it.

'Love is the one quality we have, my dear, which may be spread as thickly as we wish without being in any way diminished,' I said softly, almost unable to speak from weakness and relief.

Still clutching his hand, I climbed slowly from my bed and made my halting way to the commode.

CHAPTER THIRTY-NINE

MY universe shrank to the confines of the canopy about my bed; my room became an attic, filled with dusty stars, creation a dim light under a distant door.

I was scarcely aware whether I were moving away from the womb, or towards it; my soul was sinking into winter.

Death was upon me, the penalty for old age, the ultimate fait accompli; I was going to die because there was nothing else to do.

At least the act of dying was a positive action, to be greatly preferred to lingering in frailty, a decrepit Hamlet before an audience of weeping family.

I hesitated at the threshold of eternity for some days before I felt my time upon me; I managed to raise my hand in a final gesture, of blessing, farewell, salute to that which awaited me, and with Dimity's small hand fondling my beard, slid serenely down the chute of oblivion.

MY DEATH 1815

CHAPTER FORTY

DEATH had been a matter of the spirit leaving the body; I found now that the body had left the spirit.

I had evaporated; I was able to see and to move but not to feel. It was a world of invisible snow, muffling and distorting the nature of things, and I was a snowflake in it, that drifted and floated and rode every current of air. I moved insubstantially about, an ectoplasmic fantasy, trying to accustom myself to being merely a touch, a whisper, a thing with form but void.

The view I had of my bedroom was from an angle not entirely unfamiliar to me; it was that from a balloon as it rises from the ground. Perhaps in fact I had turned into a balloon; whatever I was I had been freed from the body of the old man lying on his bed amidst his mourners. I saw a pretty child being shooed away by a weeping girl, who rebuked him for continuing to touch the clay of the old man's cheek; the air was tense with reverence and grief.

'So there you are, begetter of bastards!'

Looking about me I saw a shimmering, luminous shape, hurried towards it with arms outstretched.

'Katie! My sweet Kate!' I stood before her, overcome with gratitude that death did not have to be a state of loneliness.

' "My sweet Kate",' she echoed scornfully. 'When I was alive you were at your lecherous frolics, and after my death you wasted not a moment before returning to them. I was with you, watching you, striving to cast a mantle of chill about you as you tumbled my trollop of a maid, but you were too hot in lust to notice. Well, there will be no work here for your outsize cod, Master Wheatcroft. Think of it, how you shall reside here for all eternity unable to cover a doxy.'

'I should find the prospect of celestial celibacy only appalling had I cod to flourish,' I told her. 'In the event, I have not. At least,' I added, peering down, 'I have the shape of one but not the substance.'

' 'Tis indeed become a wand with no magic to it,' still scornful.

'If there are to be no pleasures in ephemeral copulation, we must devise something else, my sweet.'

'Why then, wait until my maid has found another lover, which I warrant will be soon, and attend upon their wooing, as I did with you. You shall find it strange indeed, to be present at the feast yet to have no sense of taste or smell, to watch mouth pressed to mouth and ponder the reason for it, for you will find it beyond your comprehension, why two people should wish to stick together in lust.'

'Have you carried jealousy beyond the grave, Kate?'

'Jealousy? A jealous wraith? I am not jealous.'

'How beautiful you are,' I told her, and indeed we were both in the full pitch of our youth, reflections of ourselves at our most glorious. I reached out to touch my darling's face, but there was nothing beneath my fingers. We were portraits that could communicate, paintings that could speak across the corridors of their gallery but not leave their walls to embrace.

'Even as a ghost with a phantom cod you speak seductively,' Kate told me. 'I can feel you in me yet, for you were a vivid man.' She smiled. 'You used to send me spinning and whirling over the roof-tops, blazing and flinging the cinders of my passion across the world. You made of me a searing miracle, that burned and sparkled with your fire. I never knew what it was to lie abed with a pallid husband, that had other concerns than those which most concerned myself; you taught me that all were well lost if the sacrifice had to be balanced against a saucy, roistering cod that loathed to rest.'

'And are we condemned forever to talk of love without the means to practise it, like the twisted beggars who eye passing ladies to find sour fault with them? Perhaps we would do better to denigrate love, to find the dark side of it in order not to have to torment ourselves with our inability to consummate it.'

'Are you tormented?' my Kate asked me softly. 'Do you so long to touch me?'

'I long.'

'I am glad that you are here, Wheatcroft. I am sorry of course that you are dead,' hastily, 'but I am comforted by your abstract presence. I forgive you your bastard and your wenching in the dimity-room.'

'Thank you, my sweet.' I sought to console her about our state. 'It is better to be here, even as we are, than to be broiled on one of Satan's spits.'

'I have always thought the reports of hell to have been exaggerated. After all, none of those ecclesiasts who have so often threatened us with it has been there, or at least has been released to talk about it.'

I laughed. 'On the other hand, we might have been admitted to Paradise. I cannot help but feel that God is guilty of an oversight; should we not at least have been granted a vision of Him, should there not have been a hint of His presence, a few melodious hosannas sung by angels?'

'I have never been, as you know, of a musical disposition,' Kate replied. 'Save that I enjoyed the harpsichord. Choral music, I always found, depressed my spirits.'

'It is supposed to elevate.'

'I cannot help it if it provoked in me an opposite reaction,' tartly.

'Heaven for you would not then be a place of choirs, but of cherubs tinkling at their keyboards.'

'And Heaven for you would be a display of licentious wenches, whose waggling arses issued lewd invitation.'

'So long as I were able to accept such invitation, my sweet. Tell me, are we the only'—I found the word difficult to say—'the only ghosts here?'

'I have seen no others.'

'I had hoped that Hannibal might be here.'

'Hannibal did not die here. He is doubtless where he would love to be most, parading among the clouds. We are so circumscribed here,' wistfully.

'Is it not possible to leave this house?'

'We loved to be here in life, we shall spend our deaths here.'

'But have you tried to leave?'

'Once or twice I have reached the front door, but was prevented—I know not by what agency—from going farther. Gregory is become a lazy knave,' Kate added characteristically, 'that gives short measure of his virtue. Now that we are both gone he will no doubt navigate Gavin suavely to suit his purpose.'

'Gavin will require a deal of navigating. He has both mind and will, and is engrossed in our affairs.'

'Easy prey for a rascally butler, then.'

'I suppose that, if he becomes too rascally we can haunt him?' I suggested.

'I have not yet learned how to,' Kate confessed. 'Perhaps now that you are here we may practise it together.'

'We have much to learn properly to accommodate ourselves to the fashion of death. To learn the art of haunting shall be our first concern.'

I smiled; Kate eyed me seriously. 'Shall you make death into a comedy? Life should be a matter of laughter, and is life so much the opposite of death that we must now cry away the centuries? Let us make the most of death, as we did of life.'

We stood close and smiled one at the other, mingled, becoming one; I sensed Kate's tresses against my cheek, sensed the taste of her mouth, felt for a moment that we were alive and sowing the seeds of youth in springtime, instead of having traversed the divide to the other side of winter.

CHAPTER FORTY-ONE

ANCHORED in the harbour of our immortality Kate and I sought to stir our sense of purpose, lest it became barnacled by resignation. Our first endeavour was to exorcize something of Gregory's unction, for he was more and more playing the pontiff, and self-righteousness had made him vulnerable.

We learned how to startle him with the chill of our presence, how to project a faint but mocking laugh, at which Kate was especially skilled; the resultant dropping of a loaded dish, the fine lace at the neck of a silken gown awash with wine from a maladroitly tilted decanter, splendidly mortified the butler; prised from the dented armour of his dignity he was reduced.

This exercise with Gregory helped us not to become reconciled to fathomless detachment, to be entirely immune to the timeless season, to sun and storm, to passion and tranquillity. Further interest was later afforded us when Gavin brought home a wife.

Her name was Charlotte; she was possessed of auburn hair and a tilted bosom, but her nose was a trifle sharp.

I was one with the crowd that jested with the bride and groom on their wedding night and urged them to expert consummation; Kate rebuked me for my intrusion, for when the crowd at last withdrew I remained. In truth I wished not only to see how Gavin fared, but to recall through his pleasure a little of my own.

The two regarded each other delicately, she abed, he coming into the chamber and standing before her, preened and enjoying her timid admiration. Pulling back the covers, he arrived beside her and bussed her.

She returned his buss, and each examined the other's nightgown, raised it, and continued his scrutiny. Impelled yet restrained, Charlotte leant forward and thrust her sharp nose into Gavin's navel, but there her ambition halted. He seized her, after expectantly waiting, and sought to gain some definition in the matter, as to bringing her mouth up to his, or despatching it in the contrary direction to mumble his cod, but she remained frozen.

'My love,' Gavin coaxed her, 'my love, do not tease yourself. Let yourself free, my angel, let yourself find release.' She remained however as though petrified, Gavin's navel her Holy Grail, won after countless battles with her own restraint and virtue and hereafter to be pressed close.

Gavin's patience held awhile, as he stroked the hair of this mollusc at his belly, but at last the drink in him outvied his sap and withered him. He slept. Reassured by the disappearance of Gavin's proud soldier Charlotte at last moved, and lay listening to her husband's snores till daybreak; I left the marriage bed then, which might have well been a bed of death for all the exercise it had had that night, and found Kate in a rage at my curiosity.

'Must a man who becomes a ghost be present than only at his own wedding night?' I demanded. 'Am I not entitled to more than the dear memory of ourselves as we coupled and entwined and coupled again? I prized you above drink—poor Gavin has chosen a less robust way to pass the nuptial hours.'

' 'Tis merely a postponement,' retorted Kate, 'the world will not end because he did not rupture her maidenhead the moment the last guest had left.'

'If she has a maidenhead,' I answered.

'Do you then doubt her virtue?' angrily.

'Not her virtue, but her substance. I could not determine the construction of her, for she behaved so coldly, substituting paralysis for passion; I am not convinced at all that she is flesh and blood, but might have an ornamental crotch of wood and stone.' I sighed. 'And poor Gavin is like a clock, that is stopped for lack of an active pendulum.'

'No doubt he will acquit himself so well tomorrow that the clock will be some hours fast,' said Kate with loyal optimism. 'Now cease traducing your son and daughter-in-law and turn your attention to your bastard.'

'To Dimity?'

'I can still not bear to utter his name,' scowling. 'He is become a wayward child, that delights in mischief and is not restrained.'

'He is on the verge of manhood and lusty with it, but there is no harm in him.'

'I have watched him closely of late; he is a tease, that

likes to pinch the buttocks of a serving maid and run away. He is sly too; he hides in closets and leaps from them with loud cries to discomfort the maids so that they drop their trays—no doubt his birthplace has accustomed him to feeling more at home in closets than elsewhere.'

'Are you not confusing malice with high spirits?'

'I am not, Wheatcroft. That child, that brat, will bring trouble to this house if you do not curb him.' She added with a deal of malice herself: 'After all, you are his father, and ought to do a father's duty.'

'What should I do then? Turn into a bust of Socrates and fall on him?'

'Chill him a little, allow him to feel a presence for which he cannot account, as we have done with Gregory. Fear will slow him down.'

'I do not want to be feared.'

'You have a strange conception of your responsibilities.'

'You were ever adept at believing the worst of people.'

'I am talking now not of belief, but of fact. Dimity is a liar too,' she added, 'and I deplore his plausibility.'

'If I deem him to deserve it, Dimity shall suffer some sort of chastisement.'

'He must,' Kate told me, shaking her head in a way that I knew well. She stuck her lip out sulkily and drifted through the wall.

I thought of Dimity and Kate's accusation of his wickedness, but more telling than his sallies and forays against the maids was my vision of his face above mine, and the remembrance of his small warm hand against my cheek at the moment of my dying.

CHAPTER FORTY-TWO

OWNER of two hundred ships, merchant and trader, wool agent and holder of shares in a few dozen of different enterprises, my son Gavin succeeded on the third night of his marriage in penetrating his wife.

Benignly I watched him at his labours, which he had mustered in a fashion more military than amorous.

Treating Charlotte's maidenhead as an enclave that must be breached, Gavin summoned the full force of concentration to gain the stubborn stronghold, while Charlotte uttered polite screams like a barnyard at full cry.

''Tis done!' Gavin exulted at last, uttering a feral roar, and with glowing countenance fell back upon his pillows, from which he bestowed an abrupt buss on the tip of Charlotte's nose, that would have skewered a muffin.

'And did you like it, sweet?' asked Charlotte, exuding, to Gavin's evident satisfaction, the perfume of her deflowering. He played the whippet, sniffing at her before replying to her query.

'Gentle Charlotte, beloved Charlotte, to pleasure you were a way in which I could fill all my days,' with gallant exaggeration, for he was in everything a busy man.

'Thy rod and thy staff comfort me,' said Charlotte, laughing and touching, her finger curling round Gavin's supine trigger. 'To make love is to give everything a new dimension.'

'And to remove it,' looking at her playful hand.

'Thank God I was not sentenced to be all my life a maiden,' said Charlotte with satisfaction.

'There are virtuous women who believe that that on which they sit increases in value with age, and do not realize that the more closely they protect it, the less desirable it becomes.'

'My sensuous philosopher,' kissing him.

'My beautiful one,' and indeed radiance improved her greatly, although her profile had too much in common with that of a swordfish for my liking.

Gavin caressed her bosom, which responded with a twin salute; before long they were again at the thump.

Their dallying delighted me, but my witness of it augmented a wistful longing in me once again to possess a woman myself and defy Kate's mockery of my barren future.

I left the bedchamber and found her; she rebuked me as she had done previously for watching Gavin at his rites.

' 'Tis near incestuous of you, to hang over your son's marriage bed and savour his every gasp! No doubt you would change places with him, and yourself give Charlotte a hard ride beneath your prod!'

'Memories are less fulfilling than action, my sweet. I do not contemplate Gavin's ghostly cuckolding, but to assume again the canopy of a man—may I not bring that about?'

'I think not. Wheatcroft, have you lost your wits with your flesh? Do you suppose that you can arrange your own rebirth? From whose womb will you leap full-grown and lusty?'

'I was thinking not of rebirth, but in some manner to don a body.'

'Wheatcroft, death has made you mad.'

I laughed. 'Death at present has unmade me, sweet Kate. I relish not this perversity of change, that makes me neither dead nor alive but sets me gliding through the smooth halls of Purgatory.'

'Would you not rather be here in your house, than resting amidst the worms in the churchyard?'

'No doubt I am amidst the worms. My poor clay is by now quite consumed by them, but they cannot gnaw my soul.'

Kate swung about, to leave so morbid a subject. 'If this is Purgatory,' she said, 'is it not quiet? It it not tranquil?'

'We are certainly becalmed in it.'

'Then should we not be grateful? Reflect: I conceived of Purgatory as an antechamber to Hell, where we were to grovel and beg forgiveness of the sins our creation had imposed upon us, and endure the purging that gave the place its name.'

'And how did you conceive of your purging? By fire, or perhaps by emetic? Six goblets a day of salt water or sulphur, until the last evil thought that had entered the mind since birth was vomited up, accounted for and at the last forgiven?'

'I had not thought of acquiring a state of grace through emetics, Wheatcroft. Fire is surely a more probable purge?'

'If we could be set fire to, we could also feel. We could smell and we could touch, my angel. By no possible convention could we be only hurt, without capacity for being pleasured, unless Purgatory be filled with closets containing bodies, as they might be clothes, for our spirits to fit into at intervals for torment. Two hours of slow broiling, then the body carefully replaced in the wardrobe while the spirit reflects on its further punishment, as a sailor had to bear the burden of reflection on the lashes still due to him did he succumb prematurely to those already inflicted.'

'I did not expect that Purgatory would not be barbarous,' Kate said thoughtfully.

'My sweet, you gave scarce consideration to it, for you were sure that your course was set for Paradise.'

'I lived without rancour. I was no agent of misery or displeasure, delighted never in hurting——'

'My love, you were indeed a paragon,' I interrupted. 'That does not alter our present circumstances. We are now as much a part of our house as it was once of us, but we cannot summon a servant to bring us even a glass of water. We are suspended here in limbo, and if we are to escape it, must concentrate our thoughts and flex our wills.'

'My dear, you were ever an incorrigible man. Now it seems that you are an equally incorrigible phantom.'

'There must be a way,' I insisted. 'Should I feel the urge to accomplish relief, were relief impossible? I intend again to partake of corporeal pastimes, I shall not spend eternity an evanescent witness!'

'So Godspeed, sweet Wheatcroft,' mocking me. 'And when you are all clothed again in flesh, and it is young flesh, and sweet, you may incorporate me also, and dance with me back down the years, or if you have a mind to it the future, and you may buss me and sport with me also, for in that you have always delighted me.'

I smiled at her, being unable to do aught else, and was infused with the desire to be again her lover.

I moved to the window and stared out across the park, and pondered.

CHAPTER FORTY-THREE

GARTH came home, a tall, broad, bluff man that smelled of salt. He had Viking hair and resembled me as I had been before age bent my back and dragged its claws across my face.

Kate and I were present as he described to Gavin and Charlotte how he had fixed upon the whale as a source of wealth, had built up our fleet to pursue the monster through the ice blue seas. He told his tales with too much relish in gore, dwelling at length upon the blood and battle of his coursing, the great scarlet lakes which his lethal diligence created in the ocean. 'We sing a song,' he said, 'to stimulate our endeavours:

'The whale blows,
The harpoon flies;
The whale bleeds,
The whale dies.'

I did not approve of his malignancy towards the creatures, the way in which he saw himself as King Exterminator standing astride the waters with his hissing cable tipped with death.

Garth showed little interest in family affairs, and seemed restless to return to his ships; as compensation for his time spent about nautical, rather than marital, pastimes, he told Gavin, when Charlotte was in the kitchen bending the knee to Raton, he had sired children thickly upon the American coast. There he had met a senile captain, Elkan by name, who had known and loved his father.

At the mention of Elkan's name much that I had not for long remembered, returned to me, and I wondered to hear that he was still alive who had lived so boisterously, and rejoiced that he still held affection for me.

'Before I set sail again I shall visit my inheritance at Pepton Harbinger,' Garth said. 'Have you been there lately, brother?'

'I have not.' Gavin paused. 'I wonder whether you should go.'

'Should go? Is it not mine?'

'Certainly it is yours. Yet strange things are said.'

'Strange things?' Garth laughed. 'What sort of things?'

'Why, that it is haunted by a ghost so evil that none dare go near it.'

'And do you believe in this ghost, Gavin?'

'I do not believe that so many folk have dreamed of its existence. Furthermore, I know, as do yourself, something of the man alleged to have become that ghost. Our great-uncle, Sebastian.'

'We were brought up to have little faith in his kindness,' said Garth, 'but as to his possessing my house, I scoff at it!'

'He died in Pepton Grange quite alone. It was months before they found him, alive with maggots that lived in his tattered face. There was little else left of him but his bones.'

'Why then I shall go to Pepton forthwith and recapture it from this wretched carcass.'

'The house is as empty as it was. None will go near it. I suggest, brother, that you take with you a priest, if one can be found to undertake the assignment, and drench the place with holy water.'

'I have no fear of whales, that have the strength to smash a small frigate with their tails. Shall I fear this wretched and decayed uncle?' Garth filled his glass and drank. 'What is the manner of his haunting?'

'I do not know. Only that it terrifies, and is accompanied by the wailing of children.'

'All children wail. I have been many times deafened by my bastards.'

' 'Tis your bad blood,' Kate hissed at me, 'that flows in Garth! One bastard in the family cannot be enough, but must be the forerunner of an army of them.'

'I doubt your children wail in quite the same fashion,' said Gavin. 'These are, so I have heard, in torment.'

'Why then, I shall go to rescue them.'

'I will come with you, then.'

'Of course you will not. Am I to admit terror of Sebastian?'

'You know as well as I that those who have sinned are condemned to dwell here after they are dead, till they repent and are forgiven.'

'A piss-pot on such penance! England now rests under steel rails, along which steam engines will soon draw coaches. We have factories which belch their power across the sky. The furnaces we know are not those of hell but of industry. Shall old Sebastian's ghost sail with its bow-wave of miserable waifs through such times? In modern England there is no room for ghosts.'

'Ah,' I whispered to Kate, 'he banishes us from this rich technical society, if we do not run on rails behind a kettle.'

'I do not want him to go to Pepton Harbinger,' answered Kate.

'He is a stubborn man. How should we prevent him?'

'Can we not give him an inkling? Can we not find some way to change his mind?'

'There is always room in the world for things of the spirit,' said Gavin. 'What is more a thing of the spirit than a ghost? Only religion—hence, I beg you again, take with you a priest.'

'I shall go alone,' Garth responded. 'I shall show the villagers of Pepton who is master. I do not intend to take my inheritance in miserable humility, asking a phantom if I may do so. If Uncle Sebastian still resides there in the form of vapour, he shall acknowledge that he does so by my sufferance.'

'And how shall he acknowledge it? Will you threaten to loose a harpoon into him if he refuses to go? Shall you scourge him with a cat-o'-nine-tails? Spirits, if they may be opposed at all, are subject to subtlety, not force.'

'The subtlety of a priest's mumbling as he lays the ghostly dust with water sprinkled from his chalice? Gavin, we have both seen too much of the world to believe that it is not large enough for us, but extends beyond the boundaries of our conception.'

'I have seen enough of the world to beware of the vanity of thinking that I know aught but a fraction of it.' Gavin sighed. 'You are resolved to go to Pepton, then?'

'Tomorrow,' taking more wine. 'And alone.'

'I beg of you——'

'There is too much talk of begging. Begging the ghost to accept me, begging the priest to exorcize, begging me not to go.

'Dear brother,' continued Garth caustically, 'men are

my concern. To lead, to drive, to dominate with the discipline of my presence. As my crews obey me, knowing that they be lost without me and prey to every whim of man and weather, so shall the people of Pepton. I shall gather them up as the wind does a bushel of autumn leaves, and take them with me, and furbish the house and sweep it clean of the past, embroiling Uncle Sebastian's phantom in the turmoil of our industry.'

'I pray, then,' Gavin told him solemnly, 'that you come back.'

In the acute silence of the room, I heard Kate weeping.

CHAPTER FORTY-FOUR

NEXT day, Garth departed aboard a lively horse. Kate and I watched through the window as the beast frisked and pranced and Garth shouted his confident farewell.

He set off at the gallop; he was a man born to take life at full tilt. He would equip himself with clothes for his stay, on the road to Pepton, eat at inns, sleep at an hostelry, if he did not ride through the night.

Arriving in Pepton Harbinger with a cry of challenge to Sebastian's ghost, he would be embraced by the thankful villagers like a Roman despatching a Visigoth.

Afraid to go before him, strewing palm leaves, they would follow Garth as he galloped up the moss-encrusted drive and flung open the front door of the Grange, bellowed a further challenge across the hall and down the dim, dust enshrouded corridors, ran in and out of shadowy rooms shouting with his loud rich voice, commanding Sebastian to appear and, when he did not, going out again to the fearful but admiring peasantry to proclaim their release.

'I am afraid for Garth,' Kate said, when he was out of sight. 'Maybe Sebastian has learned something that we have not, and can control affairs.'

'If he has discovered how to do so, then so shall we, my sweet. We have already succeeded in creating mild disturbances to our Gregory, and so are encouraged to persist.'

'We do not have aeons in which to learn such tricks, if we are to save Garth.'

'Are you so sure that he is in danger?'

'As sure as you are yourself,' she answered. 'I do not desire to see his span cut short frivolously. There was no need for him to go.'

'He would not be deterred,' I reminded her. 'Gavin did his best to convince him that he must not toy with Sebastian. Garth was set upon it.'

'We must go to him!' cried Kate. 'Somehow we must escape this house and fly to Pepton!'

'Shall I then summon Pegasus from the Elysian fields of

mythology in which he grazes, and bid him bear me through the skies, a ghost horse bearing a ghost horseman? Shall I take my ghost sword from its ghost scabbard and smite Sebastian double dead?' Even as I spoke, in the agony of a father whose son is menaced, I was aware of feeling, conscious of a surge of blood that death could not deny.

My seed and I were still joined, the tree which I had engendered firmly planted upside down, its roots steeped in ether, its upper leaves in life.

Regarding Kate's tragic face, I cursed my impotence. 'Be damned to God! Can he not look after His own as well as Satan protects his grisly charges? Here am I, unable to act, for I know not how, while Sebastian, it seems, has learned to govern circumstances. What does he do; is he able to puncture the air about him as a rattlesnake does a man's skin, and inject his poisonous dew-drops into it, so that he moves about the halls of Pepton Grange in an aura of venom? Can he inject with it all those who come within his presence?'

Urged by my fears and spurred by Kate's lamentations, I did my best to fling myself beyond the confines of the house, strove to float from its windows or through its walls and doorways, but always I was secured by some force invisible but omnipotent.

A ray of sunlight was strong as a leash, binding me to the hallway; the sun leered again at me from an upper casement, pinning me to it at the moment that I leaped, and so I floated up and down stairways as though through water, and found walls that had admitted me from room to room grown concrete against me on the outside of the house.

I know not how long it was before Garth returned. He had galloped away in the splendour of his youth; now, tied with velvet ropes, he was borne into the house on a hurdle. Gavin and Charlotte stood mute and distressed as the footmen who had escorted him laid the hurdle on the floor, where he lay gibbering like a denizen of Bedlam.

The tale of Garth's unmanning was told by the coachman who had brought him from Pepton in the squire's conveyance.

Arrived in the village, Garth had straightway gone to see Brereton, now lord of the manor after the death of his father, and had been warned by him of the Grange's reputation. Garth had laughed, leaped again astride and ridden hard to the place to confront whatever lurked there.

When after a long time he had not reappeared, Brereton and his chaplain set out with a courageous retinue to see what had befallen him.

They had barely reached the Grange when they heard laughter, a clatter of scornful mirth all about them. They would fain have broken, but squire and chaplain held them, the latter raising his crucifix in a hand that trembled. The trembling might at first have denied the efficacy of the priest's faith, but the coachman spoke of the wonder of it, how such a holy ornament caused the laughter to turn to a snarl, the snarl to a shriek, the shriek to silence.

Clustered behind the protection of the cross, and sure that as it retreated the evil in the house would advance again accordingly, the men entered the house.

They formed a shivering cluster on the threshold, looking at Garth, who writhed and slithered and foamed on the hall's marble floor. Even when the priest had advanced, and pressed the crucifix to Garth's lips the demons did not leave him; indeed he seemed in greater torment, and sprayed his comforter with incontinent saliva.

After a while Garth was bundled up, moaning and mumbling, entrapped within the horrors of his malady, and carried hither.

Gavin rewarded the coachman and sent by him a note to Brereton, thanking him for his kindness; still bound to the hurdle Garth was borne upstairs and gently placed on a bed.

When he had been left alone, Kate and I went to him, stood beside him and tried to wrap him in the mantle of our love, but he did not see us.

Yet he had evidently seen Sebastian.

Kate placed her fingers on Garth's forehead; neither fingers nor forehead sensed each other, but were strangers.

'Wheatcroft,' Kate whispered. 'Wheatcroft, what shall be his fate? Is he damned in life as we are damned in death?'

'We are not damned,' I told her, striving to give her comfort, 'and neither shall Garth be. That which Sebastian has done, I can undo. Garth shall be my weapon against him.'

'Your weapon?' disconcerted. 'Are you yourself deranged, to speak of Garth as a weapon? How so?'

I did not answer her, not wishing her to be privy to my thought in the matter. I had for unconscious time been contemplating an act, but dared not attempt it with Gavin, lest it destroy him as Garth had been destroyed.

Now I was prepared to experiment, for Garth could be little worse off than he was now; I looked deeply into his wide and staring eyes, watched his head rolling like a ship in a savage sea, and was resolved to salvage him.

CHAPTER FORTY-FIVE

My objective was Garth's brain. I was intent upon a voyage into his mind, to spike it with my own and travel through its grey silken alleys and byways flanked by tendrilled hedgerows wrenched from their pattern by his madness.

I recalled how the rough surgery of grapeshot had smashed open the temple of a seaman, one of the earliest I saw slain, and the curiosity that grappled with my pity and disgust as his brain peered from the fissure like some soft creature of the deep.

Regrettably, I had watched other men in their turn follow along the short dark trail to violent wounding; I had seen the skull sundered often, and from my sad observations built up some knowledge of cerebral shape.

Through this mysterious maze flowed the mind, generating the lightning of thought and the thunder of action; this invisible quality it was that drew men into evil or propelled them along the avenues of good.

If I could invade the brain of Garth, to vanquish the spinning nonsense within, defy it and defeat it and control it, I would expunge Sebastian's curse, damp down my poor child's ravings, and recreate him.

He was sleeping now, occasionally convulsed against his ropes with mouth narrowed in distorting rictus; I focused my will upon him, directed myself to penetrate his head beneath the soaked fair locks and knead his disturbance from within.

'What are you about, Wheatcroft?' Kate stood beside me, so that my concentration fanned out and was lost.

'I am attempting a sublime intrusion,' I told her, satisfied at her look of bafflement.

'I do not understand.'

'Pray accept, that I may not be interrupted at present. When I am here, my eyes near out of their sockets, my mouth stretched and my forehead creased in a frown so deep that it would daunt an embalmer, accept that I am launched on serious purpose, that may not yet be explained to you.'

'Why not?' Kate asked at once.

'Give me discretion in the revealing of it, my love.'

Having failed to draw me out, Kate resorted to taunting. 'You look like a witch casting a spell. Is that what you are about, an effort to charm out Garth's devils?'

'To drive them out,' I corrected her.

'Charm, drive, expel—shall you succeed?'

'I cannot know, so long as you insist on substituting distraction for concentration.'

'Very well, but I would be more comforted were Gavin to enjoin a clerical to exorcize them. He ought to send for a bishop.'

'One does not send for bishops, my sweet.'

'A parson with some knowledge of devils, then.'

'As we are in no position to send for anybody, perhaps you will leave me to my work.'

'Very well. I shall retire to the kitchen, and stand beside the chimney, and watch the maids chattering like starlings in an elm.'

When she had gone I stared again at Garth, strove to impose my will upon him, to thrust my mind into fusion with his and straighten it, but there was naught but my outer view of him, and I despaired.

CHAPTER FORTY-SIX

It was nearly a year before I succeeded in becoming Garth. As was customary to me, I had gone into his bedroom to cast a coverlet of comfort over him, for although he was as well treated as a lunatic might be, he was for the most part deserted. Two tall and strong footmen would bring him breakfast, one to carry the tray, the other to restrain him, should he decide to be violent.

Garth slobbered down his meal, the tray was removed, and he was left alone in his chamber. The walls were all padded with thick velvet, the windows were barred that the prisoner might not break them, and so Garth remained.

'Do you realize the date today?' Kate asked, as I prepared to pay my dismal visit.

'No, my sweet.'

'Why, 'tis my death-day,' said she, laughing. ''Tis I believe eight years since I breathed my last.'

I gave her a ghostly buss, knowing not quite how to congratulate her, and left her. Arrived in Garth's velvet chamber, I confronted him, staring into his glazed eyes, and instead of being baffled by that which remained of his will, found myself aware of an extraordinary sensation.

The teeth across which my tongue passed were even but seemed thick with dust, so coated were they with matter that had not been brushed away. The mouth inside which my tongue mournfully lurked tasted like the Fleet sewer, stagnant, full of dead fish, offal and the corpses of cats and dogs. My arms were weak, for lack of exercise, and my legs could but ill support me; I was in total like a large doll that had been dragged through mire and left with twisted limbs.

The crazed melody which Garth had been humming to himself when I arrived, had ceased; I could feel his mind fluttering and fidgeting alongside mine, striving to gain control of his body, vibrating with alarm as it sensed my usurpation of its home. Ruthlessly I shut it out.

Now that I was at last in possession of Garth I was resolved not to let him go until his insanity had been cauterized, and there was but one way I knew that might succeed, albeit a way filled with danger.

Kate appeared, unable to comprehend that Garth was quiet. 'Dear God, can it be that you are cured?' she whispered, clasping her hands together.

'He shall be,' I answered her.

'Wheatcroft?' staring at her son's lips, which had not parted as I spoke.

'I have succeeded, Kate. At last I am become Garth, and shall see to it that shortly he shall be well.'

'I do not—I cannot accept that you—speak to me with Garth's voice,' disbelievingly.

'Shall I sing you then the song of the whale?' I asked loudly, feeling as I had for so long desired to feel, air filling my lungs, the chemistry of my body stirring. 'The whale blows, the harpoon flies——'

Kate eyed me disbelievingly. 'That was the voice of Garth,' she whispered.

'It was,' I told her. 'I am Garth, but fear not that I shall keep him until his time comes to die. When he has lost his demons he shall be returned to himself, I promise.'

I smiled at her, Garth's face my mask, his lips drawing back as I turnd up my own. I wanted to piss, and instead of voiding over the floor, as Garth was wont to do if the journey to the commode did not suit him, I went to it and relieved myself graciously.

'Kate, my sweet,' I said, 'the door is locked. Do you think that you could unlock it?'

'I will try.' She vanished from the room, and after a while returned, disappointed. 'I can still not impress my will upon concrete things,' wistfully. 'I cannot turn a key or so much as straighten a flower in its vase.'

'Then I shall patiently await my gaolers,' I told her.

'And you swear that you will release Garth's body to him when he is free of demons?'

'I swear it, Kate. Shall I restore to my son his sanity, that I may rob him of his being? My mind and will shall mould his and return to them their fibre; he shall be Viking Garth again, a valiant if bloody man of the sea, and will lead his own life as he led it before Sebastian distorted it and imposed on it his ruin.'

I heard a key in the lock; the door opened. The first footman bore a tray of stew, the second stood warily just inside the room.

'Good afternoon to you,' I said. 'You are called Bruce and James, are you not?'

The footman called Bruce, who carried the stew, nearly splashed it over a rug. 'Mr. Garth, sir, God be praised that you are—that you seem well!'

'I fancy I am. I am also exceeding hungry,' my appetite being now a living, physical thing.

'Then shall you have a banquet, sir!' cried Bruce, 'James, go to summon the Master!'

James hesitated, went out; Bruce slowly walked backwards, as though in the presence of the king, and stood with his back to the lintel of the doorway. Evidently he was not completely convinced that I was in truth sane; his lack of conviction made him an uncomfortable custodian.

I heard Gavin's footsteps; he hurried into the room and halted.

'Good afternoon, Gavin.'

Gavin, son become now brother to me, stared at me and into me, as though to turn over with his eyes the demons by which I was inhabited.

'Garth? Are you really Garth? Is it yourself, and not a travesty, that is restored to me?'

'It is myself, dear brother.'

'It is not possible,' softly. ''tis but a devil's masquerade!' he shouted. 'Shall you not in a moment utter a wild scream and become again a lunatic?'

'I am sane,' I answered quietly, sensing Garth's mind fluttering and swooping beside mine.

'If you are, that is God's work, come to replace Satan's. Bruce, James, take my brother to his room—the room he had before—and call Durban.'

Returned to Garth's room, I scrubbed my teeth and washed prior to the arrival of Durban, Gavin's valet de chambre, and was helped by him to dress; human form again was mine, and human substance and identity.

Kate watched me as I sent for money, and put some of it into my pocket, and a deal of it in a secret drawer, and watched me with troubled eyes, knowing my intention.

I felt no apprehension; I was a man once more, in the borrowed body of my son. All that was needed now was to bring about his triumph, his total restoration, by confronting him with the fount of his disorder, Sebastian.

CHAPTER FORTY-SEVEN

I SAW before me Pepton Grange, pinned down by moonlight; focal point of white brilliance without, it was steeped in black dark within.

The joyousness of my ride hither faded; I sat my horse stationary at the entrance to the driveway and for a brief while longer permitted the savour of my journey to remain.

To be young and on a tall horse again; to smell fragrant air and ford a stream at the gallop; to feel the touch of rain on my skin and the sun afterwards come out to mop it up, benignly playing the towel; to know live loins again, the need for a woman, had almost seduced me from my purpose, had that not been the salvation of my son.

I breathed deeply of the air of night, sweet to the nostrils; I inhaled the scent of hedgerows and small flowers of the field, the perfume of the sap in the trees, the whole rustic brew brought out by the gentle darkness.

Garth's mind bruised itself against mine, desperately seeking command; it had to be frustrated, lest it fling Garth off his saddle on to the weeds matting the drive, and drive him gibbering and shrieking like a hobgoblin across the harlequin pattern of the countryside.

I wished that I could enter the house unencumbered by Garth's sad and startled mind, to vanquish Sebastian myself, spirit to spirit; if I could but divest Garth of myself, leave him poised and motionless by the horse till I returned and infused his brain again with sanity, I would feel more at ease.

The horse reared now, and standing on its hind legs screamed like a nightjar at the stars; I fondled its ears and murmured to it, but it quivered and shivered and was reluctant to advance.

We proceeded slowly, bucking and pausing, so that I was reminded of that time long ago, when I loved Pepton Grange and from its windows beheld Squire Frayle and Brereton making their unwieldy approach.

We were before the house directly now; I held on to

Garth's mind with taut reins, knowing that if it went it went for good. I looked about me and marvelled at such desolation. The gardens and lands that I had so cherished, and that had been so well maintained, now rotted in decay, for fear had routed any who might have tended them.

Carbuncles of moss clustered on the stone seats overlooking the formal garden, but there was no sign of a beast or bird of any description, or of their mark, not a nest in a tree, not a spider's web, not the rustle of a vole.

The horse was shuddering and sweating in a fever of terror; I led him a little way off and tethered him to an elm and tried to calm him, without a deal of success.

Leaving him, I went back, grasped the handle of the front door, and turned it. The door opened; my steward had been negligent in his duty. My steward, I reflected, had been long dead, and none had come forward to take his place.

I was across the threshold, to stand still on that black and white marble floor that once had been my pride, and on which Garth had lain, reduced to a fear-soaked foetus.

Nothing at first was apparent to me; the moonlight in no wise illuminated the house, whose windows must be hiding behind their drawn curtains. Imperceptibly, the darkness took on a greenish tinge, a sinister luminosity such as I had seen only once before, when sailing through a field of ice.

With the lightness came an odour of appalling strength, so that I felt that I had been excreted by Satan, to lie upon hell's laystall.

'Welcome, greatnephew,' a sly voice said, 'I had thought you truly despatched. You have something of resilience about you, boy, to return to me, and at night.'

Clouds of vapour rolled before me; I could not be sure if they were of mist, or some other substance, for they made a sound of squelching, a wheezing and hissing, and seemed composed of that which had decomposed; the distilled juices of the graveyard.

In the midst of these juices, slowly turning as if on a spit, was a vast soft thing, that glistened and shone with pale glow, a gigantic maggot, creased in glee, something's entrails swinging through the bristles by its mouth.

'Do you admire this form, greatnephew?' asked Sebastian, his voice tinged with disappointment that he had not provoked an immediate abdication of sanity. 'Or would you perhaps prefer a creature with only twice as many legs as your own, a gentle creature of undoubted good taste?'

The maggot disappeared, to be at once replaced by a lamb, that gambolled and skipped always in the same place, and became bigger and more distorted, its eyes red, its teeth long; the lamb grew more and more malefic, its wool teeming with life, worms the size of adders, ticks as big as bats, and it mewed: Eat me, if you like lamb eat me! and showed its teeth in wicked laughter.

I remained still, even when the lamb frisked over to me and stood high above me, and bathed me in its rancid breath; it returned to its gambolling spot and changed again, this time into a spider.

The spider flexed its hairy legs and darted up the wall, to descend a moment later, obscenely dangling from the web that poured like frozen saliva from its body; the shadow of the spider was huge in the luminous haze, and it laughed with Sebastian's laugh before becoming Sebastian himself, a towering green man with festering sores that fell away one by one, leaving in the end nothing but his skull rocking on its mainspring of vertebrae.

'Ha, greatnephew, you have been tried by ordeal and this time you have survived. You may leave here without further molestation, for I shall no more addle your brain in your pate.

'Yet heed me, greatnephew: do not come hither again, or in every one of my many shapes I shall devour you, and so chew you up that what is left will not be large enough to make dung.'

Distantly I heard my horse screaming; it had, I realized, protested unceasingly since being deserted.

'Go, greatnephew!' commanded Sebastian.

'I am not your greatnephew,' slowly. 'Do you not remember me? I am nearer to you than Garth.'

Sebastian stepped back. 'Reveal yourself.'

'I am Wheatcroft, whose father and mother died mysteriously,' I said, preparing to launch myself upon him. 'Did you not have anything to do with their deaths, uncle?'

'Not with your mother's, no boy,' in the voice of a toad perched on a maiden's head. 'Your father gave me some inconvenience, so I was obliged to inconvenience him. He knew nothing, a moment of suffocation—you know how well these hands encompass a neck.' I saw them again, crawling about the neck of Squire Frayle as he knelt above me to offer succour; here they were now, settling snugly about that of my father.

'You must understand, nephew, that one does not have to be a soldier to kill another man, to enjoy killing, to feel the blood lust rise and dominate. I loved to kill, nephew, and the love is with me yet,' stretching out his arms beseechingly.

'How many more have been your victims?'

'Many, dear nephew. Not only your father, but women and children, generously supplied by your childhood friend, Timothy Spence. A good fellow, Timothy, that knew how to turn his employment at the poor house to advantage. My advantage, nephew.'

Tense in Garth's body I stood, before fleeing it, to rush upon Sebastian and grapple his will with mine.

We ran together, the contents of two paint-pots cast at a canvas striving each to eliminate the other; as blue battles yellow to result in triumph for green, and white pits itself against black in order to award the victor's standard to grey, so Sebastian and I fought to abolish each other in a welter of colour, smell and slime.

I could not grasp him, yet was aware of movement all about me, of a myriad voracious mouths that tugged and tore and sucked, seeking to imbibe all that I was and so destroy me.

I felt myself in danger of dwindling, reasserted my will and felt Sebastian in his turn begin to shrink.

Fused together in our combat, we heard voices and footsteps, and promptly disengaged. I hurried back to Garth and entered his motionless body, that had toppled and sagged against the wall. No sooner was I installed than the front door was flung open, to reveal a crowd of unhappy men holding torches, at their centre Brereton and his chaplain.

The chaplain, a big but fragile man, rendered porcelain in texture and appearance by terror, clutched a crucifix and a silver bowl. 'We are come to exorcize you,' he called, his voice hardly audible.

Sebastian laughed, the house vibrated with the malign cadence of his mirth.

Brereton caught sight of me as I stood against the wall. 'Garth!'

I could not for a minute respond, for Garth's legs were immovable. His poor brain had turned into a sponge, soaking up only fear; he was devoid of all that made man wond'rous in God's sight.

'Squire!' I forced the thick unwieldy tongue, rendered sere by the famine of thought, to pronounce the word. 'Squire.'

'What do you here?' asked Brereton, waving a pistol at the shadows.

'Why, I am come a second time to claim my inheritance. The villainous phantom that still resides here would dissuade me, lest he become homeless as a foundling, for there is no room here for the two of us.'

Sebastian's laughter echoed again through the hall, rebounded from the furthermost room. Several men turned to flee, but Brereton, evidently heir to a portion of his father's courage, bade them stay.

'This foul thing shall be driven out by exorcism,' he said. 'The screams of your horse lanced the countryside, piercing all our ears with its agony. A country fellow may not always heed the call of a man, but I have yet to meet one that does not instantly attend upon that of a horse. Thus I aroused my good chaplain here, and my servants, and came hotfoot once and for all to purge the neighbourhood of your ungodly relative.'

'Heaven aid you in your enterprise,' I answered. 'I have this evening duelled with him, but not with the aid of bible or prayer-book.'

'Bible and prayer-book are as little to me as you are,' from Sebastian, with a rasping snarl.

Brereton and his companions jumped, but did not run; I thanked them for their kindness and courage.

'Will you not stay for our service?' asked the priest. 'Abide with us as witness that your house is truly free of evil.'

'I wish that could be, but I must presently return to London.' I feared that were I to remain, I might myself be caught up in the whirlpool of his exorcism and sucked down into Hades. In that event, Garth would perhaps again have to undergo a melancholy voyage to Park Lane, and who this time would be concerned to free him from mental bondage, or be able to accomplish it?

'I shall be back, Brereton,' I said, 'and when I return, we shall toast the ghost's banishment with a decanter or two.' I clapped his shoulder and made my way through the nervous throng, forced to the brink of daring, to gain my horse.

I leaped into the saddle and galloped away from that malevolent place, and rode through Pepton Harbinger, the horse's hooves clattering on the stone pavement; I minutely relinquished my concentration on holding the fort of Garth's body, that I might feel his mind gently asserting itself, but there was no sign of it whatsoever.

Again I tried, beckoning it to cross the drawbridge to its rightful habitation, but there was nothing, no hint of Garth's mind returning to Garth's body, of which I was seemingly in total occupation.

As I rode I grew ever more distraught, as though I myself were going mad, and wept bitter moonlit tears, at the thought that I had plunged Garth's mind into limbo, and could not recover it.

CHAPTER FORTY-EIGHT

I RODE throughout the rest of that night, occasionally leaving Garth's body as far as I dared, so that it wore me like a long and luminous kerchief. His spirit and mind refused to return, the body swayed, and each time I had at once to re-enter it in order to prevent its tumbling to the ground.

Where was Garth's essence, could it be that it had entered something else? That owl yonder, that regarded me with sombre menace; it cast itself free of its branch and with lethal purpose swooped low overhead, dipped, soared moonward, a shrieking mouse held in its talons—was the owl Garth? Or perhaps he was the merry cricket that sounded like a dancing fiddle in the hedgerow.

A further appalling notion came to chill me: was Garth in the horse beneath me, were the misery and disquiet that it had suffered while tethered in the driveway of the Grange caused because Garth in his dread sought refuge in the beast?

'Garth!' I cried, and uttered his name a dozen times, expecting I know not what peculiar response: a neigh of acknowledgement, a jerking of the head, a burst of babbled human speech from equine tongue.

Dawn seeped into the sky, and still I tried to recall the mind of Garth but was vouchsafed no sign; I rode until exhausted, and stopped at an inn.

Going to the well, I laved my face, bringing up bucket after bucket in an effort to rid myself of taint, but still felt as unclean as a leper. I was not a human being but a ghost in a human being's body, a phantom jockey riding the extinct person of his son.

Having wiped my face on a cloth I once more strove to summon Garth by calling him with all my will across the void; there was no answer. His body remained awhile upright, began to fold, to crumple; I hastened back into it just in time to prevent it plunging down the well.

Slowly, I turned and made my way across the yard and into the inn. A young and comely serving wench came across to me with a smile.

'You are early, sir. Would you perhaps care for a breakfast of lamb chops and kidneys, with a flagon of good ale?'

I looked up at her bodice, whose contents leaned partly towards me, tightly wrapped as a gift. My concern for Garth, my shame and my regret, were swept away by the flood-tide that rose in my loins and engulfed all other senses.

'Or would you savour some stew, sir, that is left from yesterday?'

The wench was smiling more broadly now, with creamy satisfaction; she was a creature of the byre, large of hip and haunch, her complexion smooth, her eyes placid and brown.

She leaned a trifle lower, offering me a still more generous view of her globes, and in her eyes there was a knowing amusement as though she could see beneath the rough table my cod straining to perform its duty and pleasure.

The years of my death were discarded; I was heedless of the fact that the lust I was expressing through Garth's loins was his as well as mine, that it was his manhood that I was taking in order to gratify my own senses.

'What is your name?' I asked.

'Bess, sir.'

'For breakfast, sweet one, I would lie with you.'

She looked at me with the understanding of a country girl who has many a time seen a bull put to a cow.

'I must go to collect the eggs, sir.'

'May I come with you?'

Bess did not have to answer, but merely touched my arm with her broad, strong, gentle hand.

I followed her into the yard, matched my pace to hers as without urgency she walked past the well and cowshed towards the chickens which clamoured nearby; we entered the wooden hut that gave them shelter and fell on to the straw covering the ground, and coupled.

'My country minx, my sweetheart, my passionate jade!' I whispered, my mouth to her ear. She was not passionate, but compassionate, playing the receptacle to my agitated manhood, the smile unaltered on her face, her hips rotating now and then to spur me on, yet not so boldly that I should finish before my time.

Thus, under the beady stare of chicken witnesses, we attained our incendiary conclusion, and I fell back on the straw and pulled her close, and kissed her smooth plump cheek.

'I enjoyed being your breakfast, sir,' Bess whispered. 'You were a man in need.'

'Indeed I was, my sweet,' feeling my heart thump. Yet it was not only my heart that did so, not only my lungs that were heaving still for breath.

There was another rhythm in my body, in Garth's body; as I felt the fatigue pouring into me my mind rang as though it were a bell, whose clapper was the mind of another.

A blurred and furry fight took place within our brain, as Garth's mind nudged mine desperately, to dislodge it, and by the tenor of his persistence I judged that I had succeeded in freeing it of madness, and that it was now come back at last whence it had been banished, to claim its right to the pleasure Bess had given.

I aroused myself to quench Garth's mind until we should reach home; it protested. Giving Bess a sovereign and forgetting breakfast, I mounted my horse, as weary a beast as myself, and resumed my way to London.

As I rode I reflected: I would return Garth's body to him the moment we had arrived home. Resolutely I refused to reflect that I was making a sacrifice; I refused even to consider that I was tempted not to return to the pallid twilight existence of a ghost, but to hold on to the corporeal territory I possessed.

Therefore it was without regret that, as soon as Gregory had opened the front door and Garth and I were across the threshold, I left him.

I observed him from a distance, and prayed that I had indeed cured him, and that he would not now, the moment I had left him, revert to his former mad state.

He stood, too close to the threshold for Gregory to close the front door, and stared about him like a slave unexpectedly granted his freedom.

'Good afternoon, sir,' Gregory said, for the second or third time.

'Good afternoon,' slowly.

Garth walked a few paces into the hall, still looking about him, then let out a great cry. I thought as he did so that I had failed, that the cry was a prelude to collapse, to the foaming mouth and pitiful, incoherent cries of insanity.

Again Garth yelled, and I realized then that is was not a cry of madness but of joy, of welcome to himself for safe return from a dreadful journey.

I watched as he ran up the stairs, leaving Gregory to shake his head in wonder, and myself rejoiced that I had been able to restore my son's spirit to him.

At the same time I myself felt gratitude to that ability which had enabled me to borrow Garth's body and through its agency enjoy again a maid, to relish the country air and the excitement of the gallop.

As I wafted through the house, seeking Kate, I made a resolution that at some future time I would borrow another body, one that I would not be under obligation to yield so promptly, and that in it I would deeply, joyously, live again.

CHAPTER FORTY-NINE

CHARLOTTE was brought to bed of her first child, a daughter, two years after her marriage.

The child favoured her mother, the first feature that emerged from the womb being her small sharp nose, as though from her burrow she were sniffing the air in order to ensure that the world was fit for her to enter.

The girl was called Primula, and liked to cry a great deal, her wails sending their displeasing resonance into every ear, so that from nursemaid to pantry-boy there was much disenchantment with the infant.

Only Kate with her ethereal status was able to regard Primula with undiluted affection and to revel in her plentiful incontinence; it seemed that every laundress in the house owed her employment to the child, the generosity of whose bladder was exceeded only by that of her bowels.

Garth had wisely returned to sea, and Gavin was busy about his affairs in the city; I longed to voyage through the London streets, and experience new sensations, for from what I heard the clutch of the new century was tightening on the times.

Dimity was now become as robust as his mother was frail; I looked upon her when she came to visit him and marvelled that I had ever so desired her. Dimity, however, was dear to me, a handsome roguish fellow who intended to take life by the shoulders and shake it.

'The more I see of your bastard, the more I am affronted by him,' Kate told me. 'He should be got rid of, otherwise there will be strife between him and our sons over his inheritance.'

'He has none,' I told her, 'but his allowance, which will be sufficient to keep him, and his temperament, which will no doubt benefit him.'

'His temperament?' without a deal of charity. 'The boy's a braggart, that has grown too big for his breeches, and from frightening maids has graduated to coddling them.'

'And what else should one do to them?' I asked her. 'Is

there anything more fulfilling in life than to receive pleasure through giving it?'

She took my bait. 'Fie!' she exclaimed, 'you have a poultice for every sore. Wheatcroft. At present there is only one bastard in this house, but it will not be long before the place is teeming with them, the bastards of a bastard; Hazell House will become as prolific of them as a London stew.'

'Dimity will not spend all his life rollicking here,' I told her. 'There is, I fancy, greater ambition in him.'

'Any path he takes, inside the house or out, is bound to have the eagerly opened thighs of a maid at the end of it,' sourly.

I was about to tell her that I hoped so when there was a loud cry nearby, and a growled curse. A small boy, clad in rags and filthy, scurried past us, pursued by a villain similarly clad, carrying a sack; the sweep had arrived.

'You'll go up the chimbley when I tells yer, or your neck'll get broke quicker than it will by falling down the flue,' the sweep threatened.

'But I'm afear'd, sir.'

'Fear me, boy. Ain't I more dreadful than a chimbley, wot can't strike you?' slapping the child's face. 'Ain't I got more menace in me, than has a pile of bricks and mortar as can't move?'

'It's the dark, sir. I'm afear'd of the dark.'

'Oh, the dark is it, that frightens my poor little bird?' placing his narrow wizened face alongside the child's. 'Can the dark twist yer ears, like this?' knocking off the urchin's cap to seize a lobe.

The urchin yelled; the sweep desisted from tormenting him, lest somebody come.

'Neither yer chimbley nor your dark's as terrible as I am,' he said. 'Neither's to be as much feared as I am. Now up the chimbley with yer at once, or I'll take me fist to yer face and bash it till yer won't know what's happenin' to yer.

'And when yer does know, yer'll find yer up the chimbley, boy, securely wedged in it, and if the dark still troubles yer, why then I'll get rid of it by lightin' a fire under yer, and hearken to yer appreciation of a portion of scorchin'.'

'He berates the boy too much,' Kate muttered. 'Does a child not have the right to be afraid of the dark, without so offending its master?'

I did not answer her, but instead stared intently at the

sweep, enforcing upon him my will. Instead of pursuing the reluctant child, who had made his trembling way over to the hearth and tensed himself for further blows before being forced to struggle upwards through the sooty, narrow cavern towards the distant roof-top, the sweep remained still.

It was with triumph, mingled with revulsion, that I looked at Kate through the sweep's eyes, felt the first amazed protests of his mind throbbing with fright.

I turned to the urchin, crouched whimpering in the grate. 'Here, boy,' digging without pleasure into the sweep's pocket and finding there a shilling, 'take this, and leave the house, and seek out another, kindlier master in a less arduous profession.'

'How—how's that, sir?'

'Go now, and if you love your skin, do not work for a sweep again.' The urchin approached me on his thin and bandy legs, his face unbelieving. Surely the shilling would in a moment be thrust back into his master's pocket, and a cuff across the ear pitch him back to the line of duty.

'Be not afraid, child.'

The small, filthy hand reached out and clawed at my gift; there was a swift patter across the carpet, as though of a mouse, the opening of a door, silence.

'That was well done,' Kate said. 'Now what shall you do with this wretched fellow?'

'I think perhaps I shall take him to the kitchen, and thoroughly wash him, and steer him out into the streets, and dally a little amidst the crowds.'

'You will not greatly fancy any wench who fancies him,' maliciously.

'If you could but learn how to transmute yourself also, we could set out together,' I told her. 'Could you not exert yourself to become, as an introduction to the art of possession, a kitchen-maid?'

'I scarcely fancy myself a kitchen-maid—I would rather be dead than that,' but she spoke with a smile. 'On the other hand, knowing your admiration for maidservants, I might consider becoming a ladies' maid.'

'Were you to do so, we could love again,' ignoring her attempt to tease me.

'Do we not, as it is?'

'Not with our bodies, my sweet.'

'If I am to become some sort of a maid, I shall certainly

not consider coupling with a sweep. I counsel you to discard that horrid fellow directly—the boy by now is well escaped.'

'I have a mind to punish this sweep,' I told her. 'I shall take him for a walk.'

'Nay, do not leave me.'

'For but a short time.'

'You will find some hussy with whom to romp,' sharply. 'You will not resist any temptations that are offered you.'

'You have already said that I shall not fancy any that fancy him. What therefore are the temptations that I shall not resist? A gin-sodden crone curled in her wrapping of rags in a doorway? A cluster of sick hags cackling together as they peer over the edge of the grave, and invite me to sample their rancid privates for a penny?'

'You are ever a master of indelicacy,' said Kate.

'Very well,' I answered, 'maybe the sweep would answer more graciously, with the poetry of such a person: I seek a fair maid, that I may plant my lily in her valley. So I shall go a-planting, and send my seed shooting into a gentle wench not above an hundred years old, that has not in her life drunk above a thousand barrels of gin, and thinks that juniper is the name of a Roman god.'

Kate laughed. 'Begone with you, and come back humbled by the experience of gazing upon a desirable woman without the ability to charm her.'

'I shall prepare myself for all such disappointments, and shall return to this fellow his miserable body as Gregory opens the door.

'Farewell, sweet Kate.'

'Have a care, Wheatcroft my love,' anxiously.

'What harm can befall me? Am I not already dead?'

'Supposing that a horse should run you down, or a madman have at you with a dagger? What then would happen to the lacerated body you were in? Would it continue alive, so long as you inhabited it? Or would it die, and you with it, never to return here to me?'

'I shall always return to you, my Kate.'

We looked lovingly at each other, the face of the sweep between us; I doffed my stained and smelly cap, took some money from my drawer, and made my way to the servants' staircase.

I had descended but a few steps when I realized that the sweep's body was unhealthy. A pain assailed my side, my legs were weak, and I found myself every few moments coughing. The cough continued to shake me as I opened the street door and emerged into the London afternoon.

My eyes, confronted by the sun, puckered and watered; no doubt they could stare up the tallest chimney without faltering, but the natural golden light of a summer's afternoon was beyond their strength.

A man and woman went by, and I noted that their dress was unusual to me, especially the man's; he wore upon his head a hat different from any that I had seen, a tall, circular affair that might itself have invited the attentions of a chimney boy. His figure was elegant but without glory, his waistcoat being pearl grey but the garment he wore outside it black, as though in mourning for his missing plumage.

I walked down to Piccadilly, coughing at each step and sensing that my pleasure in being again incorporated in physical shape was gravely impaired by the wretchedness of the envelope containing me; I contrived to smile at a passing wench but was aware that my smile was a leer, and that I merited her answering regard of passionless scorn.

Humiliation seeped into me; I longed to leave the sweep for a gentleman of greater distinction, for I was not used to being ignored or despised by wenches, or glanced at with every sign of ill regard by men.

I stopped alongside the reservoir in Green Park and turned. To hasten back to Park Lane and shed the sweep's body was now my paramount ambition; coughing and spitting blood, crouched over as I walked and sure that I resembled a sickly crab scuttling blindly along the bed of the sea, I reached Park Lane, turned north, and was soon knocking at the front door of Hazell House.

Gregory opened to me, stood aghast as I hurried across the threshold.

'This is the front door!' he proclaimed, outraged St. Peter swept aside by a sinner without a passport.

I gladly relinquished the sweep's body. 'Wossat? Wot're you on abaht?' he asked, bemused.

'You have just entered this house by the front door.'

' 'Ave I now? Not sure I intended to enter it at all. Not agine—I was 'ere before, wasn't I? Where's me boy?'

'You are trespassing, fellow,' Gregory told him. 'Inebriation cannot excuse impertinence.'

'Inebriation? Gawd, I wish I 'ad a drink. I wish——'; the

sweep paused, a look of sublime astonishment on his face as from his pocket he took a sovereign.

'A thief are you, fellow?' asked Gregory. 'Or is it customary for sweeps to saunter across the thresholds of respectable establishments and toy with gold?'

'It was in my pocket,' answered the sweep defensively. He darted backwards so that he stood just without the doorway, and thus he hoped beyond Gregory's authority. 'I didn't steal it,' he whined again, 'it was in my pocket. It was in my pocket,' he repeated, thinking as is usual with his kind that repetition can be made a forcing-house for truth. 'I didn't steal it, sir.'

Gregory shut the door in his face, but the sweep knocked upon it almost at once.

'I—I've forgit me brush,' he said, when Gregory opened to him.

'If that is the case, ingress may be had through the side entrance,' Gregory informed him, age having taken away nothing of his pomposity. He closed the door again on the hapless sweep, and retired to his quarters.

Never had I thought to be relieved that I was a ghost, but to be rid of the ruined body of the sweep gave me such pleasure that insofar as I was able I capered upstairs to find Kate.

Although in my phantom's shape I could not indulge in bodily pleasures, I was compensated by the reflection that neither could I cough.

CHAPTER FIFTY

CHARLOTTE bore Gavin two more children, Saul and Tamarind, boys who favoured their father rather than their mother and were therefore less prone to puncture pillows with their noses.

The effort of producing Tamarind brought Charlotte into a decline which did nothing for her temper; she so drenched Gavin in the vinegar of her permanent displeasure that when one morning she died he was quite distraught for joy.

Death came to Charlotte as in full choler she was upbraiding Gavin for some imagined trifle; the words pouring from her ceased, although her mouth remained open as though she would still carry on with her shrew's shrilling from beyond the grave.

As the carmine of her countenance began to ebb Kate and I became aware that she had joined us.

'Charlotte!' from Kate.

Charlotte did not reply, the first time for months that she had been silent.

'The wretch shall not affect our privacy, Kate,' I said.

'How can you so speak of her, when she is but a moment since come to us?'

Charlotte stared down at herself lying still with open mouth, and began to cry, droplets of violet light running down her shimmering cheeks; they began to grow firmer now, so that her face was as it had been many years ago, when she had married Gavin and I had watched her about the business of awarding him her maidenhead.

'Who—who are you?' Charlotte asked.

'Why, had we lived you would have known us as Gavin's mother and father,' I told her.

'But you are dead.'

'Indeed, although as you see not buried. That is to say that our bodies are interred but our spirits are alive as ever.'

'Oh,' wonderingly. 'What is it like to be—dead?'

'One must always make the best of an epilogue,' I said,

'Just as one must make the most of a play. Mrs. Hazell and I find that death need not be too alarming.'

Charlotte began again to weep. 'Look at me, to die with such lack of dignity. I would not speak ill of the living, but Gavin—he was an exasperating man, that would never give an inch. I did but want him to take me to the ball at Lady Storrington's next week, but he prefers to go to the Cremorne Gardens and enjoy its raffish flavour, for he says that he is surfeited with higher society.'

'I had similar trouble's with Gavin's father,' Kate told her consolingly. 'I remember when the Prince Regent came——'

'Kate,' I said. 'Let us leave Charlotte to mourn for herself awhile,' as a doctor appeared, who closed the corpse's mouth and ran a skilled and tender finger over its eyes.

'Do not leave me,' Charlotte cried. 'I am not yet used to —to not living.'

'Of course we shall not leave you,' Kate comforted her.

'I always lived a good life,' Charlotte told us. 'Why then have I not gone straight to Heaven?'

'Kate and I have also pondered the indirect ways of destiny. We are not as it happens sure that there is a Heaven. Or a hell.'

'You shall never find Heaven by blaspheming!'

'We have found neither place,' I reminded her.

'You ought not to take a light-hearted attitude towards something as serious as salvation. Or condemnation,' looking at us as though we were sinners and she in judgement upon us.

'I relished my life, Charlotte, because I learned not to take too serious an attitude towards serious things, for that's a quick road to unnecessary misery. After all,' I continued, 'who are we, who are involved in our own affairs, to be the best judges of what is serious or not?'

'I scarcely know you well enough to argue with you, Mr. Hazell,' her nose thrust forward in quest of dispute, 'but I find your levity unseemly. After all,' in terms of self-veneration, 'we are dead, Mr. Hazell.'

'Not in spirit, as I have pointed out.'

Kate, who was bridling at Charlotte's criticism of me, desisted from her desire to comfort her. 'Come, Wheatcroft,' she murmured; together we swirled from the room.

' 'Tis usurping a woman's most prized privilege, when another criticizes her husband,' Kate said, as we found ourselves in the kitchen. We stood beside the new iron stove, an imposing item waited upon by two maids who black-leaded it each day, and told each other how much we regretted Charlotte's intrusion.

'Kate, I love you beyond all things still,' I told her. 'If only I could show you my love, take you in my arms and give you worship.'

'If only you could, my love.'

A large, handsome young footman stood talking to a pretty maid nearby.

'If you can but become that maid,' I told Kate, 'I shall become the footman.'

'But how?'

'Do as I do. Stare into the girl's eyes and assert your will. Come, my darling, try!'

Kate moved over to the maid and stood beside the footman, and stared so that I saw the girl shake her head, as if a fly were pestering her, and a new light came to her eyes. I sensed then that Kate had at last succeeded in donning human form, and I went over to the footman, who was looking a trifle puzzled at the change in his sweetheart's expression, and appropriated him.

'You leave the kitchen first,' I told Kate, 'lest we attract too much notice if we go together, and I shall follow you directly.'

'But where shall I go?' asked Kate. 'Where can we be alone, in no danger of interruption?'

'Why, my darling,' I murmured, 'there is but one place in this great house where we shall be undisturbed.

'Go you straightway to the dimity room.'

CHAPTER FIFTY-ONE

To Charlotte's rage, Gavin married again, taking to bride a saucy and comely young wench, Melinda.

'How dare he?' Charlotte asked in fury. 'I have been gone less than a year and already he is back in the bridal bed.'

I refrained from pointing out to her that Gavin's new bride showed rather more skill than the previous one. Although I witnessed that she came to her wedding night a virgin, she knew well the difference between the upper and lower parts of her husband; there was nothing here of Charlotte's sexual reticence.

Melinda was a girl unafraid to live, so that Gavin took her to places that would have outraged Charlotte, and to enjoy such excitements as the inauguration of the London to Greenwich Railway.

'I do agree with Mrs. Kemble,' Melinda said, 'that the locomotive reminded me of a little animal, with coal for oats, a dear little fire-horse with flying white breath and rhythmical, unvarying pace.'

Gavin laughed. 'It gallops along to such good purpose that the proprietors say it will save eight hours' travelling a week. What they do not say, of course, is that as there is no terminus north of the river the saving is but half as much as they claim.'

'I wish we owned a railway,' said Melinda.

'I have a substantial number of shares in the London and Manchester, my love.'

'We must sample it, then,' clapping her hands, 'although I have no wish to go to Manchester.'

'She is frivolous!' hissed Charlotte.

'We shall travel on one of these trains,' I said to Kate. 'The footman and the maid shall travel into the country with a picnic basket.'

'Each time that I become a maid I feel apprehension, lest I inflict upon the poor girl an injury. Supposing one should become pregnant? She would be disgraced through no fault of her own.'

'I have assured you before, my sweet, that I shall not so disgrace any maid in whom you reside. I would not do ill in the midst of supreme delight.'

'You did with Patsy.'

'Patsy. Never shall you forget Patsy.'

'And her bastard,' said Kate.

'Hers and mine. You must admit, my love, that he is grown a fine man.'

'That has inherited his father's sense of adventure only in the field of lechery.'

'But has further ambition.'

'So you have always said. "He shall not be content to spend all his life rollicking here," ' Kate mimicked me. 'Yet still he does naught but wench—nay, I do him an injustice—he is also a gambler.'

Further argument concerning Dimity was quenched by his appearance in the library, where Kate and I happened to be; with him was Gavin.

'Dimity,' Gavin said, 'I am a happy man. A fulfilled, though not a complacent man. I enjoy my life and I know that you enjoy yours, yet will you not do something more with it than frequent taverns and night-houses?'

'Something more?' Dimity laughed. 'I am a traveller of discernment, who, while he enjoys discovering the new, is also well content with the known. I sail from here to the Alhambra, or the Portland Rooms for an hour or so of dancing, to the Argyle Rooms, where I am much loved, or to Mott's casino, where I am highly regarded as a generous winner and equally generous loser—there are so many fellows about who are mean in both regards—I believe, in short, in treating money like love and love like money. I am a creature of abandon, as you know, in all respects, save that I do not abandon those I esteem.

'However,' Dimity continued, 'I must admit to a desire to see even more of the world. For instance, I would like to visit America, as did our father.'

Gavin did not comment on this 'our', but it was evidently not entirely to his liking, for he frowned. Dimity compounded his lack of tact by adding, albeit inaccurately: 'which art in Heaven'.

'Really, the fellow's a bore!' from exasperated Kate.

'I thought perhaps that it was not too late for you to consider a career,' Gavin told him.

Dimity fluffed out his golden red moustache. 'A career? Do you mean, brother, a career in terms of a short, sharp gallop, or a career in the sense of an opportunity for advancement?'

'In your case no doubt the two would be combined,' said Gavin drily.

'I think I have it in me to do gallant deeds, to slay dragons and rescue maidens and so add lustre to our name.'

Here again Gavin showed that he was displeased at Dimity's reference to their relationship; I was all too acutely aware of Gavin's loyalty to me in accepting Dimity as his brother, and regretted the burden I had imposed on him before dying.

'The way ahead for you is then plain, Dimity. Gallant deeds, a chance to see more of the world than the view offered by the inside of Mott's. How fortunate we are to have the Army.'

'The Army?' Dimity helped himself to brandy. 'Now that is an idea, in fact an ideal. I can salute that, brother. It was an inspiration to suggest it.'

'It seems an adequate career for a man who has no head for business, is too kind-hearted to be an executioner, and too faint-hearted to be a soldier.'

Dimity laughed. 'Too faint-hearted?'

'I do not mean that you are a coward,' Gavin assured him, 'but that you are not sufficiently convinced of the merit of anything to battle for it.'

'Have I not then battled for my portion of maidenheads?' exclaimed Dimity. 'Am I not a warrior of some renown, who has tilted his lance in the charge across many a boudoir battlefield? In the casinos and gaming-rooms have I not fought the wiles of destiny with all the vigour a man may muster? I have striven to woo chance, so that the cards turn up right, I have watched the roulette wheel with such a compelling eye that it has stopped more often than not where I willed it, so that the little ball has tripped daintily into the slot I had selected for it. On the tennis courts also, have I not many times engaged in combat, and been seldom bested?' He pouted, the embodiment of a man wronged.

'You malign me, Gavin. And now you wish to launch me into the Army under a flag of truce, as a man who has surrendered a deal oftener than he has fought.' The pout vanished as Dimity bellowed with laughter.

'You make me sound like a true commander,' he went on, 'who orders his troops to hurl themselves at the enemy in line abreast, and as soon as they have swung into the gallop turns to his mistress and carries her to couch without bothering to ascertain the results of their gallantry.'

Gavin smiled. 'I had thought of purchasing you a captaincy in a good regiment.'

'A captaincy? Surely the qualities which you have attributed to me deserve a colonelcy at the least!'

'Very well. A colonelcy.'

'And in return I shall strive to maintain your opinion of me,' slily. 'Now, what shall be my regiment?'

'I had thought of the 62nd. It has a distinguished history. And an attractive uniform,' as an afterthought.

'Ah, Gavin, you know me well; the uniform is of course more important to me than the history. After all, I did not share in that. The regiment's glory has been in deeds, mine shall be in the splendour of my appearance.

'Let me see,' thoughtfully, 'I have a number of friends among the soldiery, including three colonels with whom I toss an oyster down my throat at Barron's, which is one of the reasons why I could not accept a lesser rank. Among 'em the 62nd stand sartorially high, but not as high as the Royal Regiment of Horse, or indeed the 9th Lancers.

'For myself, Gavin, I fancy the Hussars—know a chap in the 11th. They cut a pretty dash, do they not?'

'You would make an impressive Hussar, Dimity.'

'I think so too.' Dimity drew himself up so that one could imagine the medals ranged across his chest like dishes along a shelf. 'Colonel Dimity Hazell of the 11th Hussars,' he announced sonorously, 'requests the pleasure of a charge at the foe. He will return with plumes unbent in time for supper.'

Gavin raised his glass, smiling. 'To Colonel Hazell.'

As they drank a sadness came over me, for I knew that in spite of his jesting Dimity might be called upon to fight, and I did not relish the thought of his being in danger. He was strangely close to me.

Three weeks after his conversation with Gavin he left the house in a caleche. He was in full dress uniform, glistening and gleaming and proud as a bird of prey, though in truth he resembled more a bird of paradise.

We heard his loud voice as he climbed into the carriage: 'I should not have been half so well accoutred had you entered me for the church, brother. Not even had you bought me a diocese,' and his laughter, that billowed from the caleche like an invisible sail, sweeping him down Park Lane and out of my sight, not to return for several years.

CHAPTER FIFTY-TWO

DEATH had given Kate and me eternal youth; life, abetted by a portion of ill health, was making Gavin old. Melinda still coaxed his sap's rising, and drew it off, but he was nearing the end of his magnificence.

Tamarind and Saul did what was expected of them, and grew up handsome; Saul was a boy earnest to the point of being sombre, and displayed a solicitude for money amounting to avarice, while Tamarind was his opposite, a merry fellow that loved a romp.

Feeling the call of the land and the need for a wife, Garth returned from his travels and married a wench of vivid disposition and prejudice. She was big and well-founded, a barque that sailed among men under full canvas, firing the broadside of her opinions at all and sundry as though defying them to remain undaunted.

Garth and his man-o'-war berthed in a new house in St. John's Wood, and were happy.

My poor grand-daughter Primula, although scarcely of an age, was something of a crone from the outset. She took her vengeance on the world for being born plain by inflicting good works on downtrodden women, whose virtue had tended to ease before the rigours of penury. So sere and unwholesome in appearance was Primula that it would have taken a mighty act of chivalry even to kiss her cheek.

Armoured against any gentle impulse, and bearing her heavy hymen shield as defence against assault that would never come, she walked the Haymarket each night amidst the whores, exuding the chill of her charity.

Gavin died on a Sunday morning as church bells were ringing, heralds of a new soul loosed.

I hovered above his bed, aware as I waited for him of the depth of my bereavement. Kate and I would doubtless be the richer for our son's coming back to us to be reborn in death. but the world would have lost a man of some significance.

'You have been a long time coming,' were the first words

Charlotte spoke as, bewildered, Gavin arrived in our midst. 'I suppose you were reluctant to tear yourself away from that woman,' jerking her nose in the direction of the weeping Melinda.

'Do not speak so, Charlotte,' Kate beseeched her. 'Did your parents-in-law greet you with words so sour? Gavin must be helped over this stile between life and death, not jammed through it.'

'Mother!' Gavin exclaimed. 'Father! It is worth being no more for the joy of meeting you again.'

Kate swirled over to him and raised her face for a buss. 'Gavin, my dear son.'

I waited until Gavin was used to the state that we were in, before enlightening him about the occasional escapes afforded his mother and me.

'Shall I be able to embrace Melinda?' he asked eagerly.

'Only in another's body, I fear.'

'I shall bide my time until somebody who might please her appears. Then I shall dominate him and use him to seduce her.'

'You may resent her yielding.'

'She is young; I was mature when I married her. A man must be irredeemably selfish who expects such a woman to be faithful to him till she die.'

'Some races ensure such a thing, by putting the widow to death at once.'

'I would not have Melinda undergo suttee,' Gavin said with a smile. 'I would rather she took a lover, especially if the lover were myself.'

'You are bawdy, Gavin.' Charlotte had come upon us without our knowing. 'What do I hear about your intentions regarding Melinda? Shall you haunt her, appearing to her at night, peer at her through the curtains about her bed so that she dies of fright and joins us here forthwith?

'I shall not have it, Gavin!' waving her finger at him, 'I shall not countenance anything so intolerable!'

'I fear you did not hear us correctly,' I told her. 'Gavin has no intention of so treating Melinda.'

'He had better not. Come, Gavin, I wish to talk with you about other matters. I am not at all satisfied that Melinda will not corrupt the children in your absence.'

'I can hardly help my absence, but I most sincerely trust Melinda.'

Charlotte snorted; I set out in search of Kate.

'That woman,' I said, 'must somehow be got rid of.'

'How?'

'If you, Gavin and I find ourselves hosts, hosts of authority rather than footmen or maids, we could so arrange matters that an exorcist would be summoned and pronounce against evil spirits, thus banishing Charlotte to some other place.'

'Might not the strictures of the exorcist endure, so that we could no longer inhabit the house ourselves?'

' 'Tis a risk I would be prepared to take.'

'We can bear with Charlotte awhile, my love. For reflect: shall not Primula be one day joining us? We shall, I hope, succeed in having Charlotte and herself exorcised together.'

I laughed. 'You are a very demon of ingenuity, my sweet. I confess I would ill like to have Primula set up her reformation here—how sodden with cant she is, and from what I have seen and heard is not alone in perpetrating that cruellest of practices, the implementation of her own self-righteousness on the defenceless.'

' 'Tis a vice more immoral than most,' Kate agreed. 'To be saved by such a one is to be lost.'

'I want you, Kate,' I teased her. 'There is a new housemaid that I fancy.'

'And a new footman that I covet.'

'Then we shall inhabit them this afternoon.'

Kate's face grew serious. 'The last time I possessed a maid, I was afraid. Her mind fought so against mine I doubted whether I would be able to subdue it.'

'I remember,' softly, 'was it not worth it, my sweet?'

'It is always worth it,' her mouth ghost-vapour on mine.

'Dear Kate, I see in your eyes a pageant. I look into them and behold ourselves, skipping gaily together through youth, and I imagine that our gaiety was accompanied by the merry music of fifes.

'Later we exchange their trilling for the sturdy beat of drums as, donning our dignity——'

'—And doffing our innocence——'

'—we move at a steady gait towards maturity.

'Finally, first you, later myself, hear the final trumpet, and light is washed through with darkness. Yet in your eyes I see nothing of death; death in your company is a transitory affair, eclipsed by the colour of life.

'The music and the colour are wond'rous to me yet.'

Kate's dear mouth, that had dimpled in a smile, was now taut with longing. 'Take me, my sweet Wheatcroft,' she whispered, and repeated her plea not long afterwards as we lay in love, speaking our own words with the tongues of others, the footman and the kitchen-maid the bridges to our passion.

CHAPTER FIFTY-THREE

GAVIN seduced Melinda too well, pleasuring her in the body of his closest friend, a merchant, who had come to call and been possessed for his pains.

Although, when Gavin left him, the fellow was bemused, he nevertheless collected his wits swiftly enough to take further advantage of the situation, for he had always admired Melinda. She now became enamoured of him, and to Gavin's disgust the two married, and went to live in the merchant's house in Belgravia.

Saul, Primula and Tamarind being left without adult leadership, relished it greatly when it reappeared, in the person of General Dimity Hazell.

Dimity returned from the wars forceful as an off-shore gale. There was about him a certain feline calm, alternating with the power of the storm, tranquillity the lull from which he could assert himself with renewed domination.

Kate distrusted Dimity, and resented him not a little for being my bastard, Charlotte loathed him, for he had colour, Gavin tended to be amused by him.

Primula, taking to Dimity as ivy to a wall, confided in him that she had read Mr. Russell's despatches from the Crimea, in *The Times*. 'The situation endured by the soldiers seems to have been quite dreadful,' she said. 'Only the most Christian courage could have sustained them.'

'Quite,' agreed Dimity casually, curling a whisker round his finger. 'Not a bad fellow, Russell; I met him at Balaclava. Questioned the conduct of the war—thought there was too much carnage. "I don't know how you can have a war without it," I told him, "carnage is as much a part of battle as inquisitiveness is of journalism." '

'But the Charge of the Light Brigade was unnecessarily bloody, was it not?' asked Saul, inclined to be a mental recluse, intense and withdrawn.

'The Charge was a mistake, but not a mean mistake. It was a fine mistake, a noble error, and it gave my men their chance of glory. They swept along the valley floor, straight at the Russian guns, although in fact their orders were to rescue our own. Six hundred men against several thousand —finest moment in the history of the Hussars.

'Alma, Inkerman, Sebastopol, Balaclava—all trinkets of fire to flash in Palmerston's watch chain!'

'But surely it was the act following the error that was noble, and not error itself,' suggested smiling Tamarind.

'The result of an act embraces the cause of it!' declared Dimity promptly.

'I am devoutly glad that you were not one of those slain, uncle,' said Primula.

'There would have been more than a random chance of my having suffered, like so many of my gallant men, the savage swing of death's scythe, but unfortunately I missed the 11th's moment of glory. No doubt I shall live to lament it as much as the chaps Shakespeare mentioned, who missed Agincourt. However, Lord Cardigan had charged me with a responsibility which I had to carry out.

'What was that?' asked Primula, her nose crochetting the air with curiosity.

'Why, I had to look after his mistress!'

Primula gasped, a red glow appearing at once below her gorsey hair, so that it resembled a strip of moorland about to catch fire.

'His——?'

'Nice little thing, but tended to worry too much when her lord and master engaged in combat. Had no need for concern—fellow always went into battle looking as though he'd just come straight from his tailor. Came out of battle in exactly the same style, what's more.

'His mistress was considerate of the men too, of course. In fact, spent a good deal of time with that chef fellow Alexis Soyer from the Reform Club—you probably read about him in Russell's despatches. Quitted the club and paid his own passage out to the Crimea so that he might improve army cooking. Invented a new type of stove too. God bless my soul, I thought the British soldier was about to be introduced to the joys of boeuf Wellington!'

'The plight of the soldiers attracted a great deal of attention here,' said Primula. 'And of course Florence Nightingale——'

'A dear girl. Utterly devoted to the welfare of the Army.

Nothing deterred her, and I can tell you the conditions were far from civilized.'

'Did you sleep in a tent, uncle?' asked Tamarind, 'or in the open?'

'Shared Cardigan's yacht. Dammit, I am a general; one has to have some sort of compensation for the responsibilities of leadership.'

'Did you have a mistress aboard too, uncle?' from Tamarind.

'Tamarind!' exclaimed Primula, 'Uncle Dimity would not go to war in such an immoral fashion.'

'Immoral?' loudly. 'Nothing immoral about it, my dear. Just as the coldness of the winter renders torpid the acrimonious fluids of the body, as the manufacturers of patent medicines have it, which are aroused in the spring, so a man needs a woman in battle.

'The Russians, my dear niece, were the enemy, not the temptations of the flesh. A good woman, a warm woman, has a constructive effect on a man. She calms him as much as she arouses him, bestowing each gift in its proper season. In moments of calm he is able to think and to plan; his moments of lust refresh him. A warrior refreshed is in much better condition to fight than a warrior who is stale through being deprived.'

Primula was all confusion, gurgling and blushing and no doubt wondering how it might feel to cast away the reins of restraint and fling herself beneath a busy man.

'So that, seeking refreshment, you did have a mistress aboard?' persisted mischevious Tamarind.

'Of course, my boy; she was a French girl, whom I met in the Levant. What is more, I nearly married her.'

'What became of her instead?' asked Tamarind.

'She followed the Nightingale to the bedsides of the sick and wounded, and herself perished of typhus.'

'And was she decently buried?' asked Primula.

'She lay amidst good bedfellows, for all that they were dead. A vast communal bed they shared, deep in Crimean mud.'

Primula shuddered.

'We have had some savage outbreaks of typhus here in London, and of cholera,' said Saul, 'particularly in the poorer districts, such as Bermondsey.'

'And last year the fevers and diseases formed themselves

into a vast miasma that overspread the town, and gave us the year of the Great Stink,' Tamarind put in, smiling. 'For once it was not only the poor who had their nostrils caked with unpleasant residue, but the rich also, for the stink swept in at the windows of Parliament so strongly that the curtains covering them had to be soaked in chloride of lime.'

'The trouble is cost,' resumed Saul. 'While it is of course tragic that up to four hundred souls a day are taken from us by cholera, where is the money to come from to quench it? It is said that cholera lurks in the air and feeds on filth, but how are we to pay for new drainage, to give the poor dustbins, to roof over the sewers, of which there are three hundred and ninety-nine disgorging their contents into the Thames between Putney and Blackwall?'

'I think cholera is an effluvium that rises off corpses,' said Tamarind cheerfully, 'for I can match your information, Saul, with a little of my own; namely, that 50,000 people are buried each year in the same two hundred and eighteen acres, and lie restlessly, and decide occasionally in time of flood to roam about, engaging the grave-diggers in bizarre combat.'

'As I was saying,' Saul continued coldly, 'the measures needed to purify London would cost an impossible sum.'

'Lives are much cheaper,' said Tamarind drily.

Dimity was staring at Saul intently. 'You like money, Saul, do you not?'

'I respect it, uncle, and deeply deplore the squandering of it,' gently twisting together his moneylender's hands.

'And you, Primula my dear,' turning to her with a smile, 'you enjoy morality, do you not?'

'I should have thought that immorality was more to be enjoyed,' from Tamarind.

'Aha!' bellowed Dimity, as Primula blushed and made to rebuke her younger brother. 'But one does enjoy morality, does one not? For I have heard of your good works, my dear niece, of how you spend uncomfortable hours in distressing conditions, striving to redeem the luckless wretches who infest the area of the Haymarket. Surely there is joy in being able to carry out such redemption?'

'Certainly,' Primula replied, 'although it is of course for their benefit, and not for mine.'

'Exactly, my dear, and I admire you for it.' Primula, who was not used to admiration of any sort, smiled at her uncle with fondness and humility. He benignly returned her regard, before leaning forward in his chair, his expression intent as a striking adder's.

'Morality is not merely the guarding of one's own salvation,' gently, 'but that of the salvation of others less fortunate than oneself.'

'You have a fine comprehension of morality, uncle,' said Primula.

'There are many things which are the shame and disgrace of society,' Dimity went on, 'and only the devoted efforts of people such as yourself, Primula, prevent them from becoming more shameful and more disgraceful.

'When a woman has fallen, she may continue to fall forever, she can plummet to the uttermost depths, unless some saviour should place a support under her and slowly and painfully haul her upward.

'And if you should go to that woman, and say: Enough. You shall be helped, you are going to be no longer dipped in, steeped in, squalor, that woman will look at you in gratitude, will she not?'

'Indeed I hope so, uncle,' answered Primula, much affected.

'Now you, Tamarind, you have a spark in your eye and there is a merriment in you which tells me that you are willing not only to accept life's offerings, but to offer life something also.'

'I hope that that is true, uncle.'

'I'm convinced of it. Now if I were to say to you three kinsmen who are dear to me: let us mingle the acquisition of wealth with morality, and infuse those two factors with enjoyment and satisfaction, what would you say?' rising and standing athwart a small Persian rug that I had bought from a trader shortly before Trafalgar.

'We would be most interested,' replied Saul, the others nodding in agreement.

'Excellent,' quietly. 'I have been devoting a great deal of thought to the matter!' with loud abruptness. 'We have to move in a military manner, each step carefully calculated in advance.

'What we require, my dears, is all the dash and panoply of a Charge of the Light Brigade, without the casualties.' Dimity paused, as though to send his power through the room, to lap at the cornices and envelop irresistibly his niece and nephews. I could scarce believe that this was my child, who had sat on my bed, his hand toying with my face, the day I died.

'I begin to suspect fraud,' whispered Kate. 'If need be you must inhabit your beloved bastard and sway him from his purpose, for I am near to certain that our grandchildren are about to be gulled.'

'There is one thing, a most important and respected thing, that would accrue to us together with money and morality. That thing, my dears, is society!' Dimity thrust forward a hand, slowly folded it behind his back. 'Society has many needs,' he continued. 'It needs to be led, so that others may follow it. It needs to be stimulated, in order that it may stimulate those who look to it for a measure of inspiration. It enjoys patronage, so that it may patronize those below it.

'Above all, my dears, society insists on being amused. On being diverted. The Prince of Wales said as much to me the other day.'

At the mention of His Royal Highness Primula sighed in reverence, and was not alone, for Kate was quite vanquished also. Charlotte was not, but glared at Dimity with an implacable and basilisk eye.

'The Prince of Wales feels that London, whose docks are so extensive and offer hospitality to so many vessels of all degrees, ought also to offer far more harbours than it does, for those humans who so desperately require them.

'It is, as Saul has said of a cure for London's cholera, impossible to find the money to harbour everyone in need, and therefore only a few out of the multitude may be so sheltered. We must have recourse to quality rather than quantity.

'For, my dears, London has some eighty thousand prostitutes.' He smiled at Primula. 'Of whom you during the course of your good works can have met only a handful. Am I not right?'

'Yes, uncle,' whispering in her confusion; it evidently dismayed her that the field for reform should be so vast, and the ability of the reformer to cover it so limited.

'We can offer refuge to only a few of those unfortunates,' Dimity said in tones deep with melancholy, 'but surely we shall acquire godliness by doing so? And a measure of profit,' looking at Saul.

'That will have to be carefully examined,' said Saul,

thoughtfully. 'I am not yet convinced, however, of the desirability of sharing this house with some of London's fallen, even with those of them who are still salvageable.'

'Sharing it?' echoed Dimity. 'We shall not share it with them. We shall, until such time as we feel our work is done, lease it to them. They shall not be helped entirely at the expense of society, and not entirely either at the expense of themselves. Their salvation shall be a shared responsibility, for which we may claim a fair fee.'

'It would be of great help to me, to be able to reform them here, without having to go abroad at night,' said Primula thoughtfully.

Tamarind smiled expectantly. 'Between us we shall found the finest night-house in London,' he said. 'Even though it be something of a church to boot.'

'I have great admiration for the Prince of Wales,' murmured Primula, eyes reflecting a fantasy concerning herself and the heir to the throne.

'You must stop them!' exclaimed Kate. 'I shall not have my house turned over to whores!'

'Short of taking up a permanent dwelling in Dimity, I do not see what I can do,' I told her. 'Besides, it might be amusing to see what becomes of the enterprise. I have never entirely lost my love of innovation.'

'You are incorrigible, Wheatcroft,' flouncing through the wall.

'You must stop them, Mr. Hazell,' from Charlotte. 'Can you not invade Dimity for sufficient time to force a renunciation of the project?'

I eyed her rapier nose and that of her live daughter below, preparing now to ravage harlot's consciences, and without speaking set off to mollify my Kate.

CHAPTER FIFTY-FOUR

'SHALL we put out a handbill?' bellowed Dimity, laughing as he gulped a goblet of brandy. 'Shall we advertise ourselves as the theatres do? Picture if you can delicately salacious proclamations, pamphlets hinting at delights screened by curtains: Here be seductresses, lights 'o love of delicious wantonness, guaranteed to be lubricous, lascivious and of profound sensuality.'

Tamarind, Dimity's only official audience, laughed; Kate, Charlotte, Gavin and I looked on as Dimity sketched out with sweeping gestures his intimate designs.

'Here abides promiscuity,' he went on, 'hand maiden of the deprived, here are to be found the arabesques and humours that enlightened amorousness depicts, here the jade is more valued than the emerald.' He laughed again. 'I do love a superbly writhing jade, that breathes exalted words of whoredom in my ear.'

'I fear such handbills might incur a certain amount of displeasure,' commented Tamarind. 'If we could only induce some sort of political flavour, however, they'd be fair game. Nobody considers a politician anything but a whore, with the exception perhaps of Mr. Gladstone. In his scarlet-lined opera cloak he resembles the Lord speaking from the burning bush.'

'Scarlet,' murmured Dimity, 'our lucky colour.' He shouted with enthusiasm.

'A splendid notion, politics and lewdness, with a dash of religion. Conjure up memories of the Reform Bill—this shall be an Unreform Bill, of unspeakable grandeur, luring the cuckolded who wish to avenge themselves on their errant spouses by sailing up the inlets of those well trained to give them storms that refresh but do not harm. At the same time, hypocrites and snivellers who condemn immorality because they have neither the courage nor the opportunity to practise it, shall at least be afforded the latter. Even the former may be induced, with a little skill, a slightly open mouth, an invitation demure as it it sensual.

Thus a beckoning wife may be well reclipsed by a woman more available, and morality quail in face of the common good. Now I have told you of the lady whom I collected in the Levant and who was aroused from my bed by Nightingale's ideals. In the Levant also I met a man who combines a complete lack of scruple with a considerable knowledge of art. That is to say, artistic ability. He will, my dear nephew, be here,' looking at his time-piece, 'in a few minutes. Ah, there he is now,' as the door-bell jangled and a flunkey glided rapidly across the hall in response to it.

'Good afternoon, sir. Whom do you wish to see?'

'General Hazell.'

'This way, Osman!' shouted Dimity.

Into the room flowed a short, slender man wearing a long robe that shimmered behind him like a wake in moonlight. He bowed to Dimity, then to Tamarind, at the same time contriving to raise scimitar-shaped eyebrows in reverence. Such humility, I had learned during the course of my life, usually presaged a large bill.

'Osman Osman!' Dimity introduced him. 'Architect, decorator, Furnisher Extraordinary to the Harem of the Sultanate of Ottoman. Well, Osman, does this place offer you possibilities?'

'It does not offer, sir, it implores,' looking about him. 'Take me, this palace begs, transform me. I am feminine, down to my last corridor, my most secret passageway, take me and make me over to the joys of women.'

'The house indeed has a great deal to say to this dismal charlatan, the moment he sets foot in it,' from outraged Kate. 'Possess him, Wheatcroft, and contrive that he be involved in some mischance.'

'He ought to be imprisoned,' was Charlotte's inevitable suggestion.

'I would have a word with you, father,' murmured Gavin, drawing me aside. 'I trust,' he went on, when we were standing some way away from Kate and Charlotte, 'that we shall benefit from this corruption?'

I looked at him with as little comprehension as I could muster. 'In what way benefit, my son?'

'Must I spell it out, father? If our house is to undergo the sacrilege of being turned into a brothel, in which every whoreson who fancies it may come to dip himself, and thus esteem himself a bold fellow; surely we, who have the gift of becoming men occasionally, as the mood takes us, can not remain entirely isolated from such occurrences?'

'We shall have to be exceeding circumspect,' I told him. 'Your mother would be as unforgiving as Charlotte should she detect me invading some magnificent young jackanapes in order to bed a doxy.'

'So long as she does not look into your eyes she need not know,' connivingly.

'My eyes will not for a moment be averted from the feast I shall be about,' I assured him. 'I have loved your mother in many forms, and in none more so than her own, before she died. Perhaps, only because a woman's availability is a great stimulant to a man, I shall henceforth, if only seldom, venture a loving invasion of a body whose spirit is not your mother's but its own.'

We returned to stand near Dimity, who was watching Osman Osman. The Levantine paraded about the house, measuring and calculating, occasionally nodding and winking to himself.

'I have my conceptions now,' he told Dimity and Tamarind, 'I have my grand design.

'The house shall have twenty bedrooms, a dining-room, a room for cards and a room for roulette. Each room shall be different in a subtle way from the others, and each will be allocated to a definite desire.

'Some men prefer to make love to a woman, some with a woman. Some prefer to be made love to, and some do not know the meaning of love at all, but enjoy a masquerade, in which the mask of love is torn off to reveal itself as cruelty.

'Some men burn at the sight of a woman, and some men freeze. Some are confident of conquest, others tremble with apprehension at the very thought of a woman's embrace, and are afflicted at the challenge to proof of their manhood.

'One potentate I knew could only acquit himself as a man should if, after he had been at his woman for two hours, a ram were beheaded; in came the butcher with his dagger and behold, as he struck the ram in the throat the potentate let out his shout of triumph.'

'What about the woman?' asked Tamarind.

'The woman?' Osman looked perplexed. 'The woman was delighted to have pleased her master.'

'Surely it was the ram that pleased him!' yelled Dimity, laughing.

Osman Osman frowned, offended. 'Afterwards the potentate would call for rosewater and smile as its spray gently perfumed him, and drank mint tea, and contemplated the other truths that accompany the truth of love; that is to say that love is not alone in a man's breast, but is the handmaiden of power, and of death!'

'No doubt in the case of the potentate, poor inadequate fellow!' shouted Dimity, 'but no woman in this establishment shall be affrighted by the sight of rams spilling their blood over our fine carpets. The people of England are in any case not so used to the sight of blood as of gin, which has many advantages over gore, one of them being that it does not so severely stain.'

Osman overlooked gin's particular advantage. 'Incense can also create a mood,' he murmured musingly, 'and music. We shall have a gallery on which, behind screens, musicians will play enticingly.

'Part of the house will be furnished in the eastern fashion, which will send exotic images to inflame the mind, and caress the fantasies of even the least imaginative into bloom.

'A man who wishes to be a pharaoh, shall for a short time be a pharaoh; a man who has fancied making love in a railway carriage will be able to bring about his wish through my pervasive arts. For those who believe that the sight of moon and stars is indispensable to love-making, I shall devise a luxurious planetarium, where sensual dalliance may be accompanied by the occasional glance through an azimuth at Jupiter turning in its course like a magnificent breast encircled by jewellery.

'People will recline on heavily padded cushions thick with fleece and radiant in tooled leather. Tell me,' abruptly, 'would there be any objection to slaves?'

'I fear that since Wilberforce they are forbidden us,' answered Tamarind.

'A pity. A dark, smooth, eunuch, swollen with his impotence, induces a great and inspiring gratitude in the unmaimed about their pleasures. Or a slave girl, bearing a large tray of beaten brass, at the clap of her master's hand, brings an aura of docile and complete acquiescence to the scene of love. A man likes to be tended.'

'Surely that is the whole point of our night-house?' put in Tamarind. 'The tending of men. And of women,' he added.

'I am glad that someone has mentioned women!' said Kate. 'Are we chattels, to be so little considered?'

'I'll have no male prostitutes here!' shouted Dimity. 'Nor shall I be prepared to tolerate fancy men, that mince about and oversee the profits gained by their women.

'Certain seclusives, yes; a woman who wishes to rent her own private rooms wherein to entertain. Ladies who come here to captivate the men they meet shall be welcome, and should a gentleman of eminence wish to maintain a private apartment here for his kept woman, I shall not be found objecting. But fancy men, bullies and bawds I shall not tolerate!'

'Your bastard indeed has scruples,' Kate said sarcastically. 'I am confounded to have made such a discovery.'

'I am beyond words outraged,' from Charlotte. 'That—that a kinsman of yours, Mr. Hazell, has corrupted my children. He is worse than cholera itself, for what excuse may one make to God on arrival before Him, concerning one's corruption? One is corrupted because one wants to be, do you not agree? Gavin, dispose of that monster; surely you can muster sufficient power to frighten him, so that he flees this house, or to push him downstairs so that he is injured sufficiently to lose interest in his degrading project?'

'What do you think, father?' Gavin asked me.

'I can scarcely rejoice in what is about to befall my house, but if we find that its career is too repellent to us, we can always put an end to it. In the meantime, at least we may find ourselves amused by what transpires.'

So it was that, despite, or possibly because, Gavin and I maliciously enjoyed Charlotte's disgust, we secured Kate's reluctant agreement to let the house don a new if reprehensible mantle, allowing Dimity's plans to continue.

CHAPTER FIFTY-FIVE

ALTHOUGH Robert Adam would doubtless have disclaimed Osman Osman as brother, the latter exerted himself so successfully, and was so diligent at his task of conversion, that it was not long before Hazell House was altered to his purpose.

The ballroom was made over to whist, backgammon and roulette; the other rooms were divided or enlarged, and the elegant furniture designed and built by Adam for Kate and me replaced by a vast infusion of sturdy, heavy stuff upholstered in thick velvet and stamped everywhere with buttons.

One of the drawing-rooms was adapted to a use at first strange to us, and we watched with some wonder as clusters of small divans, each big enough for two people only, were set facing in the same direction; a sheet was lowered from the cornice, and a cannon-like device, designed for no purpose that we could conceive, mounted on a table.

The device flared and threw out an image which straddled the sheet; to our astonishment we found ourselves regarding a bird, that stared back indignantly at us from its nest. The bird flickered, and now we saw a cat, and discovered that it was at that that the bird was staring, and not at us at all; we understood from Osman Osman's ensuing conversation with Dimity that the instrument was called a magic lantern, and that men and women would pay to see its wonders, and sit on the divans, in order to be gratified, not only by the knowledge presented to them by the lantern, but also by that offered away from it.

As for the chandeliers, they were replaced by others called gasoliers, that relied not upon candles but upon gas, whose jets had first blossomed along London's streets not long before my death.

Servants were hired in great number, the dimity room now so overflowed with linen that there was little room in it for love-making. Thus Kate and I had perforce to use Primula's chamber at night, when she was out reforming whores, or at least by her efforts amusing them. In short, the house approached its launching.

I recall well the date that the first ladies appeared, as though serenaded into harbour by Ulysses singing to the sirens; it was the fifteenth of April, 1858.

All was superlatively prepared; footmen stood by tables as crammed with wine and viands as the house was with furniture, whores with haughty smiles and disdainful glances extended dainty gloves and flung sweetmeats in their mouths, or took their wine at the tilt. They resembled richly caparisoned sundials, crowned by immense hats, as in heavily brocaded skirts they tacked slowly here and there and, having carefully made their dispositions, eyed the doorway for the arrival of the gentlemen.

Installed to preside over the house was one Madame LaCaille, charming but forbidding, with the aura of a virgin aunt impelled to prurience but resenting it. The lusts of the flesh, to be despised, were at the same time indispensable, morality was a casual prayer for forgiveness flung at a church altar.

Doubtless the vinegar aspect of the eyes was caused by lack of response to the prayer; how little satisfaction there is in sinning if we have afterwards to bear the burden of it, rather than sloughing it off on God.

Madame LaCaille was reputed, we gathered, to have been the best-kept, or at least the most extensively kept, courtesan in Europe; she had subsided gently on to the pertly upturned cods of kings and princes, been ravished by one or two emperors in the Palatine States, and had been induced to add her lustre to Dimity's night-house by the expectation of the presence of the English nobility.

'The shameless hussies!' hissed Charlotte, eager to quench any expression of interest from Gavin.

'I know not what inducement a man may have, to want to lie with them and be the poorer in pocket for it,' put in Kate.

'And not only poorer in pocket but in health, I should not wonder,' Charlotte returned, disapproval a ball the two could volley back and forth across the net indefinitely.

Men appeared, solemn as grouse about to be shot. They stood surveying the room as though sizing up its furnishing, without noticing that women were intent upon returning their regard.

One of the men, silver-haired and frail, approached a female clad all in dark blue, her gown as heavily engraved as a banknote. I moved over to stand beside him.

'Good evening,' he said, in a thin voice.

'Hello, sir, are you going to offer me a glass of wine?'

'Indeed, indeed,' beckoning a footman, who approached with a salver.

'You have an air of distinction about you, sir,' said the doxy, raising her glass.

'And so have you, my dear,' with a chuckle. 'You are in many ways quite different to other ladies I know.'

'Your wife no doubt is a fine lady?'

'Very fine, oh very fine.' He chuckled again. 'She has a discerning temperament, but is like most of you ladies inclined to unpredictable surges of emotion. Also, like me, she is passing thin, passing thin.' He paused. 'In fact, our friends refer to her as the chilliagon, that being a plane figure with a thousand angles, and to me, because I am a man of diverse interests, I suppose, as the chiliahedron, that being a plane figure with a thousand sides.'

Nonplussed, the doxy fanned herself. 'I'm sorry your wife is plain,' she said.

'Not plain, my dear. Flat. Plane flat.'

The girl caressed her bosom. 'I'm not, my dear, am I?' taking his hand behind her fan and squeezing it. He vibrated with joy and apprehension.

'My dear, so forward, so forward. I scarcely know you.'

'Would you like to know me a little more, sir?'

'Indeed I would, indeed I would, my dear.'

'Then shall we go to watch the magic lantern show?'

'Indeed, I doubt if I could restrain my ardour through a magic lantern show, unless it be of short duration.'

'Your ardour?' the girl smiled cheekily at him, and made a moue such as minxes are all expert at.

'As it happens, I am interested in seeing the planetarium, my dear.'

'I've never seen one.'

'A planetarium? It is of the order of a diorama, my dear, and, for that matter, has something in common with the magic lantern.'

'I do know that the planetarium here, whatever it may be, is private,' the wench told him, holding up her glass for more wine, which was quickly furnished her.

'I—I have also heard something of the sort,' confided the gentleman. 'Are you interested in the tracks made by the stars and planets?'

'I could be, sir,' again squeezing his gloved hand in hers. 'Are you?'

'I am the Astronomer Royal, my dear. I have to be,' with his thin laugh. 'Shall we then, ascend?'

'Very well. I cannot wait to see such an eminent figure in action. What shall I call you, that will sound affectionate? I can't hold you to me and say: O, Astronomer, darling!'

'Gaberdine, my love—you are discreet, are you not? I must not be discovered—Sir Gaberdine Fern.'

The doxy laughed, and rising stared in the most loving fashion into his rheumy eyes, and murmured: 'Gabby, my own sweet Gabby,' and preceded him from the room, while Madame LaCaille noted something in a book and followed them with her black eyes.

Shamelessly I stood nearby in the planetarium room as Sir Gaberdine sat down and pulled the wench on to his knee; cartilage crackled like buckshot.

'And your name, my love?' he asked.

'Sybil.'

'You seem too young to be a sibyl, my dear.'

The girl eyed him without comprehension. 'I beg your pardon?'

'The sibyls were ladies of antiquity who made prophecies. They were alleged to be able to foretell the future.'

'I wish I could do that at the Derby. Quite heartbreaking it is, to see one's horse go down. Tell me, Gabby, have you ever seen your wife undressed?'

'Well, not without her stays of course, and all that they support. Marriage is not bestowed upon us to deprive us completely of our personal privacy, do you not agree?'

'You can destroy mine, if you like. For fifty guineas?'

'Fifty guineas? But the fee agreed was twenty!'

'For twenty guineas all you can find here is supper, and a chance to lose a hundred guineas on the tables. For fifty you can go right beyond the stars, Gabby, right into Paradise itself.'

The old man hesitated but a little, before taking out his purse and counting its contents. I was desirous of inhabiting him and enjoying the wench myself, but refrained from doing so because I reflected that I would doubtless be able to accomplish little more with the Astronomer Royal's body than would he himself. Instead I determined to take the sultry young doxy as soon as I could come into possession of a body worthy of her.

'Very well, my sweet,' she said, putting the money in a purse and smiling warmly at him, 'will you help me to undress?' As she spoke she raised her heavy crinoline to reveal a firm white arse. She was unencumbered by any other garment beneath her outer covering, neither corset nor shift beleaguered her succulent flesh.

'Well, my sweet Astronomer, let me examine your telescope,' she said softly, standing naked before him and kneeling to gentle him. His offering, had it been presented to God, would doubtless have resulted in a furious thunderclap of wrath, for it was a puny thing, a cod that was too small yet to have left its mother, and too old to have abided with her. It was a thing so withered that the workmanship of it was comparable with that of the New Guinea tribes, who shrink the cut-off heads of their enemies.

'Must I undress completely too?' asked the astronomer tremulously.

'Of course, my love, I don't want to rub myself against your broadcloth, or gash myself on your scarfpin.'

Amazed that any man could be so thin, I observed the stripping of him, until the poor wishbone stood shivering in the warmth of the room beneath its canopy of artificial stars.

'Come, my sweet, caress me, show me a little tenderness,' the doxy told him, taking his hand, which in agitation had been toying with an azimuth through which he at random sighted her.

'Forgive me, my sweet Sybil. I am something of an opsimath at love-making.'

'A what?'

'One who has come late to learning, my dear. The chilliagon—my wife—and I have had little time for dallying. The production of fifteen children required more concentration than dalliance.'

'Then I shall teach you.'

I stood watching his apprenticeship, and respected the cod, petty though it now was, at having sired such a number of progeny. Guided, encouraged, strengthened by the minx's considerable arts, it gradually unfolded, a winter flower paying homage to the golden spring of lust.

Now the old man became a horse, the most ramshackle I had ever seen, that galloped along on its back, its jockey gazing down in triumph at having set the beast on course for the winning post, when all predictions would have been to the contrary.

Sir Gaberdine let out a thin wail, leaning forward to press his face to the girl's breast as though in the hour of his senility he would take suck, then fell back and lay panting, with blue cheeks, as the doxy dismounted and went to pour him wine.

'Vile,' Kate's voice whispered in my ear. 'You have been slavering at the chops like a starving wolf, Wheatcroft.'

'Possess her for me, Kate, and I shall possess for you in return the finest man in the place,' I said. 'I do beseech you. Kate.'

'Perhaps this is the finest man in the place,' gesturing at the near extinct astronomer.

'Nay, I doubt there are finer.'

'I shall possess that doxy for you, if you possess for me a poet that labours nearby. I have watched him at his work and he is charming and gentle and is being made mock of.'

'In what fashion?'

'In this devilish sewer the Levantine has built a room called the Renunciation Chamber——'

'I remember his glee as he described its creation to Dimity and Tamarind.'

'—and a young poet was brought there tonight by a jade hot as a cauldron between her legs but simulating disinterest.

'In face of her disdain the poet in desperation falls to his knees, and weeps, and recites to her a poem, whose tenor is that her relentless thighs enclose an Arctic prize, which brings bitter tears to his eyes——'

'Did you not say that he was a poet?' I interrupted her. 'Maybe I cannot possess him, for he has already been inhabited by the spirit of Shakespeare, or possibly Milton——'

'A pox on you, Wheatcroft, for you do aggravate me!'

'I will possess your poet for you,' I agreed contritely. 'Whom shall you inhabit to take him?'

'Why, yon doxy that you crave, and who is now helping downstairs the limping remnants of her conquest.' Before

I could endorse her intent, she changed her mind. 'No, I want the poet as he is, unsullied by worldliness. I will possess a wench who shall be lenient with him.'

'And I shall find a man not above ninety years of age, in whom to enter Sybil.'

'Sybil!' hissed Kate. 'I forbid it.'

'Very well. Either you renounce the poet, unless I be possessed of him, and accept that I shall not take the doxy without your being in her——'

'You will take her anyway!' snapped Kate.

'I shall let her founder on the tide of so much other temptation,' I said. 'Look about you.'

'No doubt the shopkeeper will sample all his wares,' glaring at Dimity. 'How corrupted will be my grandchildren.'

'Surely Primula's spirit is beyond corruption,' watching as our granddaughter, clad in black bombasine, as though in mourning for the lost virtue of the world, made her way with bible in her hand through the throng. She approached a whore of brazen aspect, and counselled her to renounce her unfortunate ways.

'They are not really my ways,' answered the hussy. 'For I come of a respectable family, well known in Brighton, that are fishermen. An aunt, who was desperate at the drowning of her affianced in a fishing-boat which foundered, decided to flee to London. She wanted, you understand, to leave everything which reminded her of her love.'

'I understand,' said Primula, to whom love was nothing more than a word, and furthermore a word which, when uttered by others, so often meant suffering.

'I came here to find my aunt, but could not trace her. A woman offered me her friendship one evening, as I was seeking somewhere to stay, and when I awoke in the middle of the night, it was to find——' the whore turned her head and shook—'that I was not alone. A man lay beside me, and I could not escape, struggle as I might. That was the accomplishment of my ruin, but to ensure that it was for ever, I was locked in, and another man admitted late in the afternoon, whose breath smelled strongly of drink, and bullies guarded me in the house and would not let me out until I was beyond redemption.'

'We are none of us wholly beyond redemption,' Primula told her, with the air of one confident that she had no need of it.

'The thought of Mary Magdalen,' with downcast eye, 'is my only solace.'

'Perhaps the Virgin Mary might be a happier example to you,' handing the whore a prayerbook. 'Repent of your sins, and lead a life of righteousness, and——'

'—we should have to close down,' interrupted Dimity, laughing. 'Repent if you must, my dear,' taking the wench's arm, 'but do not let it interfere with earning your living.'

'Very well, sir,' managing to quell her mirth; Primula tossed her head and made off in the direction of another hussy, as yet unaccompanied.

Thus the night house prospered, and society came to relish it. The culmination of Dimity's endeavours occurred on the afternoon of a winter's day.

A young gentleman appeared, shaking snow off his hat. He was preceded by a tidal wave of bowing and genuflecting on the part of those who affected at the same time not to recognize him, as though the Messiah were determined to pass muster as carpenter until the last possible moment. The gentleman extended his arm to Madame LaCaille, who curtsied, and was borne upstairs to the Train Room, so called because in it one might enjoy the illusion of a journey by rail. The bed was skilfully made to rock by a mechanical contrivance; at the same time, in a minute cubicle adjoining, an attendant gifted with the ability to mimic a locomotive uttered his impressions of steam gushing from a boiler. These had a quite entrancing and inspiring effect upon the Prince of Wales, bonding him to Madame LaCaille in an instant.

The prince's presence in the house, to be oft repeated, delighted Kate, who forgave Dimity much for it; both she and he were placed on pinnacles of joy when for his services to humanity generally and to the prince in particular Dimity was eventually awarded a knighthood.

One May night, when he was in his sixty-eighth year, General Sir Dimity Hazell, my beloved bastard, expired. His death occurred after dinner, as he pleasured a doxy with more enthusiasm than discretion. His end, he told me not long after it, had been exactly as he would have wished.

Saul, loving money above matrimony, had not embarked upon it, but had taken a solitary dwelling in the city, and eventually died there.

Primula, like so many reformers, became first a pest, and

later a jest. She subsided into old age and dwelled in the attic of her family's conscience, for the most part ignored but at the same time regarded as security against their own transgressions; she had never embraced aught but virginity, passion had always been a stranger to her, and in the joy of living which I still managed to sustain, there were times when I wept for her. The most barren desert ought at some time to have a taste of fertility.

It was Tamarind who restored Hazell House to its former purpose, and filled it with his children, and handed it on to them when his time came.

CHAPTER FIFTY-SIX

'AND this is the board room, gentlemen, although in view of the house's rather lurid history during Victorian times maybe one ought to spell "board" with a "w".'

My handsome descendant Vickery Hazell was showing a party of men round the house, which was by now so filled with my dead relations it seemed miraculous that there was still sufficient room for a live one.

'It seems a pity in a way, to turn this into the company's offices,' remarked a tall man in a sombre cravat, who lovingly regarded Adam's panelling.

'Well the house is too big for us to live in, and with all the complications of death duties and so on converting it to Hazell headquarters seemed the best thing to do.'

'Damn sight better than pulling it down and seeing it re-incarnated as a concrete mausoleum for the interment of typists,' said a small fat man.

'Pull it down!' exclaimed a dozen of my relatives at once. 'Outrageous!'

'We have survived assaults from the air——' from Kate.

'—Thunderbolts of the Lord,' interrupted Primula.

'—and I have no intention of permitting any rascal to pull it down. What would become of us?' Kate demanded. 'If necessary you must possess anybody who tries to deprive us, Wheatcroft.'

'Vickery has said that he is not going to pull it down, my sweet.'

'I distrust the word of any man,' said Primula.

I led the way into the board room; we sat down while Vickery was extolling the beauty of Adam's work. Nothing remained of Osman Osman's.

'We must keep out intruders,' insisted sour-faced Charlotte, nose pointing at me across the broad long table; whose polish reflected none of us.

'Seeing how the company is operated, we shall add a new dimension to our knowledge of the modern world,' I told her. 'I may even be able to take a hand with the running of Hazell Enterprises. So may you, Gavin, and Tamarind.'

'And I,' put in Tamarind's eldest son Jurgen, who had contributed little to life, in spite of his reluctance to be left out of anything.

I smiled at Kate, who was eyeing me tenderly; for two centuries we had known each other, yet were still joined in wonder.

I could possess Vickery, or Vickery's colleagues, or any man I chose; it was a matter of much assurance to me, that I was now so adept at haunting that I could project myself beyond the house, simply by despatching my will at a passer-by.

Kate was no less skilled; we had sampled the lives of many, and by our intrusion changed those of a few. In our ability to be thus able to impose ourselves there was something of godly omnipotence, tempered with human trepidation.

On one occasion, I had possessed a woman, and Kate her lover, that we might experience the difference in sensation between giving and receiving. We had each felt uncomfortable in our assumed role, and swiftly desisted.

I looked out of the window; distantly, people strolled through the park where once deer and horses had mingled, and the breeze bore through the evening air a memory of the scent of hay.

Charlotte began to speak again, and a desire for solitude overcame me; I wished to wander in the gloaming with lovers, and perhaps don a lover's mantle, that I might hold hands with a gentle stranger.

A man approached and I regarded him intently; possessing him, I turned his steps to join the distant figures beneath the trees.

A girl smiled and I returned her smile, and talked with her awhile about things of little consequence; the evening was beautiful and the maid fair and in me was the happiness and contentment of one who would know an infinite number of such evenings, and possess many more men for sweet enjoyment's sake.

You who read these words may have lately felt for a brief time different, may have mislaid your memory of a certain hour, or discovered a pleasure that was like a dream, on the fringe of recollection.

Or you may be able to remember something you did not know, glimpse for an instant down the long tunnel of history scenes jewelled in clarity but not experience; wooden ships in battle, a man before a tent, white wig glistening in the sunset, a face peering through the curtains of a sedan chair.

Maybe you sense that there is someone nearer than beside you, who without foul intent has for a spasm of eternity usurped your mind and body, and mated you with one unknown to you, whose eyes are vivid with laughter.

Have I been, am I, perhaps, in you?

If you have enjoyed this book you will also like:

FIRST DEADLY SIN
Lawrence Sanders

An astounding novel of cops and killers that carves up the neon-lit city streets of New York into the elemental forces of good and evil. A novel that has become a breathtakingly compulsive read throughout the world. A major film. *75p*

THE LIBERATED
Henry Sutton

The author of THE EXHIBITIONIST and THE VOYEUR weaves together the stories of five people as they move across the physical, political and psycho-sexual breadth of America – from a women's lib commune in New York to an orgy of devil-worshippers in Los Angeles; from New York's black ghetto to the bizarre political machinations of a Miami suburb to the mystic questing of a California collective. A *tour de force* that will totally involve, surprise and shock the reader with a shock that always comes from recognition. *65p*

PASTIME
Anthony Fowles

From dusty librarian to the most wanted and potentially most dangerous man in the country, Fowles' hero makes this the most disturbing and topical read of the year. *40p*